## Book 2

## O'Connor Girls

# RHONDA BREWER

# Dedication

*This book is dedicated to my dear friend of more than twenty years. Although we met online, she and her husband have become two of my dearest and closest friends. Thank you Audrah and Rich Gosbeth for always being there when I need a friend to vent with. I love you both and appreciate your wonderful friendship.*

# Acknowledgments

With so many people in my life to thank for making publishing this book possible, I could almost write another book on that alone. However, a simple thank you never seems like enough to convey my gratitude, but I will try to do that the best I can with this acknowledgment.

 First, thank you belongs to the many authors who have become both friends and mentors to me. Then there are the amazing ladies who help with editing and errors. A special thank you goes to Michelle Eriksen, Abbie Zanders, and Amabel Daniels for their constant support and keen eye. To my dedicated betas and dear friends, Jackie Dawe Ford, Nancy Arnold-Holloway, and Karie Deegan thank you so much for the support and constant encouragement. To my readers, you are the reason that I can continue to do this.

A very special thank you to my husband, Danny who gives me the inspiration for the romantic heroes I write and encourages me every day. To my two children Laura and Colin, both of you show me every day how proud you are and how much you love me. To my beautiful granddaughter, Emma. You may not be old enough to read yet, but your smile gives me the inspiration to keep going. I love all of you.

# Chapter 1

Jess O'Connor blew out an exhausted groan. After two weeks' vacation from the Newfoundland Police Department where she worked as a police officer, it seemed as if she would get a chance to relax and catch up on some sleep. Wrong.

September wasn't the best month to take time off. Although she had time off from her primary career, her numerous other commitments still existed.

Jess taught Karate at the Hopedale community center. Kurt O'Connor had started the dojo with his older brother Sean when Jess was little. Her dad taught Jess, her sisters, her eight cousins, as well as many of the children and adults of Hopedale and surrounding communities. Jess continued teaching when she attained her black belt. The only other instructor at the school was her cousin Ian who had taken over classes from his father, Sean.

During the summer, the dojo would be closed, but at the beginning of the school year, everyone returned to self-defense classes. So, she spent at least two evenings a week teaching and trying to arrange her schedule so that it didn't clash with work. Not to mention she kept the books for the Karate school. She'd made a mistake a few years earlier of taking over the tedious job from her dad.

Jess would also help at *Jack's Place* one evening a week so her mother and father could have a date night. Jess' mother, Alice, opened the combination diner and pub almost fifteen years earlier. It was named after her grandfather. He was there the day it opened, but he passed away not long after.

*Jack's Place* was divided into two separate businesses. The diner had some of the best home-cooked food in Hopedale and everyone in the town ate there at least once a week. The pub wouldn't open until after supper because her mother wouldn't allow it to be open during the day.

If those things had been all she did on her time off, she would've had some time to herself, but the rest of her time was spent at the flower shop she owned, *The Rose Garden*. It was just her luck that one of her employees came down with influenza and ended up in the hospital.

To top things off, once again, her car died on the way home from her shop. The worst part was the only person who answered her desperate call for help, was her father. He showed up just as the tow truck attached her car to the hook. Jess prepared herself for the long lecture on the way to the garage because it was inevitable.

She loved her father, but as the chief of police, he was also her boss. He was constantly on her case to get rid of her ten-year-old Honda Civic and get a new car. He frequently brought it up when she was at work where Jess couldn't argue with him. She could afford a new car, but she wanted to buy a house first. A car would deplete her savings and living over her parents' garage was starting to get old.

Jess slid into the seat of her father's truck and gave him a kiss on the cheek. To her surprise, he waited a whole thirty seconds before he began his rant.

"Jessica Kathleen, when are you going to get rid of that piece of shit? Don't answer that. I know the answer, but I'm telling you, little girl, I don't want to hear any more excuses about saving money for a house. Get. A. God. Damn. Reliable. Vehicle." Her dad's deep growl made it hard not to roll her eyes like a teenager.

"I know, Dad. I'm looking into it," Jess lied.

"No, you're not. You didn't even ask Wade to let you know when he came across a good deal on a used car. Since you aren't going to take my advice and buy a new Goddamn car, at least ask Wade to find you something that won't break down every other day," her dad continued to rant.

Jess understood her father's frustration because her car broke down four times in less than three weeks. Every time she'd get one thing fixed, something else would break. Considering all the money she spent on it over the last few weeks, she'd probably end up paying more on repairs then what it would cost to get a new car.

Several weeks earlier, she'd called Aaron to help her out when the car died in the city. Aaron O'Connor was the youngest of her uncle's seven sons. Although the only one who called him Aaron was his new wife, everyone else called him A.J.

Aaron drove directly to the garage without giving her a choice of where to bring her vehicle because he trusted Wade. Not only was *Wade's Auto Service* the only place Aaron would take his precious Dodge Charger, but it was also the same place where all the NPD vehicles were brought for repairs and maintenance. The problem, it was more expensive than most of the places Jess had brought her car to in the past.

It was considered one of the best repair shops in the city. According to Aaron and her father, Wade Rivers only hired the best and his reputation was impeccable. Aaron told her that business had increased so much Wade relocated his shop to a bigger location.

Jess' major problem was Wade was also the first man in a long time to kick her heart and her libido into overdrive. He stood about a foot over her five-foot, one-inch and looked as if he took care of himself. Of course, she'd only seen his well-defined biceps and forearms, but it was evident from the way his snug-fitting t-shirts hugged his body, Wade had a well-defined chest and flat stomach.

Wade had a limp that seemed to be more prominent at the end of the day. She'd never asked him about it, but her father told her Wade was injured when he was struck by a drunk driver. He'd jumped in front of the vehicle to save a little girl in the path of the car. The selfless act had caused him to be in the hospital for several months and gave him a permanent limp.

Of course, she didn't have a snow ball's chance in hell with the man. Jess didn't have any free time to put into making a lasting relationship. She hadn't dated in a long time mostly because she worked day and night. Her last relationship had been more than ten years earlier. Jess had gone so long without sex that she would probably be considered a virgin again.

Jess was forced out of her thoughts as her father pulled into the parking lot of the repair garage. After he gave her another two-minute rant, she closed the car door and made her way inside the building. Of course, she heard her father shout a warning to ask Wade to help her find a decent car.

Wade met her at the door and told her that her car had just been brought into the garage. He motioned for her to follow him to the other side of the lot. The vehicle he pointed to looked like a brand-new SUV and for a second, Jess was confused.

"This is one of our newer loaner vehicles. It's a little bigger than you're used to driving, but it's a great car." Wade handed her the keys and smiled.

The man could make a woman swoon when he smiled. Anytime he turned that gorgeous smile on her, she felt like a teenager with butterflies in her stomach.

"I've driven bigger," she retorted as she took the keys from his hand.

"Have you now? Just how big have you driven, Blue Eyes?" Wade raised an eyebrow as he used the nickname he'd started to use a few weeks earlier.

"Wouldn't you like to know?" She smirked as she got into the new Land Rover.

"You bet I would." He winked.

Jess knew she was probably blushing and quickly started the vehicle. After Wade told her some of the features of the SUV, she waved, then drove away from the sexy man.

Jess would never admit it to her father, or anyone, but driving the new vehicle home was heaven. It was comfortable, warm, and drove like a dream. She'd bought her Honda ten years earlier because it was more economical. Over the last year, she knew it was only a matter of time before it died for good.

Her dad was probably right. If she asked, Wade would be able to get her a good deal on a vehicle. It would also mean she'd have to see the hot mechanic more often. If only she had time to date because she'd definitely let Wade Rivers know she was interested.

It was a pleasure to see her bed when she got home. With a huge sigh, Jess snuggled into her pillow and closed her tired eyes. Over the last ten years, she'd watched her younger sister and seven of her cousins find love, get married, and start families. At almost thirty-five years old, Jess was practically an old maid, at least by her grandmother's standards.

It wasn't that she was unhappy, because she loved her shop and teaching at the center. The problem was Jess didn't enjoy her job as a police officer as much as she thought she would.

If she quit the Newfoundland Police Department, it would disappoint her father. He'd been so proud when she received her shield. Jess also loved working with her four cousins. John and James both ran separate units with the Hopedale division of the NPD. Nick worked with the department for special victims and Aaron was part of the homicide division. They were highly respected with the NPD and Jess hated to have them look at her as a failure.

They were also happy in their careers and all four were married with children. The little green monster of jealousy sometimes showed its ugly head when she thought about how happy they were, but she would never admit that to her family. Her father's sister would be on the hunt searching high and low for a man for Jess if that information came out.

Her Aunt Cora was known to everyone as Cora the Cupid. Cora Nightingale had an uncanny ability to know when two people belonged together. As farfetched as it sounded, she'd never been wrong. The thought of enlisting Cora to help Jess find the love of her life was humiliating.

Jess flopped onto her stomach and snatched her phone from the night table. It was a little after nine in the evening and she wondered when she became that person. The one who was in bed before ten on a Friday night.

"I really need to get a life," Jess grumbled to herself.

"Yes, you do."

Jess flipped over at the sound of the amused voice. She tumbled out of bed and her ass hit the floor with a hard thud.

"Jesus Christ, Pam. You could have told me you were here." Jess rubbed her bottom as she stood up.

"Sorry, I thought I told you I'd be staying here tonight." Pam snickered as she sat on the foot of the bed.

Pam was Cora's only child and recently started to hide out in Jess' apartment to escape her mother's matchmaking. An old flame of Pam's arrived in town a year earlier and Cora continued to invite Damon Blackwood to every evening meal without telling Pam.

Damon was a former sniper for the Canadian Army and came to Newfoundland to help out an old friend. That friend happened to be the cousin of Aaron's wife. He also started a job with Newfoundland Security Services that was owned by her cousin Keith O'Connor.

Why Pam fought the potential happily-ever-after with Damon was beyond Jess. Not only was the man completely sexy, but it was obvious to anyone who saw him with Pam that he was head-over-heels in love with her. For some reason, he always called her Trixie but neither he nor Pam would say why.

"Yeah, you did. I didn't hear you come in. I'm exhausted." Jess sat back on the bed.

"I promise I'll be out of your hair by next weekend. My furniture will be arriving next Friday." Pam clapped her hands excitedly.

"It's okay. You've only been a slight pain in the ass." Jess held up her index finger and thumb.

"Can I just say, fuck you?" Pam shoved Jess.

"Nah, but I'm sure Damon wouldn't mind you doing it to him." Jess snickered.

"Don't start." Pam flopped back on the bed and groaned.

"Fine, but you'll spill the secret on that hunk of man one day." Jess poked Pam in the thigh. "Now, get out of my room. I need to get some sleep."

"Night, cuz." Pam left and closed the bedroom door.

Jess shook her head as she snuggled into her bed and got ready to fall asleep. She closed her eyes as she imagined how she would be if she had a guy madly in love with her. There was no way she'd be hiding out. Jess would run straight into his arms and never let him go.

"Then why aren't you trying to find that love?" Jess mumbled as she drifted off to sleep.

Jess jolted up in her bed with a start. The loud buzz of the smoke detector blared over her head. She tossed the blankets off and jumped out of bed, but her feet got tangled in the sheets. She managed to make it to the door of her bedroom without falling flat on her face. With all her school day lessons of what to do in the case of a fire, she touched the door and the knob to see if they were hot. When she found them cool to the touch, Jess yanked open the door and shouted to her cousin.

"Pam, where are you?" Jess ran into her small living room where Pam usually slept on the couch.

"What the hell is going on?" Pam held her hands over her ears as she attempted to shout over the sound of the alarm.

"I don't know." Jess sprinted into her small kitchen, but there wasn't any smoke or fire anywhere.

"How do we shut that fucking thing off?" Pam yelled.

Before Jess could answer, a loud pounding on her door made her stop, but it was the panicked shouts of her father that made her heart jump in her chest. Jess rushed to the door and heaved it open.

"You've got to get out of here." Her dad grabbed her arm and tugged her down the steps behind him.

"Dad, what's going on?" Jess asked.

"Your car is on fire," her father yelled.

Jess managed to keep herself upright as her dad grabbed her arm and practically dragged her down the steps from the apartment. As she hurried down the stairs, she glanced up. For the first time, Jess noticed the black smoke swirl around from the front of the garage.

"Pam, come on," Jess yelled her.

"I'm behind you," Pam shouted.

As Jess landed on the bottom step, she could see the black smoke rise toward the sky. The vehicle she'd parked not ten feet from the garage was completely engulfed in flames. It was at that moment she remembered it wasn't her car.

"That's not my car. That's the loner from the garage." Jess glanced at her father.

"Fuck. Wade's about to get a piece of my fucking mind. Why would he give you a death trap?" Her father growled as he held the phone to his ear.

"Dad, it's…" Jess stopped when her father glared at her.

While he continued to rant about giving his daughter a piece of shit, he guided her and Pam far away from the burning SUV. Thankfully, the garage was not attached to the main house and stood far enough away that the home wasn't in immediate danger.

"Wade, what the fuck are you doing giving my daughter a piece of shit? The fucking thing is on fire in my driveway." Her dad sounded as if he was about to roar like an angry bear.

Wade wouldn't have allowed her to take the vehicle if he thought it could be dangerous. Jess knew that, and her father did as well. She'd heard her father tell people how much he thought of Wade. Her dad wouldn't trust anyone else with his vehicles.

The blaring sound of the fire engines brought Jess out of her thoughts, and she turned back to the burning car. As firefighters poured out of the vehicles to prepare to extinguish the fire, Jess felt Pam grab her hand.

"What do you mean, what am I talking about? The car you loaned my daughter is on fire in my driveway. I'm sure I'm speaking English and if you can't hear those fucking sirens, then you need a hearing aid. I came out to get the paper and it was up in flames." Her father's face was flushed with anger.

"I hope Wade has insurance," Jess muttered mostly to herself.

"The way Uncle Kurt looks right now; I hope he has life insurance too," Pam whispered next to Jess' ear.

"Well, get your ass out here. That car is not worth a piece of shit now," her father snapped and then plunged the phone back into his pocket.

Ten minutes later, her mother, her Uncle Sean, Aunt

Kathleen, and Kristy were next to her on the front step of her parents' house. The firefighters sprayed the car until the flames died and the only thing left was a charred frame of what used to be a vehicle.

"Is everyone okay?" Sean asked as he glanced around the group of people.

"Yeah, nobody was in the thing, but it looks like my garage door is fucked," her dad grumbled.

"Thank heavens nobody was hurt." Kathleen pressed her hand against her chest.

The rest of the conversation disappeared when Jess saw Wade pull around the fire truck. One of the firefighters stepped in front of the tow truck to stop him, but Wade swerved around the pissed-off firefighter and pulled the tow truck into the end of the driveway, away from the smoldering remains of the SUV.

"He got here fast." Her mom stepped behind Jess and Pam.

"I'm so damn sorry," Wade said as he stepped next to Jess and her family.

"You fucking better be," her dad fumed.

"Kurt Patrick O'Connor, watch yer language. I'm sure da young fella didn't expect da car ta catch fire." Nanny Betty whacked Jess' dad on the arm.

Jess hadn't seen her grandmother arrive, but that didn't

surprise her. The woman could be like a ninja sometimes. Elizabeth Power O'Connor, otherwise known to everyone as Nanny Betty, was the matriarch of the O'Connor family, and no matter how old any of them got, they all knew who was in charge.

"Sorry, Mudder," her father mumbled.

Jess turned back to Wade to meet his stunned expression. His jaw hung open and his beautiful grey-blue eyes widened. Jess knew the look well. People gave the same one every time they saw her father, uncle, or cousins back down from her five-foot-tall grandmother.

"Ummm… well, yeah. I'll make sure I get you another vehicle, Jess. I don't know what could've happened. This car just came off the lot two weeks ago." Wade glanced back to where one of his mechanics started to tow the burned-out car onto the flatbed of the truck.

Everett Kennedy worked for Wade. Jess had never seen him without a huge smile on his face. So when he turned around and the only expression on his face was pure rage, it surprised Jess. Without the smile, he looked mean.

"How could a new car catch on fire?" Jess asked the question but hadn't meant to say it out loud.

"I don't know, but I'll try to find out." Wade glanced back at Everett and nodded.

"Wade, what's wrong?" Her dad seemed to sense something

in the way Wade and Everett exchanged glances.

"It's nothing. Well… it could be something. We've had some strange shit happen at the new place over the last week or so. Tools broke, tires with holes in them, but this is the first time something like this." Wade's expression was filled with anxiety and Jess crossed her arms to keep from reaching out to comfort him.

"Do you want me to have John or James look into it?" Her father's anger with Wade faded.

"I don't think that's necessary." Wade shoved his hands into his jeans pockets and without thinking, Jess dropped her eyes to his zipper.

"I think it's necessary." Everett's voice had her attention.

"Everett," Wade growled.

"No, Wade. Kurt, there's been way too much shit going on at the garage over the last two weeks. Besides the stuff Wade told you, there's been more. Wade's had to shell out thousands of dollars because cars got keyed overnight, graffiti sprayed on the doors and tow trucks, but this is the first time it could have physically hurt someone." Everett's voice seemed to get louder.

"Don't you have security cameras on the lot?" Jess was sure she'd seen them there.

"Yeah, but whoever is doing it managed to get around them. The only thing we've caught was a hand with a spray paint can." Everett pulled out his phone and after he tapped it a couple of times, he held it up. "That's the video of the guy spraying the lens of the camera."

Jess studied the video as Everett restarted it several times. The only thing visible was a gloved hand spraying the lens with what looked like black paint. She raised her eyes and they met Wade's.

As if all the sound around her disappeared, her gaze locked with his and her heart thudded in her chest. She felt a familiar flutter in her belly as his eyes flicked down to her lips, and instinctively she licked them.

"Jess?" She barely heard Pam's voice but turned at the sound of her name.

"What?" She almost groaned when she saw her Aunt Cora grinning next to Pam.

"I knew he was out there somewhere." Cora grinned as she blatantly stared at Wade.

"Cora," her father growled and Jess prayed for the ground to open up and swallow her.

"What?" her aunt responded innocently.

"One girl married is enough," her father snapped.

"I'm never wrong," Cora quipped as she walked up to Wade. "I'm Cora Nightingale. I'm Kurt's sister and Jess' aunt."

Wade glanced at Jess in confusion. He obviously didn't know about her aunt's reputation, but when Jess heard a snicker behind her, she turned to glare at Pam.

"It's nice to meet you, Mrs. Nightingale." Wade shook Cora's hand.

"Call me Cora. After all, we're practically family." Her aunt cupped Wade's large hand between hers.

"Cora, Goddamn it," her father groaned.

"Me girl is never wrong." Nanny Betty turned and disappeared into the house behind Kathleen and Jess' mother.

"Shoot me now." Jess sighed as she dropped her face into her hands.

"Why should Isabelle and I be the only ones to go through this torture?" Pam whispered next to Jess' ear.

"Shut up, or I'll tell her you've been hiding at my place," Jess threatened with her teeth clenched and Pam quickly pressed her lips together.

"Wade, I'm gonna get John to send someone over to the garage to look around." Her dad seemed desperate to change the subject.

"Jess is going back to work tomorrow. Why don't you get her to look into it?" Cora glanced between Jess and Wade.

"Cora, don't you have something to do?" Her father narrowed his eyes and glared at his sister.

"Nope." Cora grinned as she wrapped her arm around Jess.

"She's a wonderful police officer."

"Cora. Go. Home," her father yelled.

"Fine, but you might as well get used to the idea of another daughter taking that long walk. Wade, it was lovely to meet you. Don't let that grump keep you from coming to visit more often." Cora winked at Wade and made her way back to her house.

Jess managed to keep from bolting up the steps to her apartment. Mostly because the fire chief hadn't said it was safe. Pam linked her arm with Jess' and didn't even try to hide her amusement.

"We should go," Wade said a few seconds later.

"I'll call John. He'll get someone out there as soon as possible." Her dad seemed to relax when Cora went home.

"Thanks, Kurt." Wade turned to Jess. "And again, I'm so sorry about all this. I'll look at your car right away."

"Thanks." Jess hated that he felt so bad. "But it wasn't your fault."

"I appreciate the understanding. I'm so glad you weren't hurt." Wade gave her a half smile as he turned and followed Everett to the truck.

"He's so gorgeous." Jess turned to where her sister leaned against the rail surrounding the front deck.

"Shut up, Kristy." Jess narrowed her eyes and turned to head toward her steps.

"She's never wrong," Kristy teased.

"Kristy, shut it." Jess chuckled at her father's annoyed roar.

Kristy rolled her eyes, but she was right. Cora was never wrong. She'd brought practically every couple in her family together. The thought made Jess' heart thud in her chest, even though she wasn't about to get her hopes up.

Jess was attracted to Wade and she sensed a hint of interest from him as he'd stood next to her in the driveway. The question was, did she have time to get to know the man Cora deemed her perfect match?

# Chapter 2

Wade stared at the remains of his two-week-old personal vehicle. He didn't permit anyone to drive it, but he wouldn't let Jess leave without something to drive. One look into those diamond-blue eyes and he would've given her his right arm if he thought she needed it. She didn't know he'd given her his personal car and he made sure nobody let it slip.

Considering her car spent more time in his garage over the last few weeks than it had on the road, Wade wondered how long before it broke down for good. He couldn't understand her attachment to the piece-of-shit, ten-year-old Honda Civic, but she seemed determined to hold on to it. Newfoundland winters tended to take a toll on cars no matter how good they were and Jess' hunk of junk was proof.

His heart almost stopped when Kurt called him on Friday to tell him the car had gone up in flames. Wade told her it was a great ride and completely safe. The Land Rover shouldn't have caught on fire, but there it was on his lot, nothing but a charred frame of what used to be a two-week-old SUV. The worst part was they'd probably never find out what started the fire.

Wade turned and made his way into the garage. Monday morning was usually busier than the rest of the week. Between appointments and cars towed to his lot, it often took the best part of the morning to get all the work orders sorted out. He wanted to make sure all his technicians had a job to work on before he tackled Jess' car. He promised to get to it as soon as possible and he wouldn't disappoint her.

"I'm guessing your car is insured." Curtis Powell, one of the mechanics, glanced up from the work order in his hand as Wade walked by him.

"Yes." Wade nodded as he took the clipboard the shop foreman handed him.

Harry Saunders was Wade's right-hand man and one of the best mechanics in the city. Wade was lucky to have the man working with him. Harry was a good friend of Wade's father and jumped at the chance to invest in the business. Wade wanted him to be a full partner, but he told Wade that he only wanted twenty percent and a job for his wife. Wade hired Josie as the receptionist and appointment coordinator right away.

"You best call the insurance company right away. They're gonna want to look at the vehicle before they pay." Harry tossed his head in the direction of the destroyed car.

"I will." Wade sighed as he handed Harry back the clipboard.

"I'm telling you something's funny with all this shit going on here lately." Logan Hutton took a work order from Harry.

"It could be a faulty starter or the remote starter could have shorted out." Dwayne Cleary stuck his head through the window that opened between the front office and the garage.

"Either way, nothing can be done except getting to work on the things we can fix." Harry waved his hand, letting the technicians know chat time was over.

"You're a fucking slave driver, Harry," Everett shouted as he made his way to his bay.

"Can't make money sitting around gossiping like old women," Harry shouted and jumped back when a slender hand reached out from behind the desk to slap his arm.

"The only ones I ever hear gossiping around here are the men," Josie retorted.

Wade loved the relationship that Harry and Josie had. The couple were married for more than thirty years but never had children. Wade wasn't sure if it was by choice or if it had been out of their hands.

"I've got you tied up with the pretty cop's car for the morning." Harry winked.

Wade didn't say a word as he took the work order and made his way to the back of the work bays. He'd put her car in the bay the day it was towed into the shop and told Harry he would be the only one to work on it.

The hood of the vehicle was already raised and the first thing he did was get into the car to start it. As soon as he eased on the accelerator, there was a pop and the car backfired. Since the car had already had a tune up the first time Jess brought it in, he had a feeling the little car was toast. Either the timing was off, or it was a more serious engine issue.

"She needs to bury that thing." Everett stepped next to the open car door.

"I know, but she has some weird attachment to this piece of shit." Wade got out of the car and walked around to the front.

"Might be the timing belt." Everett rested his hip against the side of the car.

"We both know what it is. The fucking engine is shot. It's going to cost more to replace it than what the car is worth." Wade sighed.

"I guess you'll have to call her and see what she wants you to do." Everett grinned. "Or I can call her."

"I'll call her. You hit on her enough when she comes in here, asshole. Besides, I'm pretty sure Harry gave you a job to work on." Wade glared at Everett.

"Waiting on Harry to bring me a fuel pump." Everett chuckled.

"Harry got the fuel pump, Kennedy. Now stop teasing him about his sweetie." Harry snorted when Wade tossed a rag at him.

Wade stalked to his office and shoved the door open. The sight that greeted him made him roar with anger. The entire office was a complete disaster with papers and file folders scattered over the floor as well as file cabinets tipped over. Everything that was on his desk the day before now sat on the floor. The sight of his cup and framed pictures shattered against the wall made him clench his fists. Wade's daughter gave him the mug for Father's Day three years earlier and had been so proud that she'd bought it herself. Then there were the pictures of his family that he'd proudly displayed all around his office. Now they were in a broken heap on the floor.

"Wade, what's… Fuck," Harry growled next to him.

"How the fuck did they get in the building?" Wade shouted.

"I don't know. You were the last one out of here Friday," Harry yelled back.

Their back and forth was halted by the buzz of the main entrance. Before he had a chance to say another word, Josie called out to him. Wade slammed his office door and clomped to the customer area with Harry behind him.

"Hey, Wade." James O'Connor leaned on the counter.

"I'm guessing Kurt sent you?" Wade reached out and shook James' hand.

"Yeah, John's off today and I needed to come to town anyway." James glanced around the front.

James was one of Kurt's seven nephews. John, James, Nick,

and Aaron were police officers, while Ian followed in his own father's footsteps and became a doctor. Mike was a lawyer, and Keith owned a security company and construction company.

All the brothers brought their personal vehicles to Wade, which was why he knew them. It was also how he met his favorite O'Connor.

Jess made him feel like a teenager from the moment he'd set eyes on her. His heart thundered in his chest and it was almost impossible not to be hypnotized by her natural beauty. He'd get sweaty palms whenever she was near him, but thankfully, he managed to speak like a normal person when she was around.

Wade had never experienced that instant attraction to anyone in his life. It was why the effect she had on him threw him for a loop. He didn't believe in love at first sight although his mother described it as having the wind knocked out of you but still being able to breathe.

Wade never had an issue getting a date in the past. He had his fair share of one-night stands, a fact of which he wasn't proud of. One of those evening romps resulted in his daughter, Ocean.

Wade met her mother at the university bar the week they graduated. Wade and Sky both completed degrees in business. A little too much rum, two oversexed twenty-three-year-olds, and nine months later, Wade was a father.

Wade wanted to help support his child, but Sky Pushman

didn't want to be a parent. She warned Wade if he didn't take the baby, Sky would give her up for adoption. He immediately went to his parents and asked them what he should do. They told him they were behind him whatever he wanted to do.

Sky signed away her parental rights without hesitation and hadn't looked back. Wade raised Ocean with the help of his parents and his sister. When he opened his repair shop, he bought a house with an in-law suite for his parents and a small apartment in the basement for his sister.

People thought it was strange, but it worked for them. The thing that bothered him the most was Ocean never met her mother but only asked about her once. Wade told her that her mom wasn't prepared to be a parent and she hadn't asked about Sky since.

"Uncle Kurt said you've been having some issues." James' voice brought Wade out of his thoughts.

"We just found another one." Harry leaned on the counter next to Wade.

"Want to show me?" James nodded toward the back.

"Someone trashed my office." Wade motioned for James to follow while Josie dealt with the customer that entered.

Wade pushed open the office door and was about to walk inside. James grabbed Wade's arm to stop him. James shook his head as he pulled out his phone.

"Hey, send a team over to Wade's Auto Service on Torbay

Road. I need to check for prints in Wade's office because someone trashed it over the weekend." James used a pen to pull the door closed.

Wade couldn't believe someone would do this. His garage was one of the best in the city and had gotten so busy over the last few years he'd had to move to a bigger building. He'd also hired more technicians and was in the process of adding extra ramps. If someone was out to sabotage his business, then they were off to a good start. He started to regret the move.

"Do you need to go into the office for anything?" James asked after he ended the call.

"I was about to call your cousin to let her know her engine is toast," Wade explained.

"She's not going to be happy with that news." James chuckled.

"What is it with that car? She doesn't want to part with it no matter how much trouble it is." Wade shook his head.

"I think it has something to do with it being the first vehicle she bought herself." James crossed his arms over his chest.

"That would do it." Wade forced half a smile.

"Yeah, I still have the hood ornament off the first car I bought." James laughed.

"I still have the first truck I bought and she runs like a

dream." Harry cut in.

While they chatted, James made his way around the garage, taking pictures of the things Wade hadn't fixed yet. Two other officers from the forensics team checked his office for evidence and fingerprints, but Wade was overwhelmed with it all.

"By the way, I told Jess what you said. I've never heard her curse so much in her life." James shook his head as he clicked a few pictures of the graffiti sprayed on the back of the garage.

"Did she say what she wanted to do?" Wade walked with James, but he was disappointed he didn't get the chance to talk to her.

"No, but she'll probably get back to you." James held out his hand.

"What do I do now?" Wade shook James' hand.

"Keep track of anything that happens and call me right away." James handed Wade a card. "That's my personal cell phone number. Use it if anything happens."

"I could just call the station." Wade was surprised James would give out his personal phone.

"I was told you're practically part of the family or you will be." James winked.

"Wait? What?" Wade stared at James.

"I heard you met Aunt Cora Friday." James grinned.

"Yeah, so?" Wade shrugged.

"She's known to our family as Cora the Cupid." James shoved his phone into his pocket.

"I don't get it." Wade shook his head.

"Oh, trust me; you will." James smirked as he walked through the exit.

"What the fuck?" Wade stared at the back of James' head as he walked away.

After lunch, Wade headed to the office to clean up. Harry had the mechanics under control, which gave Wade time to take care of his office. Knowing the room was a disaster irritated him because he usually kept it in perfect order. Until he cleaned up, Wade wouldn't be able to concentrate on anything else.

Wade had just started to pick up the papers from the floor when the door of his office opened and his sister entered. Carla graduated from university at the beginning of the summer and was in the middle of a job search. While his sister waited for the perfect job, she helped him out with Ocean and some things around the garage.

"Josie told me what happened. I thought since Ocean is at her friend's I'd come back and help you clean this mess." Carla tossed her purse on top of the desk.

"I'd appreciate it. I'll pay you for your time," Wade said but turned when something hit him in the back.

"I'm not helping to get paid, jerk." Carla glared at him.

"I know, but you're not working and I'm sure the extra money won't go astray." Wade picked up the balled-up piece of paper she'd tossed at him.

Carla plopped down on the floor as she started to pull all the papers toward her. At twenty-six years old, his sister was ready to start a career as a teacher, but except for a few days substituting, she wasn't having any luck.

Carla had been a surprise to his parents almost ten years after Wade was born. They didn't think his mom could have any more children. After his birth, she'd suffered several miscarriages and had all but given up. Then almost exactly ten years later, Carla was born.

Both of their birthdays were in March with his on the second and Carla's on the first. His parents always made sure they both felt special on their birthdays growing up, but he didn't care. He loved Carla and would walk through the fires of hell for her.

"You'll never guess who I saw at the mall today," Carla chattered as she organized the papers.

"Who?" Wade asked distractedly.

"Sky," Carla gagged on the name.

"I thought she left for the mainland." Wade didn't care one way or the other if Ocean's mother was back in Newfoundland.

Sky made it clear she didn't want anything to do with her

daughter. It wasn't that she was a bad person; she just didn't have a maternal bone in her body. Sky was all about her career. When Wade left the hospital with Ocean two days after she was born, Sky had wished him good luck and that was it.

"I still can't believe she gave you custody of Ocean and walked away," Carla continued.

"Some people are just not meant to be parents." Wade placed the last of the file folders into the cabinet.

Carla piled the rest of the papers in the to-be-filed basket and blew out a breath. Wade glanced around his office, impressed that they practically had everything back in place. His mood dived when he glanced at the broken mug that he didn't have the heart to throw away.

"I'll get some new frames for you and see if I can find another cup like that online." Carla interrupted his thoughts.

"I know, but I'll know it's not the one Ocean gave me." Wade placed the broken pieces on the cabinet behind his desk.

He didn't want to think about how upset his daughter would be to know the first thing she'd bought him with her own money was broken.

"Ocean said her friend's mom would drive her home around eight. I guess we can go now." Carla picked up her large purse.

Wade couldn't understand why such a tiny woman would need a purse she could use as a suitcase. Carla would spend most of her time searching through the damn thing when she looked for her keys or phone.

"Yeah, I'm going to make sure everything is locked up first. Wait out front." Wade closed his office door and for the first time, locked it.

Wade walked through the service bays and gave each of the doors a shake to make sure they were locked. When he was satisfied everything was secure, he started to leave the garage area, but a prickle at the back of his neck caused him to spin around. There was nothing behind him. Wade shook his head as he limped back to the front of the building.

Carla sat behind the counter with her phone in her hands, probably checking out social media. She was obsessed with it. Snapchat, Instagram, Facebook, and his sister was a pro with all of them.

"Ready?" Wade asked as he made his way to the front exit.

"Yep." She smiled and hopped down off the stool.

Wade punched in the alarm code, then walked outside and locked the door. He shook it several times to make sure it was locked and opened his phone to check the security monitors. All of them seemed to be working, not that it helped, but he hoped it would discourage the assholes screwing with his building.

"I'll meet you at home," Carla shouted as she hopped into her car.

Wade watched as she drove out of the lot, but another chill skittered up his spine and he casually turned to check the lot. The only things he saw were cars and an older couple stroll down the street.

"Okay, go home, Wade," he whispered to himself.

Wade limped toward his truck and cringed in pain as he climbed into his pick-up truck. He hadn't had a chance to rest his leg all day and knew he'd probably suffer for it all night. Wade lived with pain since he'd been hurt eight years earlier. He did all the therapy, but because of the severity of the injury, he'd always have a limp and discomfort.

Wade didn't regret what he did to be in the condition. If he hadn't run into the street to push the little girl out of the way, she would've been killed by the drunk driver flying down a residential street. It was much better for Wade to get hit by the car than the six-year-old girl.

The only thing it cost Wade was an artificial hip, a rod in his femur, several ugly scars on his leg, and months of painful therapy. All that was nothing compared to a little girl's life. The insurance settlement also helped him with his dream of opening his own garage, so Wade figured it was a win for him. The man who'd hit him lost his license for the rest of his life and that was the best thing that could have happened.

Wade pulled into the driveway of his two-story home fifteen

minutes later. It was on the outskirts of the city of St. John's with plenty of land for his dog to run and play. It was great for his parents as well because they loved to garden.

"Wade, I've put supper in the microwave for you. Carla told me you were on the way home." His mother sat on the front deck in the swing Wade and his father had installed for her.

There were even times during the winter she'd sit outside in it with a blanket wrapped around her and a hot cup of tea. It was the only thing she ever asked for and Wade made sure she had it.

"Thanks, Mom." He bent down and kissed her cheek.

"You're limping a lot today." His mom raised an eyebrow.

"I was swamped today and never got a chance to sit." He smiled down at one of the most important people in his life.

Renee Rivers worked hard her entire life as a housewife and mother. She left her teaching job to raise her family and she was always there for them when they needed her. His dad worked as a fisherman and retired two years earlier after he'd suffered a mild stroke.

Seamus Rivers was a hard man to convince to slow down, but after the stroke, he was scared. He never ate properly but since he'd always been active, the man was in good shape. When he had to slow down and give up his boat, depression set in for a short time. It was only thanks to Wade's mom that he snapped out of it.

She introduced him to gardening when Wade built a

greenhouse in the back of the house. Since then, his mom and dad grew fresh vegetables. What they didn't use, they donated to food banks.

"You're just like your father." His mom shook her head.

"I love you too, Mom." Wade chuckled and walked into the house.

Wade finished the left-over supper and was in the middle of cleaning the plate when a car pulled into his driveway. His heart almost stopped when he realized it was a police cruiser.

"Now what the fuck happened?" He grabbed the dish towel and headed out of the house.

# *Chapter 3*

"I can't believe the dresses you have here." Isabelle gasped as she turned around in another dress she had added to her list as her future attire for the fundraiser at the end of September.

"My sister is the best and now that she's partnered with Pam, we'll be the best-dressed women at this shindig." Emily grinned while she held up a dress in front of Jess.

Great, another dress to add to her closet full of dresses she'd never wear again. Jess was probably the only one of all the women roaming around Pam's shop who didn't want to wear a dress. Well, except for Sandy. Ian's wife wasn't happy about the whole dress situation either.

The fundraiser was usually held during the end of July but had been delayed because the usual venue had been overbooked. They moved it to the end of September instead of canceling it because it raised a ton of money for the children's hospital.

Jess glanced around the large dressing room at the women in her family. Her sisters Kristy and Isabelle continued to search through the racks, full of excitement. Emily, Keith's wife, thumbed through a book Elaine handed her. James wife Marina stood at the mirror scanning the beautiful green dress she wore.

"This color would be so great for you." Pam held a dress up in front of Jess.

"It is, but that style doesn't suit that incredible body." Emily's sister, Elaine, tilted her head as she scrutinized the dress.

Elaine Bradshaw followed her dream of designing clothes several years earlier. She opened an online store and her business soared. After Pam opened her store, Elaine approached her about forming a partnership. Elaine took care of the online shop and Pam ran the store. They were doing great and had named the company *Cupid's Closet*.

"Jess, I really need you to train me." Emily sighed.

"Your body is perfectly fine," Jess assured the woman.

"I know I'm not overweight or anything, but since I had Noah and Patrick, I'm jiggly where I wasn't jiggly before." Emily plopped down on one of the overstuffed chairs in the dressing area of the store.

"Is my cousin not giving you enough hot and sweaty sex? If he's not, I'll knock him over the head." Kristy sat next to Emily.

"No, Kristy. I'm getting plenty of that." Emily rolled her eyes. "I just think I need to work out more. I've got a two-year-old and a three-year-old to run after. By the end of the day, I'm exhausted."

"Yep, that's the way it works." Sandy walked out of the dressing room with a beautiful red dress that clung to her every curve

Sandy, like Jess, worked out six days a week. She was a police officer, but her principal employment was with Keith's security firm. Sandy was also the mother to four children which was probably why Sandy worked so hard to stay in shape.

"You're a big help." Isabelle snorted.

"She's not wrong," Stephanie agreed.

Stephanie was married to John. Stephanie had struggled to get pregnant at the beginning of her marriage, but the doctors couldn't find anything wrong. So, when a doctor suggested they take a vacation to relax, they made a trip to Hawaii. It worked because nine months later, they had a baby. The couple now had a three-year-old boy and a seven-year-old girl.

Billie, Lora, and Bethany were in the dressing rooms changing. The three women were married to Mike, Nick, and Aaron respectively. Jess loved every one of the women in her family, but she felt out of place when they talked about their individual families.

That was the way it went when they all got together. Kids, men, and relationships. It was something Jess had almost given up on. Jess had a successful flower shop, Karate classes she loved to teach, and the fact she'd made it through the police academy, but she would give it all up to have what they had.

"Guys, I need to get to work." Jess hadn't expected to take so long to pick out a dress.

"Okay, honey. We'll pick out your dress on your next day off." Kristy hugged her.

"You're telling me I'm going to have to do this again, aren't you?" Jess groaned.

"I love you, Jess." Kristy smiled as Jess rolled her eyes.

"We love you too," Sandy called as Jess walked through the door into the warm fall breeze.

She adjusted her bag on her shoulder and made her way across the street. Pam's shop was almost directly across from the station, which was the only reason she'd allowed herself to stay so long dress shopping before heading in for a twelve-hour shift.

Jess' shift was slow, but she knew it wouldn't last long. She'd knew between six and ten she'd get called into St. John's a lot. It was why she started to make her way out of Hopedale and toward the city to grab a bite to eat.

At ten minutes after six, Jess pulled into the parking lot of the local Dollar Store and started to fill out a report for a traffic stop when a call came over the radio. A local Piper's store had nabbed a shoplifter and had the person detained until the police arrived.

Jess was practically on the doorstep of the store, so she took the call. According to the dispatcher, the shoplifter was a minor. Jess hoped it wasn't one with a major attitude.

"I'll probably have to bring some bratty kid home to parents that probably won't give a shit what their kid did." Jess stepped out of her cruiser and placed her cap on her head.

The store manager was a major asshole. The first thing Mr. Edgar Barter complained about was how long it took for the police to get to the store. Jess managed to apologize but inwardly rolled her eyes because it had only been a little more than ten minutes since he called.

"The brat said she wasn't stealing, but I caught her hauling this chain out of her pocket." He held up the tackiest necklace Jess had ever seen.

"She was alone?" Jess asked.

"No, there was another little bitch, but she ran off before I could grab her," he spat.

Edgar walked into the office ahead of Jess and immediately started to berate the young girl inside the room. The girl was probably no more than twelve or thirteen years old. She sat with her feet propped up on the manager's desk as she played with her phone.

"Get your dirty shoes off my desk, brat," Edgar shouted.

"Sir, there's no need for name calling." Jess couldn't hold her tongue after hearing him already say the other girls were bitches.

"I call it like I see it." He stomped behind his desk and plopped down in the chair.

"What's your name?" Jess asked the young girl.

"Didn't you hear Fat Ass? It's brat." The girl glared at Jess.

"Watch your mouth, young lady. If you don't give me your name, I'll have to take you to the station until we find out who you are," Jess warned.

Jess could tell the kid wasn't as badass as she put off. The flash of fear in her eyes when Jess mentioned the police station was evidence of that. It was probably a situation where the girl wanted to show off for her friends.

"My name is Ocean Rivers." The young girl dropped her head.

"Ocean Rivers?" The manager laughed. "That can't be true."

"Mr. Barter, please." Jess wondered if the name was real.

"It is my name," the girl snapped at the manager.

"Are you pressing charges?" Jess asked the manager.

"No, but she's not to come in here again." He dragged his fingers through his thinning hair as he stood up.

"Fine, come on. I'm going to bring you home to your parents." Jess opened the door.

She kept a close eye on Ocean as she slowly walked out of the office. Jess had her fair share of runners over the last year, including one who stomped on her toe. He'd practically knocked her down before he ran off. Her foot was bruised for days.

"I only have my dad." Ocean walked by Jess with her hands fisted at her sides.

"I need your address, and I need to know if anyone is at home now." Jess' heart went out to the young girl and wondered if this would be one of those situations where she brought a kid home to a drunk, unemployed dead beat who didn't give a damn about his kid.

"Yeah, he usually gets home around six." Ocean stood by the cruiser as Jess opened the back door.

Ocean hesitated and stared inside the back seat. It was another clue that she wasn't a girl who got in trouble with the law before. Without a second thought, Jess slammed the rear door and smiled at Ocean.

"Why don't you hop in front with me?" Jess opened the front door and Ocean quickly got in.

It was against protocol to allow the girl in the front seat, but something told her Ocean wasn't a bad kid. She looked nervous, but Jess didn't think it was because she was afraid to go home.

"How old are you?" Jess asked several minutes later as she turned onto the street where Ocean said she lived.

"I'll be thirteen in June." She stared out the window.

"It's just you and your dad?" Jess hated to pry.

"No. My Nana, Pop, and aunt live with us too." When Ocean

crossed her arms, Jess knew that was the end of the conversation.

The house wasn't what she expected. It was well maintained with two rose bushes on either side of the front steps that had lost their blossoms for the year. A double garage was on one side of the house and a covered porch ran all the way across the front of the house. She loved the style of the house and if it were in Hopedale, she'd love to own it.

Jess stepped out of the car and walked around the front to let Ocean out. When she opened the door, the girl hopped out like she'd been sat on hot rocks.

"Can I help you, Officer?" Jess turned and all the breath in her body whooshed out.

"Dad, she brought me home." Ocean sauntered by Jess and made her way toward the house.

"Stop right now, young lady." Wade's tone was calm but firm, reminding Jess of her own father.

"Dad," Ocean groaned but stopped next to him.

Ocean's last name finally clicked in Jess' brain. *Rivers.* Considering how much the man entered her thoughts, the last name should have given her a clue. Then again, she didn't know Wade had a daughter.

"What did she do?" Wade's eyes met hers and Jess found it hard to answer.

"I didn't do anything," Ocean whined.

"Quiet." Wade didn't look away from Jess.

"But, Dad…" Ocean pressed her lips together and stopped talking when Wade glared at her.

"We got a call that the manager of Piper's caught a shoplifter," Jess started.

"I didn't steal…" Ocean stopped again.

"For what it's worth, the other girl ran, but Ocean stayed." Jess felt terrible for the young girl.

"Ocean, what happened?" Wade did sound calm, but Jess could see the clench of his jaw.

"I can talk now?" Ocean snapped.

"Look here, little girl, you're lucky Sergeant O'Connor didn't drag you off to jail. Now, what happened?" Wade crossed his arms over his chest, and Jess bit her lip to keep a sigh from escaping.

"Kaylee wanted to go to Piper's. She said she was looking for something for her dad for his birthday. I didn't know she was going to steal it. Honest, Dad. When I told her she was going to get in trouble, Kaylee put a chain in my pocket. The manager walked up when I took it out to put it back, but Kaylee ran off and left me." By the time Ocean stopped talking she had tears streaming down her cheeks.

"Ocean, did you tell the manager that?" Jess asked.

"Yes, he called me a liar." Ocean sniffed. "He wouldn't let me call my dad or my nana. He kept telling me I was going to end up in juvenile detention."

Jess couldn't help but feel sorry for Ocean. She really seemed genuinely upset by her friend's actions. For some reason, Wade didn't seem affected by his daughter's confession.

"I thought you were supposed to be going to Addison's house?" Wade glanced at Jess then back to his daughter.

"We were at Addison's, but she didn't want to go to Piper's." Ocean wiped her hand across her cheeks.

"No, because she knows she's not supposed to be with that girl because she's bad news." Wade held out his hand.

"What?" Ocean glanced from her father's hand to his face.

"Phone." Wade wiggled his fingers.

"Dad," Ocean whined and stomped her foot.

Jess wanted to laugh because she, Isabelle, and Kristy had pulled that move more than once as teenagers. It never worked and only made matters worse most of the time.

"Phone, young lady," Wade ordered.

"This is so unfair." Ocean pulled her phone from her pocket and slapped it into her father's hand.

"iPad." Wade held out his hand again after he shoved his daughter's phone into his pocket.

"Dad." Ocean dropped her backpack on the ground and angrily yanked out an iPad.

"Now, inside and get ready for bed. No television, no computer, and you're grounded for two weeks." Wade pointed to the house.

"I didn't do anything." Ocean stomped her foot again.

"You may not have stolen anything, but you lied and were with someone I specifically told you to stay away from." Wade turned back to Jess and winced as he stumbled.

"I hate my life," Ocean shouted as she ran up the driveway to the house.

"She really didn't do anything." Jess felt the need to pick up for the girl.

"She did. She was supposed to be at Addison's house and Mrs. Fry was supposed to drive her home." Wade smiled. "She's twelve and likes to test me to my limit sometimes, but she's a good kid most of the time."

"My mom said my sisters and I were lucky we made it to adults. Nan told me once that girls are the most emotional children to raise." Jess hooked her thumbs into her Kevlar vest in an attempt to look casual.

"Great," Wade groaned.

"I bet she's still daddy's little girl," Jess teased.

"My little hellion too," Wade grumbled.

Her radio crackled, and the dispatcher called for an officer needed for a disturbance not far from Wade's house. Although she hated to leave, she knew she had to because she was technically on duty.

"I need to get going, but don't be too hard on Ocean." Jess smiled.

"I'll try not too." Wade's eyes dropped to her lips and Jess held her breath.

Every time she was near him, she wished she could read his thoughts. Did he want to kiss her? God, she was so pitiful. She was almost thirty-five, but whenever she was around Wade Rivers, she felt like an awkward teenager.

"Jess, I'm really sorry about the fire," Wade said as his eyes met hers.

"It wasn't your fault, Wade. Besides, nobody was hurt." Jess hated that he seemed to feel guilty about the car fire.

"I don't know what I would've done if you'd gotten hurt because of that car." Wade's voice seemed to drop into a whisper.

"I didn't, Wade." Jess took a step toward him but stopped when he moved back from her and reached into his pocket.

"By the way, I may have a car for you." Wade cleared his throat and glanced back at the house.

"What?" She had no idea what he was talking about.

"Your dad asked me to look for a good used car for you because he said you won't spend money on a new one." Wade smirked.

"I'm going to kill him." Jess clenched her teeth.

"I don't think that's a good thing for a police officer to say about the Chief." Wade chuckled.

"It is when he's my father," Jess returned.

"Jess, your car is toast. It will cost more than the car is worth to fix it. Even if you did fix it, I can't promise how long it will last. You could be stuck out in the middle of nowhere." Wade held out a card. "This is the guy selling the car. It's in great condition and the price is a steal for a five-year-old car with barely thirty-thousand kilometers on it. That's if you don't want to actually take your dad's advice and buy a new one."

"Don't you start too." Jess took the card.

She looked at it for several minutes before she raised her head again. It was difficult to maintain her composure around Wade, and Jess didn't like the out-of-control emotion.

"Thanks." She shoved the card into her back pocket.

"Let me know what you want me to do, but take my advice. Your car is not worth fixing." Wade gave her half a smile.

"I'll call you tomorrow and let you know what I'm going to

do." Jess sat in the cruiser.

"I'll look forward to your call. By the way, thanks for bringing Ocean home." Wade's hand was on the top of the car door.

"You're welcome." She smiled as he closed her door.

Jess backed out of his long driveway, but before she drove off, she glanced back. Wade stood in the driveway staring after her. She couldn't remember ever feeling the magnetic attraction she did with Wade. She'd once been madly in love with Jason Brenton, or at the time she thought she was, but even Jason didn't make her heart flutter the way Wade did.

Maybe she should take a gamble and ask Wade out. After all, it was the twenty-first century. She was a strong, independent woman and although she wasn't all soft and girly, she knew men found her body attractive. At least she'd been told that by her sisters and cousins' wives.

The problem was she wasn't that type of woman. As independent as she seemed to everyone, Jess wanted to be treasured in the same way her dad cherished her mom. Her father held doors open, pulled out chairs, and brought her little gifts. They weren't expensive, maybe a flower he picked from the garden, a cupcake he bought while he was in St. John's, or serving her breakfast in bed. They were affectionate and never missed a moment to tell the other how they felt. Jess and her sisters found it embarrassing as kids, but as an adult, Jess thought it was beautiful.

Her parents' love was timeless. They had mutual respect for what the other thought and felt. They weren't the only couple she looked up to in her family. Her Uncle Sean and Aunt Kathleen, and Uncle Brian and Aunt Cora were equally as in love. Then there were her cousins and her sister. They'd all found those fairy-tale loves Jess dreamed about.

"How weird is it that the tomboy slash flower-child wants the fairy-tale ending?" Jess muttered to herself as she pulled into the address of her next call. "Very weird."

Midnight felt as if it would never come, but when it did, Jess got tied up on a call at an apartment complex with a woman who'd been attacked by a neighbor. Thankfully, the lady's son stopped the assault before it went too far, but both were shaken.

"You don't need to stay." The woman gave Jess a weak smile as the paramedic checked her.

"I don't mind. Once your brother comes to get you, I'll head home," Jess assured the woman.

"Thank you, Sergeant O'Connor." The woman's voice was barely above a whisper.

"Call me Jess, and you're very welcome." Jess stepped back to allow the woman to be checked.

"How's she doing?" Jess turned at the familiar voice of her cousin Nick.

"Shaken but luckily the son stopped him before he could rape her." Jess held back the shudder that came over her at the thought of what the bastard tried to do.

"Fucking bastard," Nick growled through gritted teeth.

"That's a good name for him, but his actual name is Morton Gibbons. He ran off when her son ran after him with a bat," Jess explained as she kept her eye on the young boy who still looked ready to kill someone.

"Did they catch him?" Nick asked.

"Yeah, Blake just left with him," Jess said referring to one of her co-workers, Blake Harris. "I doubt it would be a good idea for him to come back to his own house any time soon." Jess nodded toward the boy.

"What's his name?" Nick was good with kids and Jess hoped he could talk some sense in the boy.

"His name is Raymond and the mother's name is June Higgens." When Jess glanced at her watch, she almost cursed when she saw it was almost one in the morning.

"Weren't you supposed to be off duty at midnight?" Nick turned back to her on his way to talk to Raymond.

"Yeah, but I didn't want to leave until her brother got here." Jess gave him half a smile.

"I got this, cuz. Go home and get some rest." Nick winked and then motioned his head toward the door.

When the man walked in, Jess recognized him immediately. He worked for Wade, but she didn't know his name. He looked completely frazzled as he rushed to his sister.

"June," he said as he pulled his sister into his arms.

"Logan," June choked.

"I told you to move away from that creep. I knew he would do something like this. I didn't like the way he leered at you." Logan held her tight against him.

"I know." June sobbed.

"Hey, Logan." Nick held out his hand.

"Nick, I'm glad you were on duty." Logan shook Nick's hand.

"Actually, I just got here. Jess was first on the call." Nick nodded toward her and Logan glanced in her direction.

"You own that frequent flyer piece-of-shit." He didn't release his sister, but he held out his hand to her.

"Yes, that's my car and it's not a piece of shit." Jess sighed.

"It's a ten-year-old Honda Civic that breaks down every week." Logan raised an eyebrow.

"Definitely a piece of shit." Jess and Nick turned to where Raymond sat on the sofa.

"See, even the kid knows." Nick laughed.

"On that note, June, I'm going to head off now. Nick will stay until you decide whether you're staying or if you're going somewhere else. You've got my card if you need anything or just need to talk." Jess ignored the snickers from Nick.

"She's coming with me," Logan answered.

"Logan." June pulled away from him and turned to Jess.

"Thank you so much." June wrapped her arms around Jess and hugged her. "I appreciate how sweet and compassionate you've been."

"You're welcome. If you need to talk, call." Jess smiled as she stepped back from June.

"Thank you, Jess." Logan held out his hand again. "By the way, Wade's a great guy."

With that statement, Logan walked his sister out of the living room, leaving Jess with her mouth hung open. She stared after him for several minutes before she heard Nick's chuckle.

"What?" Jess snapped at her cousin.

"I guess what A.J. told me was true. You got a little crush on Wade," Nick teased.

"Shut up, asshole." Jess spun around and practically stomped out of the house.

By the time she completed her last report and got back to her apartment, it was almost three in the morning. Being a police officer wasn't a regular job where employees could leave right at the end of a shift.

As she opened her apartment door, she felt her phone vibrate in her pocket. Jess pulled it out as she closed the door behind her. It was a text from Isabelle and Jess' guard immediately went on high alert. Not only because it was unusual for her sister to be up so late, but the message contained only one word in all capitals.

*Isabelle: HELP*

Jess tapped her sister's number as she unbuckled her utility belt and made her way to her bedroom. Isabelle's phone rang several times and then went to voicemail. Jess called her back a second time and after the third ring, Isabelle picked up.

"Oh my God," Isabelle whispered.

"What's wrong?" Jess dropped her utility belt on her dresser but waited before putting her weapon away because if her sister were in trouble, she'd need it.

"Jess, I did something really, really, really, bad. I mean colossally stupid." Isabelle's voice was barely audible.

"Okay, first, why are you whispering, and second, what the hell did you do?" Jess rolled her eyes.

Isabelle tended to be too hard on herself, so the situation probably wasn't as terrible as her older sister thought. As a perfectionist, Isabelle thought anything that wasn't done correctly would be considered a disaster.

She put her phone on speaker and stripped off her uniform after she locked up her weapon. She figured if she needed to go help her sister, she should probably change. Jess quickly pulled on a pair of yoga pants and an oversized t-shirt.

"I'm whispering because I don't want the person that's here to hear me." Isabelle kept her voice quiet.

"Who's there?" Jess was extremely tired and Isabelle had her utterly confused.

"Hold on a second," her sister grumbled.

Jess waited patiently as she listened to see if she could get some idea of what was going on. The only thing she heard for several minutes was the click of a door and what sounded like bare feet hitting the hardwood floor.

"Isabelle, what's going on?" Jess asked impatiently.

"Okay, so I've been really stressed at the restaurant because some weird shit happened. Mostly stuff that's just annoying and nobody seems to know what's going on," Isabelle explained.

"Go on." Jess flopped down on her bed.

"Anyway, tonight one of the fryers mysteriously started to leak out through the drain. The only way that would happen is if someone didn't close the valve all the way, but I know for a fact that I closed it tight. I always double-check after I clean them." Isabelle's babbling had to be going somewhere.

"Isabelle, get to the point," Jess grumbled.

"I slept with Roman," Isabelle spat out.

"Your chef? Ethan's best friend?" Jess almost choked on her laughter as she sat up straight in the bed.

Nick's wife introduced Isabelle to Roman Young a couple of years earlier, but Isabelle hadn't hired him right away. If Jess remembered correctly, he'd been working there for almost a year. Isabelle constantly told her how great he was in the kitchen.

Lora and her brother grew up with Roman. When Lora found out Isabelle needed a new chef, Lora suggested she call Roman. He'd moved back to Newfoundland after his mom passed away.

"Yes, that Roman," Isabelle snapped.

"Didn't you go out on a date with Ethan a little while ago? I didn't know you and Roman are seeing each other." Jess tried not to laugh at the panic in her sister's voice.

"That wasn't a date with Ethan. It was a… dinner and I'm not dating Roman. It's just that we were the only two left after everything was cleaned up. I was so damn pissed I had a shot or two of Newfie Screech. Okay, maybe six, and he did too, and then he walked me back to my house, and well, he's really hot, and it's been way too long, and…" Isabelle's voice trailed off.

"And you like him," Jess finished.

"Yes. No. Yes. Shit. I don't do one-night stands and I don't do my employees." Isabelle sounded as if she was going to burst out in tears.

"Isabelle, calm down. First of all, maybe this won't be a one-night stand, and you actually did do an employee." Jess snickered.

"Not. Helping." Isabelle groaned.

"I know. I'm sorry, but if you like him, what's wrong with you two going out?" Jess stifled a groan as she looked at her watch again.

"Because he's a big flirt. He reminds me of A.J. and Nick before they got married. He keeps calling me Tiger, but I have no idea why," Isabelle continued.

"Does he flirt with all the women at the restaurant or just you?" Jess knew Isabelle didn't like playboys.

"I don't know. I just know he does it with me. A lot." Isabelle sighed.

"Is he still there?" Jess asked.

"Yes, that's why I had to leave the bedroom," Isabelle responded.

"Look, you have a hot man in your bed and I'm assuming the sex wasn't awful." Jess laughed.

"So not awful. Amazing. Incredible. Freaking mind-blowing." Her sister sighed.

"Then don't complain. Just go with it." Jess rolled her eyes as she realized she probably should be taking her own advice.

"What if people find out?" Isabelle whispered.

"Isabelle, you're a thirty-seven-year-old adult woman. Who the hell cares if people find out?" Jess shook her head.

Growing up in a small Newfoundland community, it was hard to keep secrets. There were people in Hopedale who made a life of starting gossip and before all her cousins got married, the biggest gossip about the O'Connor family was the boys' playboy ways. Of course, that was only partly true. John, James, Ian, and Keith dated but not often. Mike, Nick, and Aaron were the ones who caused the story to spread.

Jess, her sisters, and Pam managed to keep their names out of the rumor mill. Of course, Jess wouldn't care about it anyway, but Isabelle seemed to be terrified that her name would be brought up in some sort of rumor that would ruin not only her reputation but her restaurant's as well.

"I don't need it getting out that I slept with one of my employees." Isabelle sounded so defeated.

Jess heard a soft gasp from Isabelle, then the deep chuckle of a male. Jess pressed her lips together to keep the snicker from coming out.

"Oh, umm. Gotta go," Isabelle stammered, but she didn't hang up her phone, so Jess listened to make sure her sister was okay.

"I woke up to an empty bed, Tiger." Roman's deep voice

echoed into the phone.

"Umm… sorry. I was… ah… thirsty," Isabelle stumbled over her words and it surprised Jess how Roman affected her confident sister.

"Did you have to order some water?" Roman chuckled.

"Huh?" Yep, Isabelle was head over heels by the sound of her.

"You were on the phone, Tiger." Roman's voice sounded louder.

"Stop calling me that, please." Isabelle groaned.

"Why? The name fits you." He must have moved closer to Isabelle because his voice was clearer.

"Why does that name fit me, Roman?" Isabelle practically whispered the words.

"I've watched you every day since I started to work for you. Not only because you're incredibly sexy, that's just a bonus. From what I see, you meet every characteristic of a Tiger person." Roman's voice sounded so seductive that Jess bit her lip.

"What's that supposed to mean?" Isabelle scoffed.

"You've got this air of authority when you walk into a room. I feel it every single time you're near me. You're calm and warm, but you're courageous and fearless. You're always in a hurry to get things done, and I've noticed you like to work alone. You're sensitive, passionate, and I would bet my last dime you're a romantic at heart." Roman sounded in awe of Isabelle.

Jess felt guilty listening to such an intimate conversation between Isabelle and Roman and quickly ended the call as she fell back on her bed. What she wouldn't do to have a man speak to her like Roman did to Isabelle.

She'd never had that hot romantic love that made her toes curl. Jess did love Jason, but if it had been real, she wouldn't have ended the relationship when he told her he'd leave if she joined the NPD. She knew at that moment they weren't meant to be.

Jess lay on her bed and stared at the ceiling. It was almost five in the morning and she was still wide awake. How that was possible, she didn't know. Jess needed to get some sleep because she'd be useless on her shift later in the day.

"I should have taken another week of vacation time." Jess sighed as she flopped over on her stomach.

As she closed her eyes, Wade popped into her thoughts, making her wonder if she should take a chance. After all, it wasn't the dark ages. Perhaps she should bite the bullet and ask him out for a drink.

"What's the worst he could say? No?" Jess whispered and snuggled into her pillow.

As much as she liked people to believe she was a modern woman and didn't need to be romanced, Jess wanted a man to sweep her off her feet and make her feel beautiful. The problem was, she could never see that happening for her.

Jess had never been a spontaneous person. It took her almost eight years to take the plunge and go into the police academy. However, she had decided to meet with John in the morning to make some changes in her life.

Jess thought being a police officer was something she wanted, but she'd come to realize that she was already doing what she loved. She needed to take her life back and get back to doing what she loved. Maybe then she'd have time for a love life.

# *Chapter 4*

Wade tossed and turned the entire night. Not only because he worried about his daughter, but because nightmares plagued his dreams. He'd been told it would subside over the years and they did for the most part. The problem was, whenever he was stressed or worried, they came back with a vengeance.

Then there was the pain in his overused leg. He refused to take the pain medication because they muddled his brain. The other problem was when he was in pain and didn't take the pills, he didn't sleep well. It was the reason he stood in his bathroom fresh out of the shower, coating his leg with the cream the therapist gave him to help with discomfort. He hadn't done any yoga for a few days, which was part of the reason he'd been able to maintain his pain over the years.

He stared at himself in the mirror. Wade's hair was wet and disheveled after he gave it a quick rub with the towel. His hair had receded a little, but at nearly thirty-six years old, he was probably lucky he still had any.

Wade scrubbed his hand over his cheeks and chin. He really

needed a shave, but he didn't have the energy and using a blade probably wouldn't be safe in his condition.

"Wade, are you up, son?" His father's voice floated into the bathroom from Wade's bedroom.

"Yeah, Dad," Wade called out as he wrapped the towel around his waist.

"All right, just checking. It's almost six." His father was always up before the sun and made sure nobody ever slept in.

As a former fisherman, his father found it hard to get out of the habit of being up at four in the morning. Wade knew as soon as he made his way to the kitchen, his dad would've coffee brewed, and his mom would have breakfast on the table.

Wade was spoiled, but it wasn't because he didn't want to do things himself. When he was laid up after the accident, they'd moved in and taken care of everyone. Once he was back on his feet, he'd convinced them to give up their house and he bought a house they could all live in.

"Wade, you look tired," his very observant mother said as he entered the kitchen.

"I'm fine, Mom." Wade forced a smile as he kissed his mother's cheek as he took the cup of coffee she held out to him.

"I heard you up at five this morning. That's not like you at all," she pushed and Wade stopped the urge to roll his eyes.

"Just getting an early start, Mom." Wade smiled at her when she placed the plate of boiled eggs and bacon in front of him.

"I heard you shouting, Wade." His mother crossed her arms over her chest like she did when he would get in trouble as a kid.

"It's just a nightmare." Wade winked at her and dug into his breakfast.

"Which only return when something has you stressed. That accident was the most stressful time of your life, which is why you relive it in your dreams when you're worried." His mother could read him like a book.

"Renee, leave the boy alone. He'll be fine," his father said with a mouthful of oatmeal.

"You used to say that about yourself, too, Seamus. What did that get us? You a stroke, and me more grey hair." His mom turned and pointed her finger at her husband.

"You only look more beautiful with that silver in your hair, my darling." His father grinned.

Wade put his cup to his lips to hide the smile at his father's attempt to calm his mother's rant. It worked every time because even at the age of sixty, his father knew exactly how to make his mother swoon.

His parents' relationship was probably one of the best he'd ever seen. They never went a day without telling the other how much they were loved and appreciated. They rarely argued but when they did, it was worked out at the kitchen table, even if it took all night.

Wade knew he was privileged to grow up with parents who were still in love. He yearned to find that kind of love himself someday, but at the rate he was going, he'd probably die alone.

"By the way, Ocean is grounded for two weeks and she's not allowed to have her phone, her tablet, computer, or video games." Wade pulled on his jacket.

"Is she allowed to breathe?" Wade turned at the sound of his sister's voice.

"I'm still considering that." Wade pointed his finger at Carla.

"Aren't you being a little hard on her, Wade? I mean it's those awful girls that put her in that situation." His mother was a marshmallow when it came to her granddaughter.

"Have you noticed how soft she's gotten with Ocean but if one of us did it we'd be locked up for a year?" Carla scoffed.

"That's what nanas are for. We spoil and parent's discipline." His mother smiled.

"I've shelled out the discipline and I expect you to support me." Wade knew she wouldn't go against his wishes.

"You know I will." She waved him off as she filled the dishwasher with dishes.

"I'll see you later. I'm hoping to be home the usual time today," Wade called as he walked out of his house.

Those words disappeared as he drove on to the lot of his shop. Everett and Logan stood next to one of the large bay doors. All the windows in the door were shattered and half of the windows on the other bay door were too.

"You've got to be fucking kidding me." Wade growled through his teeth as he slammed his gearshift into park and got out of the vehicle.

"Before you ask, there's nothing on the video. The only thing we saw were bricks being lobbed at the door until all these windows were broken." Everett looked about ready to kill as he pushed the broken glass onto a large pan Logan held.

"Wade, you might want to think about hiring security after we close." Logan dumped the pan full of broken glass into the large garbage bucket.

Two of the newer technicians walked out from the side of the building pulling a bucket with them. Dwayne Cleary and Cody Oates were only part-time until the other ramps were ready. Both Dwayne and Cody were in the same class with Wade when he completed his Automotive Technician Certificate after he finished his Business degree at university.

The two men looked as if they were ready to kill someone. Probably because they knew this would put Wade behind in getting them on the schedule full-time. He'd already put them off for two months because of the other incidents. He just wasn't willing to put any of his guys in danger.

"Is anything missing?" Wade ignored the question but knew Logan was probably right.

"Not that we saw. Besides, if they went inside, they'd show up on camera." Dwayne crossed his arms over his chest and shook his head as he scanned the front of the building.

"Wade, if you can't afford security, I'll stay here all night to beat the little bastards doing this." Curtis stomped out of the main entrance.

"Look, I'm going to call James to let him know what happened. I'll give Keith O'Connor a call about the security." Wade fished his phone out of his pocket and headed inside the reception area.

Hiring security would put a little dent in his savings but what choice did he have? It would cost him more in the long run if the bastards kept vandalizing his building.

While he waited for James to answer, he made his way to his office and unlocked the door. It pissed him off that someone was out to screw with the garage's reputation. When he'd first opened, Wade worked his ass off to build a business that he could be proud of. Now six years later, several companies depended on his garage to fix and maintain their vehicles.

Four years earlier, Kurt contracted Wade's Auto Service exclusively for all maintenance and repairs on Newfoundland Police

Department vehicles. Wade was proud of that and hoped the vandalism didn't fuck that up.

"James O'Connor," James answered after several rings.

"James, it's Wade Rivers." Wade eased down in his chair and rested his leg on the stool next to his desk.

"Wade, what's up?" James asked.

"I hate to bother you, but we had another incident." Wade puffed out an exasperated breath.

"What happened?" James sounded as if he was almost as pissed off as Wade.

"Someone tossed bricks through the windows of several of our bay doors." Wade flipped open his laptop and turned it on.

"Anything on the security video?" James inquired.

"Just the bricks hitting their targets." Wade signed into his computer.

"Of course," James grumbled. "I'll get someone out to take your statement and check around."

"I guess I should tell you we've already cleaned up the broken glass." Wade scrolled through his email.

"That's fine. Just keep the bricks. Not sure what we can do with them but maybe we can find out where they came from," James told him.

"We have it all in the buckets next to the door," Wade said.

"Good, I'll get someone by ASAP," James said.

Wade thanked James and hung up. His full inbox was mostly from customers looking for appointments for the vehicles. Although he knew Josie would bitch at him later for sending her so many at one time, he forwarded all of them to the feisty woman. Maybe she would give him a little slack since he'd been distracted the last few days. He suddenly realized it was only the middle of the week.

He sat back in his chair and tucked his hands behind his head. His mother was right. Wade only had nightmares when he was stressed, but how could he not be tense? His business was being vandalized by someone, his daughter got brought home by the cops, granted a hot cop, but it still wasn't a good thing.

He closed his eyes as he tried to remember what happened in the dream. A therapist once told him that if he could go through what happened in the nightmare, he may be able to figure out precisely what his subconscious wanted to work out while he slept.

Before he had a chance to think about it, a loud crash followed by several shouts echoed in from the shop. Wade jumped to his feet and hurried out of the office. He made it to the entrance of the service bays to see Harry run toward him. Wade couldn't remember Harry looking so pale.

"What was that racket?" He glanced over Harry's head and Wade's heart practically stopped in his chest.

One of the lifts had tipped, causing the car that was hoisted on it to fall to the floor. Wade knew which bay it was and he didn't wait for Harry to tell him what happened.

"Curtis? Curtis, are you hurt?" Wade shouted as he hurried toward the destroyed vehicle.

Curtis stepped out around the side with a cloth held to the top of his head. Wade's stomach lurched as he saw the blood on the side of the technician's cheek.

"I'm okay. I didn't get hurt by that. When I heard the lift crack, I ran out of the way and smacked my head off the garage door." Curtis pulled the cloth away and tossed it in the bucket.

"Go get that checked." Wade nodded toward where the blood oozed out of the side of his head.

"I'm good." Curtis grabbed another cloth from Everett.

"Go. Now. Curtis," Wade roared as he turned to look at the car.

He breathed a sigh of relief when he saw it was the burnt-out frame of the car he'd loaned Jess. He turned to ask Curtis why he had the heap on the ramp in the first place, but Harry stepped behind him.

"James asked us to have a look at it. He wanted to see if we could find out what started the fire," Harry explained.

"Fine. I just want to know what the fuck happened to the

ramp." Wade walked around the lift and studied the cracked mechanism that raised the lift.

Wade was meticulous when it came to inspections on his equipment. They were done every six months, and it only had been a little over two months since they were checked. It was impossible for it to wear so much in such a short period.

"I don't know, Wade, but it looks like someone fucked with the bolts up there." Everett pointed to the ceiling above the ramp lift where it had once been attached.

"Fuck. Fuck. Fuck." Wade turned to the other ramps. "Okay, guys. Bring down your lifts, shut everything down, and go home. I'm calling someone to come and check these things before we do anything else under them."

"What about the customers?" Logan asked.

"Harry, tell Josie to call them and let them know that we need to close for the day because of an incident with one of the ramps. If they can come to get their cars, tell them to do it. If we can't give them their cars, get them a rental." Wade didn't wait for Harry to answer as he stalked toward his office to call James.

Two hours later, inspectors, the police, and his sister stood in the front of the garage. James had several of his officers going through the broken lift with a fine-tooth comb, and the inspector confirmed that the lift didn't break because of normal wear.

"Wade, can you think of anyone who would be out to destroy

your reputation?" James asked.

"Not off hand. I mean, I've had pissed-off customers because we couldn't fix their car, or they didn't like the price of the repair, but I don't think anyone would do something this dangerous. Curtis could have been killed." Wade swallowed the bile that rose in his throat.

"Not to mention you or that pretty cop could have been burned alive," Everett reminded everyone.

"Look, the broken windows, graffiti, your office being torn apart, that's all annoying shit that will cost money to fix, but the ramp and the fire is pure evil." Josie shook her head.

"It's costing money, too," Harry snapped.

"Harry, money isn't everything." Josie swat her husband on the arm.

"It is when you have several people depending on your business for a living." Wade plowed his fingers through his hair.

"I've called Keith. He's on his way," James informed Wade as the chime of the front door went off.

Wade turned to see who'd entered, fully prepared to tell the person they were closed for the day. The woman who entered made his frayed nerves ease and a calmness came over him. Jess seemed to make his problems seem not so big.

"Jess, what are you doing here?" James gave her a side hug

and kissed her temple.

"I was at the station talking to John and he told me what happened. Is there anything I can do?" It was obvious she was talking to James, but her eyes bore into his.

"I've got things under control here," James responded as the rest of the officers walked out of the garage bays.

"I'm going to make sure everything is locked down before we leave." Harry winked at Wade and nodded his head in Jess' direction.

"I'll help you, honey." Josie smiled and followed her husband.

When Wade glanced around, it seemed everyone had made themselves scarce, leaving him alone in the front lobby with Jess. He turned back to her when he heard her laugh.

"Do I smell or something?" Jess chuckled.

"No." Wade studied her face.

"Are you okay?" Jess' smile faded as she stared up at him.

"Except for being pissed, frustrated, and worried, I'm fine. Luckily, nobody was seriously hurt. Curtis got a gash on his head, but he's fine." Wade scrubbed his hands against the stubble on his face.

For the first time in a long time, Wade felt self-conscious about how he looked. He probably looked like a bum after the day he had.

"I like the way your beard is coming in." Jess smiled as she leaned her back against the wall.

"I wasn't growing one." Wade had never found a police officer's uniform hot, but on her, it was sexy as hell.

"You should." Jess tilted her head and narrowed her eyes as if she tried to picture him with a beard.

"Maybe I will." Wade gazed into her eyes.

"Not too long. A little longer than you have now but you know, not like Santa Claus or anything." Jess winked.

"So, are you saying you like men who have beards?" Wade raised an eyebrow.

"No. I'm saying I like you with a beard." Jess' eyes dropped to his lips.

"You won't like me if I shave?" Wade grinned, hoping it hid the way his heart thudded in his chest.

"I'd like you either way." Jess lifted her gaze to his.

"Good to know." Wade took a step closer to her and tucked a stray hair back behind her ear.

"Would you go to supper with me?" Jess spoke so quickly that Wade wasn't sure he'd heard her correctly.

"What?" Wade's hand froze next to her cheek.

"I know it's not conventional for the woman to ask the man, but it's the twenty-first century and I like you. I understand if you aren't interested…" She pressed her lips together when he put his finger to her lips.

"Yes." Wade ran his knuckle down her cheek.

"Really?" She seemed so unsure.

"Really, Blue Eyes. I've been trying to build up the nerve to ask you for weeks, but I wasn't sure a woman like you would be interested in an ugly mug like me," Wade admitted.

"You're not ugly," Jess insisted.

Before Wade could respond, James and another of the officers walked into the lobby. Jess pressed her lips together and suddenly found her utility belt very interesting.

"I sure picked a heck of a time to make a move," she whispered and glanced back up.

"It's a perfect time," Wade said low enough that only she could hear.

Jess smiled when he stepped back from her as James approached them. Wade barely heard anything James said because it was hard to concentrate on anything other than the excitement of finally going out with Jess. As old-fashioned as he was, it didn't bother him that she'd asked.

With the terrible day he had, the thought of a date with the beautiful Jess O'Connor made it all a little easier to deal with. He couldn't wipe the smile off his face if he tried.

# Chapter 5

Jess shook while she waited for James to finish talking to Wade. She hadn't gone there to ask Wade out, but when he touched her, the words flew out.

She would've laughed at the stunned expression on his face if she hadn't been so shocked herself. If he'd said no, or worse, laughed at her, she didn't know what she would've done.

"Is that okay, Jess?" she heard James address her.

"Huh?" She hadn't heard a word her cousin said.

"I asked if you could stay here until Keith gets here." James smirked.

"Oh. Yeah. Sure." Jess knew her face had to be red.

"Not get enough sleep last night, Jess?" James teased.

"I got enough sleep. I…" Jess was cut off when she heard her father's voice behind her.

"You're quitting the NPD?" Her father didn't sound pissed, but he did seem surprised.

"What?" James and Wade said at the same time.

"Yeah, but this isn't the time or the place to talk about this." Jess turned around, expecting to see disappointment on her father's face.

At first, she couldn't raise her head to meet his eyes. She hated when he looked at her with displeasure even if she was an adult. Jess always wanted her family to be proud of her.

Her father put his finger under her chin and lifted it until she raised her eyes to meet his. He didn't look angry or upset. He almost seemed relieved.

"I'm so glad you finally dropped something. You were wearing yourself too thin, Pumpkin. Between your shop, the Karate school, and the department, I was waiting for you to drop down of exhaustion." He wrapped his arm around her shoulder.

"You're not mad that I quit?" Jess asked.

"No." Her father looked over her shoulder, then back to her. "We'll chat later about it."

"Uncle Kurt, what are you doing here?" James said, but his eyes were focused on Jess.

"I was at Keith's when you called. He's just outside checking for weak points." He continued to talk to Wade and James but kept his arm wrapped around Jess' shoulder

Wade stared at her for several minutes. She wondered what he thought about her life change. Jess had gone back and forth on it all night. At one point, she almost canceled her meeting with John.

As she was getting ready to leave, she finally made her decision.

John seemed surprised, but when she explained why she needed to leave, he understood. She told him she'd work until the end of the month, but John wouldn't hear of it. He was also concerned about how much she worked and told her after her shift Thursday, she'd be free.

Her father was right, Jess spread herself too thin. Everything in her life started to suffer, and it would catch up with her eventually. Even her morning workouts suffered because she was exhausted. If she continued to work as a police officer, she'd probably get killed or get someone else killed. That would be something she'd never be able to live with.

Jess made her way out of the garage. As the door closed, Keith stepped out from the side of the building. He tapped something into the tablet in his hand and glanced up to the camera hung near the corner of the building.

Jess waited for Keith to finish his inspection of the property before calling out to him. Her cousin was diligent in his business and would check every access point before he would move to the inside. Kristy's husband, Dean "Bull" Nash told her once that Keith had taken over the inspections since he didn't do any more security himself.

Dean was Keith's partner in the security firm. Newfoundland Security Services had gained respect across the province and the country. Keith had employees who traveled all over the world to protect people, and Dean said they were looking into hiring more staff.

"Hey, Jess." Keith hugged her as he stepped next to her.

"Hey." Jess smiled up at him.

"I heard you're turning in the badge." Keith raised an eyebrow as he glanced down at her.

"Yeah. Are you disappointed in me?" Jess didn't want anyone in her family to be upset about her decision.

"No, cuz. I'm proud of you. If you don't like what you're doing, what's the point of doing it?" Keith smiled.

"It's not that I don't like it. It's just that teaching kids, and running my shop, I love. I want to do something I love." She returned his smile.

"You're a great cop, cuz, but you're right, you make a great instructor. I've seen you with the kids. They love you. I also know that shop of yours is one of the best in the city to buy flowers." Keith winked as he raised his eyes to look over her head. "I should get this finished. I'll see you later, Jess."

Keith quickly made his way inside and when she turned, Wade was behind her. She hadn't heard him come out of the garage, but she was glad to see him.

"You asked me out, but you didn't tell me when or where."

Wade smirked.

"We kind of got interrupted." Jess raised an eyebrow.

"True, so when are you free?" Wade asked.

"I'm working tonight and tomorrow night, but then my evenings will be free until Monday. How about Friday?" Jess realized that after she ended her shift on Thursday, she wouldn't be a police officer anymore.

"Sounds perfect. If you want, we can meet at my house around seven," Wade suggested.

"Sounds great." Jess walked back a couple of steps and turned after he waved.

She wanted to squeal and jump in the air, but she kept composed as she made her way to the cruiser. As she opened the door, she glanced toward the entrance, but he'd gone inside.

Jess sat in the car and managed to keep from squealing until she was on her way back to Hopedale. Things in her life were beginning to look up.

Three hours later, Jess wanted to toss her phone through the window of her cruiser. News in a small town got around fast, but with her family, it went faster than the speed of light. She'd lost count on the number of family members who called her but as her phone vibrated again on the dash of the car, she groaned.

"Hello?" Jess tapped the earpiece without checking to see

who was calling.

"Jess?" a male voice she recognized echoed in her ear.

She wanted to hang up right away. Especially since she was leaving the NPD. It was the reason she'd dumped Jason in the first place.

"Hi, Jason." Jess sighed.

"I have a question for you." He chuckled.

"If the question is about me leaving the NPD then I don't want to hear it," Jess returned.

"What? You're leaving the NPD?" Jason sounded surprised.

"That's not why you're calling?" Jess hoped he wouldn't tell her he was right when he told her it wasn't the right career for her.

"No, but why are you quitting?" Jason had become a good friend after she allowed herself to get over the anger of his refusal to support her decision to join the department.

"I want to concentrate on the Karate school and my shop," Jess explained.

"Good for you. Mike told me he was worried you were taking on too much." Jason and Mike had gone to law school together.

They formed a band after law school with John, Nick, Aaron, and Cory Flemming, another police officer. *Rockin' the Law* played mostly at fundraisers to raise money for different charities. The name was a play on the fact that the members were lawyers and police officers.

"It's a great job, but I feel more fulfilled when I'm teaching or surrounded with flowers." Jess was at her best when she was in the middle of a flower arrangement.

"The flower child who can kick my ass." Jason laughed.

"As long as you remember that." Jess chuckled.

"I'm glad we started talking again. I missed that sassy mouth." He wasn't the only one, because she missed talking to Jason.

When they'd dated, they would talk for hours but something in the back of her mind nagged her constantly back then. It took her several years before she could be in the same room with him. That's when she came to terms that she and Jason were never meant to be more than great friends.

"I'm glad, too. You had a question to ask me." Jess glanced at her watch to see she only had another hour for supper.

"I was wondering if you were hiring at your shop," Jason said.

"Not making enough money as a lawyer?" Jess snickered.

"Not for me, smart ass. My niece is looking for work." Jason's niece was in her last year of high school and was the only child of his brother.

"I'd love to have her for a couple of hours in the evenings, but I need to check the schedule." The shop was busy, and the girls who currently worked for her mentioned getting someone in part-time.

"Sounds good. Give me a call when you know for sure, and Jess, good luck with the life change," Jason said.

"Thanks," Jess replied.

"By the way, I heard you got the hots for Wade Rivers," Jason teased.

"Mike has a big freaking mouth." Jess groaned.

"Mike didn't tell me, A.J. did." Jason laughed.

"His mouth is even bigger. I'm going to have to get Bethany to keep him occupied so he doesn't have time to gossip." Jess hated being the subject of gossip even if it was true.

"Just so you know, Wade's a good guy. Anyway, thanks again, Jess. I got to get back to court." It didn't surprise her that he was in court at four in the afternoon.

"I'll call you. Good luck in court." Jess tapped her earpiece and dropped her head back against the headrest.

She only had one more shift to work, and she was excited about her date with Wade. Jess hoped he didn't expect her to be a girly girl, because she wasn't. She wore dresses on special occasions, and she wanted to look good for Wade. It just wasn't something she wore all the time.

She was never so happy to see midnight. Luckily, she'd had a slow night and got off duty on time. She'd just made it to the top of her steps when she heard her mother's voice.

"Jess, can I talk to you?" Her mother stood at the bottom of the steps.

Jess couldn't put off a conversation with her mother, especially if she waited up until midnight. She suddenly felt ill at the thought of her mother being disappointed with Jess' decision.

"Sure, Mom. Come on up." Jess unlocked her door and stepped into her apartment.

She made her way to her bedroom, stripped out of her uniform, and threw on her comfy pajamas. When she walked back into the kitchen, her mother was in the process of preparing tea.

"Mom, what's wrong?" Jess sat in the chair next to her small dinette table.

"I wanted to talk to you about your decision." Her mother didn't turn around as she poured water into two cups.

"Mom, can't this wait until tomorrow?" Jess was tired, and the last thing she wanted was a lecture on how disappointed her mother was.

"No." Her mom placed a cup of tea in front of Jess and sat in the chair across from her.

"I've made the decision, and it's the best one for me, Mom." Jess wrapped her hands around the cup.

"I know, and I wanted to let you know I'm proud of you." Her mother reached across the table and placed her hand on top of Jess' arm.

"You're proud I quit?" Jess wasn't sure she understood.

"Not that you quit, I'm proud you realized what you truly love to do." Her mother smiled.

"I enjoyed being a police officer, Mom." Jess did but not as much as she thought she would.

"But you love teaching Karate. You love your flower shop. I think in the back of your mind you thought because your father was a police officer who taught Karate, that you needed to follow in his footsteps." Her mother sipped her tea.

"Maybe, but I'm glad I had the experience." Jess smiled.

"Good, and I don't have to worry about you killing yourself. Maybe now you can get yourself a social life," her mother teased.

"As a matter of fact, I took that step today." Jess winked.

"Oh, is it that nice man from the garage that Cora accosted last week?" Her mother laughed.

"Yes, I asked him to supper on Friday." Jess sat back in the chair and chuckled at her mother's shocked expression.

"Good for you but I'm not surprised, you always go after

what you want." Her mother stood and placed her cup in the sink.

"Not as much as I should have, but it's a step in the right direction." Jess stood and wrapped her arms around her mother.

"Yes, it is. Maybe we'll have another wedding soon." Her mother smirked.

"Goodnight, mother." Jess guided her mother toward the front door.

Jess made her way to her bedroom, shaking her head. Her mother seemed set on having all her daughters married off much to her father's dismay.

Jess yawned as she climbed into bed. She wouldn't have any issues falling asleep. She closed her eyes, and for the first time in a long time, she felt as if her life was going in the right direction.

# Chapter 6

Friday morning seemed to drag on forever. Mainly because he was slowly losing his patience with the customer in front of him at that moment. The idiot didn't understand why he couldn't drive his car with the rear axle cracked.

"Can't I just take the car? I'll bring it back Monday to get it fixed. I can't go all weekend without my car," the young man whined.

"The axel is cracked. That means it can't be moved. It's why it had to be brought in on a flatbed." Wade spoke slowly to keep from shouting.

The guy was in his early twenties and Wade could see he was one of those overprivileged assholes who thought the world revolved around him. One of the perks of having a good reputation was you got customers who would pay big money to fix their vehicles. One of the downfalls was some of them thought they were the only customers.

"I was told you could fix it right away." He slapped his hand on the counter.

"You were told if it was something small, we could fix it by the end of the day, but you need a new axle. The only place we can get that is the dealer. It's why I originally suggested you bring it to the dealership." Wade shoved his hands into his jeans pockets and squeezed them into fists.

"I can't bring it to the dealer. They will call my father," the guy complained.

"Look, I can order the part, but it won't be in until Monday. Once it comes in, we'll fix it," Wade explained.

"What am I supposed to do until then? I need a car." The guy's whine started to get on his last nerve.

"Maybe you should call Daddy. I don't have a car for you," Wade snapped.

"Fine." The guy turned on his too-expensive shoes and stomped out of the garage.

"I fucking hate brats," Harry grumbled.

"That guy looks old enough to have better sense." Wade shook his head as he handed the work order to Harry. "Order that part for that asshole, please."

"Will do." Harry's voice trailed off behind Wade as he made his way to his office.

The entire day had been one asshole after another and he didn't want to be in a bad mood when he had supper with Jess. He figured a short text to confirm their date would distract him.

*Wade: Have you changed your mind about tonight, yet?*

He stared at his phone for several minutes, almost willing her to text him back. Wade was about to slam the phone on his desk when he saw the little dots that told him she was typing a message.

*Jess: Did you think I would?*

*Wade: I hoped you wouldn't. I figured you might realize you could do a lot better than this ugly mug.*

*Jess: You're not getting out of our date that easy, buster. By the way, you are far from ugly.*

*Wade: I would never want to get out of a date with a hot cop.*

*Jess: LOL I'm not a cop anymore.*

*Wade: You still have the handcuffs, right?*

*Jess: That's a secret.*

*Wade: I like mysteries.*

*Jess: I'm sure you do. Can we keep the dress casual?*

*Wade: Aww, I wanted to wear my tuxedo tonight.*

*Jess: If you still want to wear it that's fine with me, but I'll be in jeans.*

*Wade: Won't you get cold in just a pair of jeans. It's awfully bold of you to go out topless. Not that I'd complain.*

*Jess: LOL perv. I will be wearing a top.*

*Wade: Darn. I gotta get back to work. I'll meet you at my house around seven.*

*Jess: Looking forward to it.*

*Wade: Me too. Later Blue Eyes.*

Wade could feel the anger dissipate with a few flirty texts and it amazed him. They'd sent little texts over the last couple of days, but mostly to ask how their day was going. He hoped after their date, things would move in the right direction.

The rest of the day dragged on but there were fewer jerks to deal with, and except for two cars, the mechanics managed to get all the vehicles done before they closed at five. He was proud of the guys who worked for him and thankful they got along well. Of course, they were like family to him and had disagreements, but they always worked it out.

At ten minutes past five, Wade and Everett were the only two left in the building. They had a customer who got held up at work and practically begged them to wait for him so he could pick up his car. Since he was also the man who'd sold him the new building, Wade didn't mind waiting for him.

Everett offered to stay with him, but after a quick chat, Wade convinced him to leave. It wasn't like he didn't know the guy coming to pick up the car.

Wade was in his office when he heard the chime of the front entrance. He stood up and made his way out front to hand the keys over and head home. He had a little over an hour to get ready for his date.

George Crocker stood on the other side of the counter, panting like he'd run all the way to the garage. He gave Wade a relieved smile as he pulled out his wallet to pay for the service on his car.

"Wade, you're a gem. I would've been screwed all weekend without my car. The wife would've had my nuts in a sling." George handed Wade a credit card.

"Can't have that." Wade chuckled as he rang up the invoice.

"It's our anniversary on Saturday and I promised her a weekend at a little bed and breakfast in Heart's Delight." George grinned.

"Sounds great. Happy anniversary, George." Wade slid the pin pad across the counter to George and waited for him to tap in his number.

"Thanks, twenty years, and five kids. She deserves a weekend away." George chuckled.

"You both do by the sound of that." Wade handed the receipt to George and gave him his keys.

"How're things going here with the new place?" George asked as Wade walked him to the exit.

"Busy, but we've had a little trouble with graffiti." Wade didn't have time to go into the whole issue.

"I saw that outside. Damn hoodlums." George shook his head.

"We got the police looking into it." Wade smiled.

"Good. Anyway, thanks again, Wade. I'll see you again in November for my winter tires." George waved as he headed out through the door.

Wade locked the front door and completed his usual check around to make doubly sure the building was locked up tight. He wished Keith had been able to have security start before Monday, but unfortunately, all his guys were tied up on jobs.

James assigned an officer to stay on the lot and Wade saw the unmarked car parked in front earlier that day. He took a quick glance through the window to confirm the car was in the same place. When the officer waved, Wade felt a little more at ease about leaving the building.

Wade grabbed his phone from his office and had just locked the door when a loud clang echoed through the building. He spun around and made his way through the door leading to the service bays.

The eerie silence made him edgy as he slowly made his way through the garage. It always seemed odd to walk through the bays once everything was shut down. It was so quiet that his footsteps echoed through the area.

"Hello?" Wade shouted as he slowly made his way to the back.

His voice reverberated back to him, but nobody answered and nothing seemed out of place. He continued to the back and walked around each of the lifts. The only thing he found that could have possibly made the loud sound was a torque wrench that lay next to one of the ramps.

Wade picked it up and glanced at his watch. He had an hour to get home and get ready before Jess would be at his house. He tossed the wrench on top of the tool bench and shrugged as he started to head out of the service bays.

As he passed by the last one, a dark figure stepped in front of him, but before he could utter a word or react, something struck the side of his head. Wade fell to his knees and cringed when pain shot through his leg. He shook his head and tried to stand, but something hit him again, knocking him back to the floor and leaving him dazed.

Wade tried to lift his head from the concrete floor and covered the side of his head with his hand. He turned to see where the figure had gone, but the only thing he saw was something coming down on top of him.

Wade didn't have a chance to move before it hit him in the forehead. Wade's world spun and blurred then faded into blackness. The last thing he saw was a large figure over him holding something over his head.

# Chapter 7

Jess checked herself once more in the window of her sister's car before she climbed out and made her way toward the front door. She didn't see Wade's truck in the driveway, but there were a couple of other cars.

Jess' hand shook as she lifted it to knock on the door. She was so nervous that she was startled when the door opened. A pretty woman squealed as she grabbed Jess' hand and dragged her into the house.

"You are just as pretty as Ocean said you were." The woman grinned.

"Ummm, thanks," Jess said as the woman closed the door.

"I'm Carla, by the way. I'm Wade's sister." Carla beamed.

"It's nice to meet you." Jess could see the family resemblance since both Wade and Carla had the same grey-blue eyes and brown hair.

"Carla, for goodness sake let the poor girl get inside the house before you scare the life out of her." Another woman appeared in the foyer and Jess knew instantly she was Wade's mother.

"Sorry." Carla smirked. "Jess, this is our mom, Renee, and the man over there in the rocking chair is our dad, Seamus." Carla pulled Jess further into the house.

"Wade must have gotten held up at the garage, but he should be here shortly," Renee said as she glanced through the window.

Something in the way Renee held herself told Jess Wade's mom was concerned that he wasn't home. Jess was a little early, but the garage closed at five and it was almost seven. Jess noticed Seamus tap something into his phone and he furrowed his brows as he stared at the screen.

"Seamus, could you say hello to the lovely young girl?" Renee sat on the arm of the chair next to her husband.

"Sorry, it's nice to meet you, Jess." Seamus nodded at Jess.

"It's lovely to meet you both." Jess clasped her hands in front of her as she stood in the doorway of the living room.

"Sit down, my dear." Seamus motioned toward the large L-shaped sofa in front of the window.

After she was practically forced to have a cup of tea, Jess glanced at her watch. It was getting close to eight, but Wade still hadn't arrived. His father had called the garage and Wade's cell several times, but he didn't get an answer. Jess sent a couple of texts herself without any response.

"Why don't I take a drive over to the garage to see if he's there?" Jess stood up and shoved her phone into her back pocket.

"I'll call Harry and have him to go over." Seamus held up his phone.

"Mr. Rivers, I'd rather go check myself. I know he's been having some issues and I'd rather not send anyone into a situation that could be dangerous. It may just be Wade got lost in work, but I would rather go check myself." Jess turned and made her way to the front door.

"Call us as soon as you know something." Renee followed her with her arms wrapped around herself.

"I will, Mrs. Rivers. I promise." Jess pulled open the door and ran to Kristy's car.

Wade wouldn't stand her up and the fact that he was late gave her a bad feeling in the pit of her stomach. Jess wasn't careless either, so while she drove to Wade's garage, she called James.

"Hey, Jess," James answered the phone after several rings.

"James, I'm on my way to Wade's garage. He was supposed to meet me at his house at seven, but he didn't show up. His family has tried calling him, but he's not answering. Can you get someone to meet me there for backup?" Jess gripped the steering wheel tightly as she waited for a light to change.

"I've stationed a guy there. Hang on, let me give him a call and ask if he's seen Wade." James asked Marina to borrow her phone.

Jess slammed on the gas when the light changed as she waited for James to come back on the phone with her. She was almost to the garage by the time James spoke to her again.

"He's not answering either. Jess, be careful. You're still on the roster until Monday, but technically you're not a cop anymore. I'm sending another car over there." James sounded concerned. "I'm leaving the house now. Don't do anything stupid."

"I won't." Jess ended the call and turned onto Torbay Road where Wade's Auto Service was located.

She pulled onto the lot and immediately looked for the unmarked car James had stationed at the garage. She saw it parked in a dark part of the lot with the driver's door opened.

Jess pulled next to the unmarked car and scanned the lot before she got out of the car. She probably should've waited until the backup arrived, but she had a bad feeling that something wasn't right.

Jess held her phone in her hand as she carefully walked to the car. She was around the vehicle before she saw the shattered phone next to the car. There was no sign of the officer and she didn't know who James assigned to the area, but the sight made the hair stand up on the back of her neck.

Jess ran toward the entrance of the garage. She pulled the door, but it was locked and all the lights were off inside. She turned around and scanned the parking lot. It was probably a dumb move to walk around the building to check for another way in, but she was worried about Wade and the missing officer.

As she walked by each garage door, she peered in to see if she could see anything inside. She walked around the back of the building and saw one of the doors opened enough for someone to crawl under it.

She tapped the flashlight app on her phone and crouched to look inside. She could see a light at the other end of the service bays and she called out. When nobody answered, Jess lay down on the ground and rolled quickly under the door.

"Wade?" Jess called out again as she got to her feet.

When she didn't hear anything, she slowly made her way to the other end of the large garage. The eerie silence caused a chill to skitter down her spine. Jess realized if anyone was inside, she had to be prepared to defend herself.

"Wade, it's me, Jess," she called out.

Jess pushed open the door leading to the front of the building and was about to call for Wade again when she heard a soft groan. She stopped to see if she could pinpoint where it came from and turned back to the garage. She heard the moan a second time and lifted her phone to illuminate the area. She saw something move next to one of the lifts and slowly made her way closer.

After three steps, Jess could see it was a person. She ran toward the lift, and it shifted. It wasn't the sound of the metal scraping that made her heart pound, it was the agonizing roar coming from the person trapped under it.

"Oh my God, Neil." Jess recognized her co-worker immediately.

Neil Simms was with the St. John's division of the NPD. They'd crossed paths a few times on cases and he was one of the officers who'd responded to a shooting Aaron's wife witnessed.

"Jess, I'm jammed under the lift." He groaned in pain.

"What happened here?" Jess asked as she tapped nine-one-one.

"I thought I saw someone walk around the building. I…" Neil gasped in pain. "I made my way around and saw one of the garages opened. When I got inside, I saw a guy beating the shit out of another. I don't remember what happened, but someone hit me from behind."

Jess stopped him as she spoke to the operator and scanned the area for any sign of Wade. When she didn't see him, she felt anxious.

"Neil, did you see Wade?" Jess asked as she ended the call with the emergency operator.

"I didn't see anything until I woke up here." Neil shifted and groaned.

"I know it's probably difficult, but you've got to try to stay still. I'm going to go open the main door so the paramedics can get in." Jess hated to leave him, but she needed to find Wade.

There was no sign of him anywhere as she made her way to the front of the garage. She flicked the lock and switched on the light in the reception area. It was empty.

"Wade," she shouted as she made her way back through the building.

She saw two closed doors on her way back to Neil and tried them both. They were locked, but something in the pit of her stomach told her to get into the room with the word *office* written on it. There was a large window next to the door and she tried to see through it, but the room was dark, and the blinds were drawn. She shouted to Wade again, but she didn't hear a response.

"Fuck it," Jess grumbled.

She ran back into the garage to find something to break down the door. Several seconds later, Jess found a large mallet that felt about a hundred pounds, but knew she was strong enough to swing it a few times.

After several unsuccessful attempts to break down the door with the mallet, she smashed the window with it. Jess cleared away the glass and carefully climbed through the window. As she landed on the floor, all the air whooshed out of her.

"Wade." Jess fell to her knees next to his motionless body and she pressed her fingers to his neck.

She let out a sigh of relief when she felt a strong pulse, but he was face-down on the floor and unconscious. The fact that he didn't respond made her uneasy and she carefully rolled him over on his side.

"Wade, honey. I need you to wake up," Jess whispered as she ran her hand over the top of his head.

Her hand swiped against something wet and sticky on the top of his head and she quickly pulled it away. When she saw blood covering her hand, she slowly rolled Wade onto his back.

"Wade, please open your eyes for me. I need to see you open your eyes now," Jess called to him again.

He didn't move, but she heard several footsteps and shouting outside the office door. She jumped to her feet and immediately unlocked the door to allow the paramedics into the office.

"Wade, help is here, but I need you to wake up," Jess shouted as she fell to her knees next to him again.

"Jess?" James's voice echoed through the building.

"In here, James. Wade won't wake up." Jess didn't know when the tears started, but she felt one run down her cheek as she held tightly to Wade's motionless hand.

"Jesus, what the fuck happened here?" James appeared in the door of the office.

"I don't know, but Neil's trapped under one of the ramps in the back, and Wade won't wake up. James, he's bleeding." Jess tried to keep the sob from escaping, but she couldn't.

"I need a paramedic in here," James shouted.

Two minutes later, Jess was pulled back from Wade while two of the paramedics assessed him. James pulled her out of the office as several firemen headed into the garage.

"Are you okay?" James wrapped his arm around her shoulder.

"I'm fine. The place was locked when I got here, but one of the garage doors were open, and I crawled under it." Jess wiped her fingers under her eyes.

"You should've waited for us before you came inside," James chastised.

"I couldn't. I had to find Wade." Jess sniffed.

James didn't say a word as he guided her out of the building to wait for Wade and Neil to be loaded into the ambulances. She was outside for several seconds before she pulled out her phone and tapped in the number Wade's mother had given her.

"I need to call Wade's family." Jess held the phone to her ear.

"Jess, wipe the blood off your face and hands." James handed her a paper towel and then he headed back inside.

Wade's mother answered on the second ring and Jess quickly explained what happened. Renee told her that they would be at the hospital. As Jess ended the call, the paramedics brought Wade out on a stretcher, but he was still unconscious.

"Can I go with him?" Jess asked James.

"Where's your car?" James escorted her to the ambulance.

"I've got Kristy's car, but I'll get someone to come get it." Jess climbed into the back of the ambulance.

"I'll take care of it." James squeezed her hand and stepped back.

"The keys are still in it," Jess shouted as the door closed.

Jess sat as much out of the way as she could while the paramedics monitored Wade. He looked so still and even with the monitor beeping a steady rhythm of his heart, she worried about the large gash on his head.

While she stared at him, Jess realized she was falling for Wade. They hadn't had their first date, they'd never even kissed, but Jess knew deep down Cora was right about him. Wade was meant for her. The magnetic attraction she had to him was something she'd never experienced in her life. She didn't know if he felt it, but there was no way she would ignore the signs anymore. She reached out and grasped his free hand.

The ambulance turned into the hospital parking lot when Wade began to move for the first time. He rolled his head back and forth but winced when he tried to lift his head.

"Jess?" His voice was barely above a whisper as he squeezed her hand.

"Wade, stay calm. We just got to the hospital," Jess whispered next to his ear.

"I'm sorry." He sighed.

"For what?" She cupped his hand between hers.

"I think I missed our date." Wade's eyes fluttered open.

"You found a hell of a way to be late for it." Jess brought his hand to her lips and kissed his fingers.

"You're so fucking beautiful," he whispered.

"Shhh." Jess pressed her finger to his lips.

"She's beautiful, isn't she?" Wade asked the pretty paramedic seated next to Jess.

"She is." The woman smiled.

"My head hurts like hell." Wade squeezed his eyes shut.

"Someone gave you a pretty hard crack to the head, Mr. Rivers," the paramedic told him.

"I'm pretty sure someone broke into the garage again. I just couldn't see who it was." Wade's voice was low.

"Don't worry about that now. Let's get you fixed up first." Jess tried to release his hand, but he gripped it tightly.

"Don't leave," Wade begged.

"I'm not going anywhere, but they need to bring you into the hospital." Jess kissed his cheek.

Jess leaned against the wall outside of the emergency trauma room. They'd wheeled Wade into the room almost an hour earlier and nobody had come to tell his family anything.

"Here."

Jess turned to the sound of the voice. Keith stood next to her sipping coffee and holding another cup in front of her. She gave him a weak smile and although she didn't want it, Jess took the cup to give her hands something to do. The only thing she wanted to know was if Wade was okay.

"I'm really starting to hate this place." Emily stepped next to her husband and tucked herself under his arm.

"I think we all have one bad memory or another from this place." Keith kissed the top of Emily's head.

Jess' family had several bad memories in the emergency department. James' first wife lost her battle with breast cancer eleven years earlier. The day of her funeral, John hit a moose on the highway and almost died. Six years later, Keith almost died when he was shot by a man obsessed with Keith's wife, Emily.

"There are also good memories here, too." Emily gazed up at Keith.

"All the babies that keep popping out." Keith smirked.

Jess stared at him for a moment and tried to read his expression as he smiled down at his wife. She'd seen that look before on all of her cousins.

"Are you pregnant?" Jess turned her attention to Emily.

"Yes, I found out this morning." Emily's smile could have lit up the entire floor of the hospital.

"Isn't that five babies due in the spring?" Jess snorted.

"Actually, it's six. Bethany called Kathleen this morning to tell her she and A.J. are expecting." Emily tucked herself under Keith's arm.

Jess was happy for all of them. Besides Emily and Bethany, Stephanie, Billie, Lora, and Kristy all announced they were expecting the following year. It sounded like if everyone went by their due dates, between mid-April and late May, a new O'Connor baby born each week. Jess envied all of them.

With that thought, her attention went back to the emergency room doors. Why did it take so long for them to report back on his condition? She turned to see Wade's family paced around the waiting room and hallway. Renee, Seamus, Carla, and Ocean had to be going through hell. Her heart broke at the sight of Wade's daughter with tears in her eyes.

"Jess, is he going to be okay?" Renee asked Jess when she'd arrived shortly after Wade was brought in.

"We have to think positive," was all Jess could say without bursting into tears.

Jess didn't know what to do with herself. Technically, she and Wade were nothing to each other. They never got to have their first date, so she couldn't say she was his girlfriend.

"What about the police officer?" Keith asked.

"He's been brought into surgery. His lower leg was crushed under the lift." Jess turned at the sound of James' voice.

"Dear, God." Emily covered her mouth with her hand.

"Is my dad going to be okay?" Ocean grabbed hold of Jess' hand and looked up at her with hopeful eyes.

"Of course, he will, sweetheart." Jess pulled Ocean into her arms and kissed the top of her head.

At first, Jess felt as if she overstepped with the young girl, but Wade's daughter clung to her as if she'd known Jess all her life.

"Daddy almost died when I was six. He was in the hospital a long time." Ocean sobbed against Jess' shoulder.

"Ocean, your dad is tough. He'll be just fine." James placed his hand on Ocean's shoulder.

"Ocean, this is my cousin, James. He's a police officer." Jess turned and nodded at Keith and Emily. "That's my cousin Keith and his wife Emily."

As Jess tuned out the conversations going on, her thoughts went to Wade. How did he burrow into her heart in such a short period of time? Sure, she'd seen him almost every week for nearly three months, but it wasn't as if they were dates. He was the guy who fixed her crappy car, but he called her himself about the repairs and he served her when she went to the shop.

Her thoughts went to the trouble at Wade's garage. Wade told her about the vandalism at the shop, but whoever was doing it was getting more aggressive, and dangerous. Between the fire, the ramp cracking, and the attack, it was a wonder nobody was killed.

"Boy, did you pick the wrong time to quit the force," Jess whispered to herself.

Twenty minutes later, the waiting room was filled with Wade's family and his staff. Most of her family had arrived a short time later and did their best to keep everyone calm. Jess hadn't moved from the wall across from the trauma room door.

She'd almost talked herself into stomping into the room to see what was taking so long when the door opened, and a familiar face smiled at her.

"Well, if it isn't the O'Connor clan again." Doctor Adam Cramer chuckled.

"Hey, Adam." Jess shook the doctor's hand.

Adam Kramer was an ER doctor and always seemed to be on

duty when one of her family ended up in the hospital. He was well liked by her family and trusted.

"I'm guessing since I don't have a patient with the last name O'Connor then either I have a husband or friend of your family." Adam sauntered into the waiting room.

"Wade is Jess' boyfriend," James answered and Jess wasn't about to argue.

"Damn, you mean I lost another chance with one of the beautiful O'Connor girls?" Adam pushed out his lower lip into a fake pout.

"Adam, is Wade okay?" Jess wasn't in the mood for Adam's flirting.

"You don't have to worry. He has one hell of a headache and it looks like whoever hit him gave him a few jabs to the ribs because his side is bruised. What I'm mostly concerned about are the bruises on Wade's hip and thigh. With his previous injury, I'm going to do an MRI to make sure nothing is reinjured." Adam might be a flirt and a joker, but he was a good doctor.

"Can we see him?" Ocean pushed between her grandmother and Jess.

"Adam, this is Wade's daughter," Jess explained when Adam seemed confused.

"He's groggy and I'm going to keep him here for a day or so, but you can definitely see him." Adam smiled at Ocean.

"Can Jess come with me?" Ocean had already dragged Jess across the hall toward the door.

"I'll bring you both in." Adam winked.

"Ocean, I think your grandparents and aunt may want to go in with you." Jess stepped back.

"Don't be ridiculous. My boy is probably waiting for you." Seamus held the door open for Jess and Ocean.

Adam led them down the hall to one of the trauma rooms. He nodded toward the closed door and continued down the hall. Ocean grasped Jess' hand and held on as they walked into the room.

She knew his eye and jaw were bruised. Jess saw that in the ambulance, but she didn't expect to see Wade's naked chest or the black and blue marks on his left side.

The sheet lay across his flat stomach showing the hint of a six-pack and dark hair across his pectoral that ran down his stomach and under the sheet. She mentally slapped herself for gawking at him while he was laying in a hospital bed, but the man was beautiful.

"Dad, it's me, Ocean." The young girl cautiously stepped next to the bed.

"Honey Bunch, I know who you are." Wade chuckled then winced as he covered his daughter's hand with his.

"Your dad will be fine, Ocean." Jess wrapped her arm around the young girl and for the first time, she realized she was only an inch taller than the twelve-year-old.

"This wasn't the date I had in mind for tonight." Wade slowly turned his head and his eyes met hers.

"What? Are you kidding? I was just about to tell you how much fun I'm having." Jess winked.

Wade laughed but quickly grabbed his side and grunted. It was clear he had some bad bruising around his ribs. She could see his discomfort and hurried to the side of the bed.

"Shit. Don't make me laugh," Wade grunted.

"Sorry." She glanced at Ocean who seemed amused by the banter between Jess and Wade.

"Don't be. I like your sense of humor." Wade tapped the other side of the bed and motioned for Jess to sit next to him.

"I don't think I'm supposed to sit on your bed." Jess felt a little uncomfortable with the way Wade looked at her since his daughter was in the room.

Before Jess could respond, Ocean pushed Jess to the other side of the bed and rolled her eyes. She didn't seem to be the least bit uncomfortable with Jess.

"Sit down, for goodness sake," Ocean said as she walked back to the other side of the bed.

"I shouldn't stay too long. Your parents are outside and I'm sure they want to see you." Jess sat on the edge of the bed.

"I think Dad needs to plan another date because this one is kind of a disaster." Ocean pointed her finger at her father. "I'll let Nana and Pop know you're planning your next date and when you're done, let us know."

"Ocean, we can do that later." Jess stood up.

"Nope. Dad, I'm so glad you're okay. I'll be back." Ocean turned and was out through the door before Jess could protest.

Jess stared after the young girl until she felt a warm hand wrap around hers. She looked down at Wade and swallowed down the lump in her throat. The sight of his injuries and the memory of what Adam told them about his leg made her stomach clench at the thought of what he endured.

"I'm fine, Blue Eyes." Wade tugged her closer so she could sit next to his hip.

"You're not fine. You've got a lot of injuries," Jess reminded him.

It was hard to concentrate with his grey eyes staring into hers and his finger gently gliding back and forth on the back of her hand. His touch was both soothing and exciting at the same time.

"I'm alive." Wade tugged her hand toward his lips and pressed them against her knuckles.

"Yes," Jess breathed.

"Thanks to you." He kissed her fingertips.

"Wade," Jess sighed his name.

He aroused her with the kisses to her hand more than any other man had with actual sex. Jess licked her lips when he reached up and cupped her cheek. His thumb ran over her lower lip and she held her breath.

"I wanted the first time I kissed you to be romantic, and sweet, but I crave you right now." Wade tried to sit but winced and eased back on the bed. "So much for romance."

Jess leaned closer until her lips hovered over his. Wade ran his finger down the side of her cheek and her eyes fluttered closed. She'd dreamed of his kiss for months, but when he touched her, it felt so much better.

"Kiss me, Jess." Wade's warm breath feathered against her cheek.

Jess trembled as she leaned closer and touched her lips to his. They were warm and soft against hers as she lightly brushed a small kiss across his mouth. Before she could pull back, Wade slid his fingers behind her head.

"Really, kiss me, Jess," Wade growled as his mouth engulfed hers.

His kiss was demanding but gentle at the same time. Their lips moved against each other and Jess tried her best to remember he was in a hospital bed. That was a little difficult, especially when his tongue glided across her lower lip as if asking her to open for him.

She did.

Jess moaned when his tongue slipped inside her mouth and swirled against hers. The man knew how to kiss, and she was lost in it. So lost that she almost didn't hear a throat clearing.

Jess pulled back and ducked her head, too embarrassed to turn toward who entered the room. Wade chuckled as he kissed her temple.

"I'm sorry to interrupt." Renee grinned and Jess felt the heat rise in her cheeks.

"It's okay, Mom." Wade winced as he tried to sit up straighter in the bed.

"I'll go out so your mom can visit." Jess tried to ease off the bed, but Wade grasped her hand and practically begged her with his eyes not to go.

"You stay right there, young lady." Renee pointed her finger at Jess as she walked toward Wade's bed. "That's the kind of medicine he needs for a quick recovery."

"You couldn't be more right, Mom." Wade gently squeezed her hand and Jess gave him a shy smile.

She sat on the bed next to him while his parents, sister, and daughter continued to parade into the room. Adam came back a couple of times to check on Wade and explained that Wade would be sent for an MRI in the morning.

Wade wasn't happy about the overnight stay, but when Jess agreed to stay with him, he was more receptive to the idea.

Before Adam left, he ensured there was a recliner brought in for Jess to get some sleep. She insisted she didn't need to sleep, but Wade had made her promise to at least sit in the chair.

It was a little after midnight when the nurse came in to check his vitals and gave Wade some pain medication. Jess knew the nurse through her sister. Kristy met Leah Sellers when she worked at a long-term care facility. It was the job that finally brought Kristy and her husband together, but it wasn't without danger and death.

"Here's an extra pillow and blanket." Leah crouched next to the chair when she returned a few minutes later.

"Thanks, Leah," Jess whispered.

Jess curled up in the chair and watched Wade as he slept. How was it possible to have such deep feelings for a man she'd only met a few months earlier? She shouldn't be surprised since her sister fell in love with Dean the first day she saw him. Most of her cousins fell in love with their wives the same way.

The question was, did she love Wade? It was too soon to know that. They hadn't even gotten to go on their first date, although the kiss was the best she'd ever had. She couldn't imagine it getting better than that.

"What have you got going through that pretty head of yours?" Wade said quietly.

"That you should be sleeping." Jess smiled.

"I don't sleep well in hospitals. Besides, I'd rather watch you. Did I tell you how beautiful you are?" Wade lifted his head and turned, so he was looking straight at her.

"Yes, you did in the ambulance." Jess met his eyes.

"I guess our date got kind of screwed up." Wade snorted.

"What are you talking about? This was an awesome date." Jess winked.

"Well, we are spending the night together." Wade wiggled his eyebrows.

"Yes, we are." Jess stood up and made her way to the side of his bed.

"I haven't thanked you." Wade reached for her hand.

"For what?" Jess threaded her fingers with his.

"Finding me and getting that cop to the hospital. Dad says he's going to be okay, but his leg is in pretty bad shape." She saw Wade's Adam's apple bob up and down as he swallowed.

"Yeah, his leg was crushed under the lift. Whoever knocked him out dropped the lift on his leg," Jess explained.

"I owe that guy my life." Wade blew out a breath.

"Why do you say that?" Jess asked.

"He walked in on the guy beating me. I managed to crawl out

of the garage and into my office while they fought, but I must have passed out before I got to my phone. When he grabbed the guy, he told me to run. Everything after that is a little fuzzy." Wade ran his finger slowly up and down her thumb.

Neil had said he thought there were two men. Was it possible Wade didn't see the other man, or was Neil confused? She found it hard to believe that one man would be able to overpower Neil.

"You're sure it was just one guy?" Jess knew she probably shouldn't be questioning Wade, but James told her he'd wait until the morning to interview Wade.

"That's all I saw, but it was definitely a man." Wade shifted in the bed and clenched his teeth.

"James will be by in the morning, so anything you remember, make sure you tell him." Jess was moving into cop mode.

"Yeah." Wade shifted again.

"What's wrong, Wade?" Jess could see he was more uncomfortable.

"I need to use the washroom." He glanced around the room.

"They left a bottle here for you. You can't get out of bed." Jess handed him the blue urine bottle that Leah had placed on the side of his bed.

"I hate those fucking things." Wade groaned but reluctantly took the bottle.

"I'll wait outside." Jess stood and left the room before he could respond.

She made her way to the vending machine to grab something to eat. The cafeteria was closed at night, so she was stuck eating the stale food from the machine. When the sandwich fell into the slot her stomach rumbled and Jess realized she hadn't eaten since lunch.

As she made her way back to Wade's room, her thoughts went through everything Wade had told her as well as what she'd seen at the garage. Between that and the amount of shit that happened over the last few days, she knew someone was after something.

She itched to ask Wade more questions, but she knew James would be pissed. It wasn't her job anymore. She leaned against the wall outside his room.

Who was out to destroy Wade's business, or was it something else they were after?

# *Chapter 8*

Wade woke the next morning and turned toward the recliner. Jess was curled up in the recliner with her arm tucked under her head and the pillow tossed to the floor.

Wade stared at her and took in her beautiful face. She'd removed the tiny bit of makeup she'd had on the previous day. Not that she needed any of that shit. Jess had a natural glow on her skin that made her look radiant. Her long eyelashes fluttered as she slept, and he would give anything to know what she dreamed about.

Her slender nose fit her face perfectly and her plump lips were as soft as he'd imagined. When he'd kissed her, it was clear to him that Jess O'Connor was the woman he wanted for the rest of his life. Love at first sight wasn't fiction because Wade knew he'd fallen in love with her that first day she'd walked into his repair shop with Aaron.

He wasn't about to tell her that, though. She'd probably run for the hills. No. Wade would romance her and hopefully, she'd fall in love with him. He wasn't dumb, he could see she was attracted to him and that was a step in the right direction.

"Why are you staring at me?" Jess said as she tucked her beautiful auburn hair behind her ear.

"Why wouldn't I? You're the best-looking thing in this hospital." Wade smiled when she rolled her eyes.

"How do you feel this morning?" she asked as she folded the blanket.

"With my hands," Wade said as he wiggled his fingers.

"Smart ass." Jess narrowed her eyes as she walked toward him.

"You don't like intelligent men?" He raised an eyebrow.

"Wade, how are your injuries today?" Jess sighed.

"I'm a little sore, but I'll survive." Wade reached for her hand and tugged her closer.

"That's right, you owe me supper." Jess smirked and he cupped the back of her head.

"I do and as soon as I'm out of here, I'll be paying that debt." Wade pulled her face down until her lips were a hair away from his.

"I haven't brushed my..." Jess tried to pull back but he didn't give her a chance to finish the sentence as he silenced her with his mouth covering hers.

Jess whimpered but cupped his face between her hands as he devoured her mouth. The feel of her lips against his had his dick hard and when she slipped her tongue into his mouth, he groaned.

He was about to tug her on top of him when he heard a voice outside the room. Jess pulled back quickly, but he saw the arousal in her eyes.

"Kissing you is addictive," she whispered.

Before he could respond, the voice outside the room entered. His doctor and James stepped into his room. From the smirks on their faces, they'd been in the room and stepped out to give them privacy.

"Did we interrupt something?" Dr. Kramer wiggled his eyebrows.

"Yes," Wade growled as he lifted his good leg to hide the semi-erection showing through the thin sheet.

"Too bad." The doctor chuckled and made his way to the side of the bed.

"Adam, you're such a shit." Jess laughed.

"Is that any way to talk to the doctor who's going to get your man here back in peak form?" Adam pressed his hand against his chest.

"He's already in peak form," Wade retorted.

"I'll be the judge of that after your MRI." The doctor pointed his finger at Wade.

"When is he going for the test?" James asked as he wrapped his arm around Jess.

"In about an hour," Adam responded while he examined Wade.

"Good, gives me time to talk to Wade before he goes." James kissed Jess on the temple and sat in the recliner.

After he told James what he remembered and had the MRI, Wade sat on the edge of the bed, praying Adam would say he could go home. He hated the hospital and wanted to get out sooner rather than later.

His leg ached, but that was nothing new. He'd managed to put weight on it as he made his way to the washroom after his test, so he knew it wasn't broken again. His ribs hurt and he still had a bitch of a headache, but he wanted out. He also needed to figure out how much business he was about to lose.

"Why are you not in bed?" Jess walked into the room in a pair of jeans and a dark-green sweater, looking so damn sexy he ached for her.

"I just came back from the bathroom." Wade smiled and held out his hand.

"I'm not kissing you again until you are out of this place." Jess narrowed her eyes.

"Why?" Wade chuckled.

"Because people keep walking in." Jess sat next to him on the bed.

"I'm waiting for Dr. Kramer to come in and tell me I can leave." Wade glanced toward the door.

"You feel good enough to go home?" Jess ran her finger across his cheek where he'd seen the bruise on his face earlier.

"I'm fine, Blue Eyes. I'm in no more pain now than any other day," Wade lied.

"That's not true. You don't have hurt ribs or bruises every other day." Jess stood up and stepped in front of him.

"This is nothing compared to what I went through eight years ago." Wade rested his hands on her hips. "I want to go home so I can finally take you out."

"Hey, I asked you, remember." Jess wrapped her arms around his neck.

"Yep, but you said that we had that date here at the hospital. So, this will be our second one and I'm planning it." Wade tugged her between his legs.

"Okay." She smiled and pressed her forehead against his.

He could smell the flowery scent from her hair, and Wade smiled. It shouldn't surprise him Jess would use something with a floral scent.

"Are you ready to get sprung out of this place? Oops." Adam chuckled.

"I'm more than ready." Wade smiled as he tipped his head back to look up at Jess.

"Your leg looks good and everything else will heal. Try to take it easy for a few weeks. I've got a prescription here for pain…" Wade stopped Adam before he continued.

"Don't need that medication," Wade interrupted.

"Wade, it's not going to hurt to have it," Jess complained.

"I don't need it. I have medication at home that I use when the pain gets too intense." Wade wasn't lying.

He did have it home, but he just never used it. He couldn't remember the last time he'd taken one. Wade used meditation to help him deal with pain. Also, the yoga he'd started a couple of years earlier helped him more with the pain and discomfort than any medication he'd ever taken.

"Take it anyway. If you don't fill it, that's your choice." Adam held out the paper.

When Wade didn't take it, Jess huffed and took the paper from the doctor. After a few more ridiculous instructions about taking it easy and no heavy lifting until his ribs healed, Wade was on his way home.

When Wade walked outside, he took a deep cleansing breath. It hurt to do it, but it was so good to not be inhaling the antiseptic scent. His relief was short lived when he glanced at the car Jess parked in front of the entrance. It wasn't her old car and it wasn't one of his loaners.

"It's Kristy's car," Jess answered his unasked question.

What concerned him was how the hell he would squeeze his body into the front seat of the tiny vehicle. Jettas weren't built for men of his size, but he would force himself into the car just so he could get home and spend time with Jess.

"Ready?" Jess asked.

Wade could feel the ache in his ribs even at the thought of trying to fold his body into the car. Jess was so concerned about him, she probably didn't even realize how small the car was. Wade slowly made his way to the passenger side of the car and reached for the handle.

"Hey, Grease Monkey. Get away from my baby." An amused female voice behind him made him turn.

Kristy leaned against the front of an SUV with a huge grin on her face. He glanced back at Jess who looked equally amused at his confusion.

"You didn't think we'd make you squeeze into that tiny car, did you?" Jess smirked.

"Well, you pulled up in it." Wade shook his head.

"What are you, six-foot-two?" Kristy stepped in front of him and looked up at him. "My husband says getting in my car is like trying to fit into a sardine can."

"That sounds like an accurate description." Wade laughed.

"Hey, that's my baby." Kristy pointed her finger at him and narrowed her eyes.

"And you're just the right size for it." Wade chuckled.

Kristy hitched her thumb over her shoulder in the direction of the SUV. She gave them a finger wave as she got into the smaller car and zoomed away from the entrance of the hospital. Wade walked to the SUV and opened the door.

"That wasn't funny." Wade raised an eyebrow at Jess as she hopped in the truck.

"It was a little funny," She snickered.

"I'm just glad I didn't have to squeeze into that front seat." Wade sighed as he pulled the seatbelt around himself.

Wade made himself as comfortable as he could on the ride back to his house. He asked Jess to take him to the shop, but after she glared at him, he decided that it wasn't going to happen. It was kind of a stupid request, but he wanted to see what was going on.

She pulled into his driveway and before the vehicle was shut off, Ocean yanked it open. She wrapped her arms around him, and he winced but as much as it ached, he wasn't about to tell his daughter her hugs hurt.

"Dad, I'm so glad you're home." She pulled back as he smoothed his hand over the top of her head.

"Me too, baby." Wade kissed her forehead.

"Nan cleaned your blankets and made your bed. She has supper started and said Jess had to take you to bed when you got home." Ocean babbled as she stepped back for him to close the door of the SUV.

"Jess has to take me to bed, does she?" Wade glanced to the front of the vehicle where Jess stood smiling at Ocean.

"Eww, Dad, don't be gross." Ocean gagged.

"What?" He feigned innocence.

"I'm twelve, Dad, I know what you're insinuating." Ocean rolled her eyes.

Wade hated the thought of his daughter growing up. He missed the little girl who would run to him when he got home. The sweet little baby who begged him to play Barbies with her or take her out to play with the toy trucks she'd wanted him to buy for her.

Ocean loved to play with dolls when she was younger, but she also used to like playing with toy cars and had a huge box that she would pretend was a garage where the cars went to be fixed. He still had that box and all the little cars tucked away in the attic.

"You're staying for supper, right, Jess?" Ocean asked as she ran toward the house.

"Yes, she is," Wade answered before Jess could respond.

"I didn't agree to that." Jess narrowed her eyes.

"Then you'll miss out on my mother's beef stew with pastry." Wade winked.

"I can't miss out on that." Jess walked next to him while they made their way to the house.

When they stepped inside, his mother met them in the foyer and pointed to the stairs. It seemed as if his mother wasn't going to let him do anything either.

"Get upstairs. I'll bring you both supper when it's ready." His mom turned and made her way back to the kitchen.

"You must be special because she'd never let me take girls to my room when I was a teenager." Wade slowly made his way up the steps to his room.

"Ocean's a teenager. Would you let her take boys to her room?" Jess teased as they stepped inside his bedroom.

"Ocean isn't allowed to have a boy within a thousand feet of her room." Wade placed his phone and bag on the dresser next to the door.

"You sound like my dad." Jess leaned against the doorjamb.

"I'm sure I sound like every dad who has a daughter." Wade eased down on his bed and braced himself against the headboard.

"Do you need anything?" She suddenly seemed nervous and he didn't want that.

"Just you to come over here." He slapped his hand against the mattress next to him.

"Wade," Jess warned.

"Jesus, do you think I'm a pervert? I was going to put on a movie." Wade motioned toward his fifty-inch screen mounted on the wall opposite his bed.

"Oh." Jess blushed as she moved toward the bed.

"Do you really think I could do that right now?" Wade could barely breathe let alone make love.

Not that he didn't want to because he'd never wanted anyone or anything more. Jess had a sweetness about her that drew him in, but that didn't take away from her smart-ass attitude, her intelligence, or that killer body.

They were two episodes into repeats of an American police show when he heard a light knock. He shouted for them to come in and the door opened slowly. Jess moved closer to the other side of the bed as his mother stepped into the room carrying a tray.

"Mom, I could've come down to eat," Wade complained.

"Jess told me what the doctor said. You're supposed to take it easy for a few weeks." His mother placed the tray across his lap.

"Traitor," Wade grumbled when Jess giggled.

"There's plenty left downstairs if you want more and Ocean is on the way up with dessert." His mom kissed the top of his head and smiled down at him.

"Thanks, Mom." Wade knew how lucky he was to have a family like his.

"Thanks, Mrs. Rivers," Jess said as she picked up the other bowl of hot stew.

"It's Renee, and you're welcome. If that boy of mine gets out of hand, you just come tell me." His mother winked and left the room.

"Jesus, do all the women in my family think I'm some sort of horn dog?" Wade grabbed a thick slice of his mother's homemade bread.

"I'm starting to wonder about you." Jess chuckled as she lifted a spoonful of stew in her mouth and moaned.

That didn't help at all. Wade wondered if she'd sound the same once he got her naked in his bed. Wade still had pain, but his dick didn't seem to care when Jess was close. The thought of having her under him made him painfully hard.

Wade shifted and was glad the tray covered his growing erection. Maybe his family was right. He was a pervert, but it wasn't like that was the only reason he wanted to be with Jess. No. He loved her and that was the one thing he was sure of.

Monday morning, Wade made his way downstairs, ready to head to the garage. He remembered what the doctor said, but he wanted to get there and see what damage the intruder had done. Josie and Harry spent the entire weekend calling customers booked for the first part of the week and getting them either in with other garages or rescheduling appointments.

Harry insisted the garage be closed until the whole place was inspected yet again. Wade agreed and wanted to figure out what to do about security. Harry was enraged that Wade and the police officer got hurt. Wade was angry, too. The police officer was still in the hospital. According to Jess, the lower part of his leg was broken, but he would recover.

Jess spent the weekend with him watching television and talking about their lives. The more time they spent together, the more he wanted to spend with her.

He didn't like the idea of her going home at night, but she was stubborn. When his mother suggested she stay in the spare room if she wasn't comfortable staying in the room with Wade, Jess assured her that wasn't the reason she couldn't stay.

Wade was about to go through the door when he heard a car pull into the driveway. He didn't know who would be coming to his house so early in the morning, but when he opened the door, he tensed at the sight of Kurt O'Connor walking up the steps to his house.

"Kurt, is Jess okay?" It was the first thought that came to his mind because the only time Kurt had ever come to Wade's house was when they signed the contract for his shop to exclusively perform service on the cars for the NPD.

"My daughter is fine," Kurt growled through clenched teeth.

"Okay, good." Wade took a step back and allowed Kurt to enter his house.

"We need to talk." Kurt poked Wade in the chest and he was glad the man hadn't poked lower on his injured ribs.

Wade motioned for Kurt to follow him into the kitchen. Monday mornings were quiet at his house because his father and mother did aquafit. Carla would drop them off and she and Ocean would go to breakfast at one of the fast food places. It was why Wade knew he could sneak out to the garage.

As they entered the kitchen, his dog bounded toward them and stopped in front of Kurt, blocking his entrance to the kitchen. When Kurt tried to step around Rufus, the dog would whine and block again.

"Does your dog sense that I want to kick your ass?" Kurt grumbled.

"Maybe." Wade glanced down at the normally playful dog. "Why do you want to kick my ass, exactly?"

"You need to ask?" Kurt snapped.

"Isn't Jess an adult? I'm pretty sure she said she was almost thirty-five. She's the first woman I've ever met that admitted her age." Wade poured himself a cup of coffee and held the pot up to Kurt. "Want one?"

"Call off the dog, Rivers," Kurt growled.

"Rufus, here," Wade ordered and the black Labrador sniffed Kurt once more before he bounded over to Wade.

"Now, I'll have that coffee." Kurt sat on the kitchen chair and slapped his hand on the table.

Wade limped to the table and placed a cup of coffee in front of Jess' father. He knew Kurt had coffee black since he'd been in his garage so often. What he didn't know was why he was at Wade's house.

"So, what's up?" Wade asked as he eased into the chair across from Kurt.

"How are you feeling, by the way?" Kurt asked after he sipped the coffee.

"Good," Wade lied.

He wasn't good. His leg pained almost as much as it did when he hurt it the first time. He had trouble sleeping because it was hard to get comfortable with the bruised ribs and the headache still plagued him.

"Liar." Kurt snorted.

"You didn't come here to check on my health, Kurt. What's wrong?" Wade wasn't one for beating around the bush.

"First, I'm glad you weren't hurt more than you were. John and James are trying to figure this shit out. I'm concerned about your intentions with my daughter." Kurt stared him directly in the eyes.

"Do you think I'd hurt her?" Wade felt wounded that a man who knew him for so many years would think so poorly of him.

"No, I know you won't because she'd drop you like a bag of shit. What I'm concerned about is if you're willing to commit to her." Kurt tapped his finger on the table top.

"Kurt, I care about your daughter. We've only known each other for a few months, as you know, but I've never met a woman that I've wanted to be with as much as Jess." Wade figured honesty was best.

Kurt stared at him for several minutes before he dropped his head and blew out a huge breath. The man looked distressed, making Wade wonder if there was something Kurt wasn't saying.

"Kurt, I won't hurt Jess. Not intentionally, but I am a man and you know how stupid we are. I'm bound to do something dumb to piss her off." Wade leaned his elbows on the table.

"Yep, I do that on a daily basis, and I've been married for almost forty years." Kurt chuckled.

"So, you're well aware of how stupid we are." Wade laughed.

"I just want to make sure you're not going to play with her heart. Jess puts off as being this tough cop, or former cop, but I know my little girl. Her heart will break like a piece of glass. If she gives it to you, you better guard it with your life. You got me?" Kurt stared straight into Wade's eyes.

"I got you." Wade held out his hand and Kurt shook it.

"By the way, where were you going when I got here? Jess said you're supposed to take it easy." Kurt smirked.

"I just need to get out of the house for a bit." Wade sort of told the truth.

"Probably take a little trip to Tim Horton's and then casually drop by the shop." Kurt raised an eyebrow.

"You're going to rat me out, aren't you?" Wade laughed.

"Hell no. I'll just file this away in case I need to use it at a later date." Kurt grinned.

Wade rolled his eyes and he followed Kurt out of the house. He had about twenty minutes before his parents returned. He'd deal with that rampage later. Jess told him she'd be at her shop until five and would drop in before she went home for the evening. He wondered if he could convince her to go out that evening.

Wade walked into the shop and got several lectures from Harry, Josie, and Everett. They were the only three in the building except for the inspectors who were in checking all the equipment. Keith and two of the guys who worked for him were installing high-end security locks on all the garage doors and windows.

Wade watched Gage "Smash" Hodder and Caden "Rex" Dixon as they attached one of the motion sensors in the corner of the reception area.

Wade thought it was funny how all the men who worked for Keith had nicknames. He didn't know the reason for most of their names, but Smash told him the reason he got the name was because he could smash the keys on the computer like nobody. Keith had stood behind Smash shaking his head, so Wade wasn't sure that was the truth.

Rex wasn't from Newfoundland, that was obvious by his American Southern accent. He told Wade he was from a small town in Georgia and Rex met Keith when a mutual friend introduced them. Wade had no doubt that the man was also former military because of the way he held himself, as well as the tattoo on his bicep.

The only one of Keith's employees who didn't have a nickname was Sandy. She was married to Keith's brother and was one of the best computer analysts in the country. The few times Wade met her, he could tell she was a woman who didn't take any shit.

"Rusty, check the app on Wade's iPad," Smash shouted to Keith, who was in the office.

Keith's nickname was obvious since he had red hair. Most of the O'Connors had the auburn in varying degrees. Although, none of them were as sexy as Jess.

"Got all the cams showing," Keith yelled back.

Wade didn't know if all this was necessary or if it would help, but he couldn't afford not to try it. He was on his way back to talk to Keith in the office when his phone rang in his pocket.

"Hey, Blue Eyes," Wade answered when he saw Jess' number on the phone.

"Why are you not at home?" She didn't sound pissed, but he was sure another lecture was coming.

"I am at home." He chuckled.

"Oh, really? Then why am I looking at you walking to your office." She chuckled when Wade spun around.

Jess stood by the main entrance with her phone to her ear, her other hand on her hip, and a beautiful smile on her face. His heart flipped in his chest at the sight of her.

"I could ask you the same thing." Wade kept the phone to his ear and leaned against the door jamb leading to the back.

"I went to your house to surprise you because I finished early, but you weren't there," Jess spoke into the phone.

"It was a nice thought and I'm delighted to see you now." Wade smiled.

"Are you two just going to talk to each other on the phone when you're in the same room? Go kiss the girl for Christ's sake," Everett grumbled.

"Sounds like a plan." Wade shoved his phone in his pocket and stalked toward her.

He stepped next to her and cupped her beautiful face in his hands. He brushed his lips across hers once, then did it a second time. Jess smiled as she rested her hands on his chest.

"You're still in trouble for not listening to the doctor. You should be home resting." She narrowed her eyes.

"If I go home and stay in bed then I guess that means I can't take you out tonight." He grinned.

"Not if you're in pain. I saw you wince when you walked toward me." Jess smoothed her hands across his chest.

"Blue Eyes, I'm always wincing. My leg has been like that for years. I promise it's nothing new." Wade brushed his thumbs across her cheeks.

"Then take something for it," she whispered.

"I'll be fine." Wade kissed her forehead.

"If you don't like medication, why don't you try yoga?" Jess raised an eyebrow.

Wade stared at her for a moment, then it suddenly hit him that she knew. The corner of her lips quirked, but she didn't say another word.

"How?" he asked.

"I saw your mat," she whispered.

"I usually do it in the morning and before I go to bed I meditate," Wade admitted.

"I love yoga," she whispered.

"I'd love to watch you do the downward dog." Wade wiggled his eyebrows.

Jess laughed and shook her head. The sound was like music to his ears. He would tell jokes all day long if it kept that beautiful smile on her face.

"How are things going here?" Jess asked as she waved to Smash.

"Good, the inspectors are meticulous, or if you listen to Harry, a pain in the ass." Wade took her hand as they walked toward his office.

"Hopefully, we catch the guy." She seemed distracted. "I mean they."

"You seem unsure about quitting." Wade glanced down at her.

"No, I'm sure. There's just something about this whole situation that I can't put my finger on." Jess glanced through the window that looked into the garage bays.

Wade stood behind her and watched the inspectors. They were completed with the older ramps and started on the newly installed ones. They hadn't even been used yet and one of them already put someone in the hospital. Not that it was his fault.

Wade didn't know why someone was trying to put him out of business. He started to regret moving from the old building, but he'd hoped to really increase business by moving to a busier part of St. John's. The problem was, the move might cost him and Harry their business.

# *Chapter 9*

Jess couldn't shake the feeling something was staring them right in the face. She scanned the garage area, taking in each of the ten lifts. It didn't look any different than any other repair shop except it was a lot neater than most.

She watched the two inspectors as they meticulously checked every section of the garage. Jess scanned up to the ceiling and down the walls. Something was out of place, but she couldn't tell what it was.

"Jess, what are you looking at?" Wade wrapped his arms around her shoulders and pulled her against him.

"I don't know. There's something there, but for the life of me, I can't figure out what it is. Did you ever feel like the answer was right in front of you, but you didn't see it?" Jess turned her head so she could look up at him.

"Yeah, but I don't see anything out of place. I don't know how these bastards are getting into my building or why they're out to destroy me and Harry." Wade squeezed her gently and she placed her hands on his forearms where they lay across her chest.

"At least with all this new security equipment and security here every night, it might stop, or at least catch them." Jess turned in his arms and rested her hands against his chest.

"I'm sorry." Wade cradled her head in his hands.

"For what?" Jess had no idea why he'd be apologizing to her.

"I wanted to romance you, treat you like you deserve to be treated, and make you feel like you're the most important person in the world, but instead our first date starts with you finding me unconscious on the floor and ends in the hospital." Wade's forehead furrowed as he gazed into her eyes.

"I thought that was a great first date. I can honestly say I've never been on a date like that." Jess smiled.

"Jess, I don't want to lose you because of all this shit that's happening. I know you can do way better than me ..." He whispered but Jess pressed her fingers to his lips.

"Stop right there. I don't know why you keep putting yourself down, but I don't want to hear you do that anymore. Wade, I've had a better time with you over the last few days than I've had in the last ten years. Sure, it wasn't the dining and romance you think it should be, but you know what?" Jess placed her hands on his cheeks.

"What?" Wade stared into her eyes.

"Watching movies, talking, playing twenty questions with you all weekend while we hung out in your room were the best dates

I've ever had. Don't you get it? I want to be with you because of you. I enjoy spending time with you. It doesn't matter what we're doing, who we're with, or where we are. I. Like. Being. With. You." She smiled.

Jess wanted to tell him she was falling in love with him, but she didn't think either of them were ready to say those words. She hoped he felt the same way, but she didn't want to be the first one to say it.

"You are one amazing lady, Jess. How nobody has snatched you up before now is beyond me, but I'm one lucky son of a gun that you were available because let me tell you something, I'm not going to be stupid enough to let you get away. I'm yours as long as you want me." Wade pressed his forehead against hers.

"You two are sickly cute." Sandy's teasing made Jess laugh.

"Yes, we are." Wade kissed Jess' forehead and turned around.

"It's about freaking time you two got together." Sandy winked.

"I didn't realize you were here." Jess felt a little embarrassed with the way Sandy grinned at them.

"I'm everywhere. By the way, what's this shit about you quitting the force?" Sandy narrowed her eyes.

"Don't start on me, Sandy." Jess sighed.

"I'm kidding. I'm glad you made a decision before you dropped down in a heap." Sandy pointed at her. "I'm still not happy you didn't tell me first. I had to hear it from my husband. What happened to the woman club?" Sandy complained.

"Sorry, I didn't know there was a club." Jess chuckled.

"There is, and you better remember that." Sandy walked toward Jess and turned to Wade. "And you better not hurt my girl here. If Kurt doesn't kick your ass, I will."

"I wouldn't think of it." Wade held out his hand and Sandy shook it.

"Good. Now, I was sent to get you so I can show you how to work this security system. How computer savvy are you?" Sandy turned the laptop toward him.

"I get by." Wade bent down to look at the screen, but his arm remained around Jess.

"Well, you're about to have a crash course on one of the best systems in the country. Created by me and Smash, patent pending, of course." Sandy motioned for them to follow her into Wade's office.

Two hours later, Jess could only shake her head at Sandy as she tried with great difficulty to show Wade, Harry, Josie, and Everett how to monitor and work with the system.

Jess wasn't really paying attention, and what she did hear confused the hell out of her, but Wade seemed to understand. Sandy surprised her because she was so patient with everyone. She had the idea that maybe Sandy should work with the senior citizens at the community center teaching them the basics of computers.

The inspectors left, but something still needled at her. Jess probably should've stayed out of the garage, but she shook that thought out of her head as she made her way through the door.

It didn't seem as creepy as it had on Friday. The scent of oil and gas was strong, but it was a garage, so that was expected. She stood still and scanned down one side then up the other.

There were six lifts in the front of the garage area that were accessed from the front of the building. Four lifts were on the left and could only be obtained from the back of the building. To her immediate left was a wall with a large bulletin board. Under it, a large stainless-steel counter ran the entire length of the wall.

It hit her like a slap in the face. That part of the garage didn't have an entrance from the outside. She stepped toward the counter and scanned the wall behind it. The lift next to that section of the garage was where Neil had been trapped.

"What is it? There's something here," Jess murmured to herself.

After ten minutes, she still didn't know what drew her to the area and she spun around in frustration. She stopped when she noticed the corner of where the two walls met. It appeared as if the two walls were separated.

As she walked closer, she realized it was an opening. Jess pushed the wall and it moved inward. She gave it another push and it opened enough for her to look inside.

"I wonder if Wade knows about this room." Jess pushed the makeshift door all the way open.

There weren't any windows, but it was surprisingly clean. In one corner was a mini-fridge covered in dust but it didn't look ancient. She opened it and closed it quickly as a foul odor emanated from inside. Something inside had gone rancid.

The room was lit by the overhead lights, but she could tell that when they were turned off, the place would be pitch black. Since there was such a thick layer of dust on the floor and fridge, it appeared that Wade and Harry weren't aware of the extra space.

She scanned the room as she slowly walked further inside. The only other thing in the room was an old mattress on the floor in the far left-hand corner. As she got closer, there was a strong smell of dirt. The bed was stained and a dirty blanket was balled up in the middle of it.

It appeared as if someone had lived there at one time. Considering the state of the mattress and the blanket, she hoped there wasn't anyone still living there. If this was the reason Wade had issues, then someone was pissed because Wade took over the building.

She hurried out of the room to go tell James and Wade about the hidden area. When she turned, she bounced off a chest and someone gripped her arms. Jess gasped.

# Chapter 10

Wade blew out an exhausted breath as he finally figured out how to maneuver around the system that Sandy set up. It wasn't really that difficult, but it was new and trying to learn it with Harry gave him a headache.

"You can check it from home, too. I've put the program on your laptop and hopefully, soon we will have an app that you can put on your phone. Smash and I are working on that," Sandy said with pride.

"You're so smart, Sandy." Josie was obviously impressed with the spunky brunette.

"I've been told that once or twice." Sandy laughed.

"Yeah, also that she's a smartass." Keith chuckled.

"That too." Sandy grinned.

"So when can we open again?" Harry asked.

"We can open the day after tomorrow." Wade stood up.

He noticed Jess leave the office shortly after the inspectors finished. Wade wanted to get out of the garage and spend the evening with her. It was about time he gave her the romantic date she deserved.

"Sounds good to me. Another day off sounds like heaven." Everett grinned.

"Another one on the hook, Kennedy?" Harry chuckled.

"I never kiss and tell." Everett winked and stood up. "I'll see you all Wednesday morning."

"Wade, Trunk and Rex will be on security tonight." Keith handed Wade a piece of paper.

Ben "Trunk" Murphy stepped into the office a scowl on his face as he shoved his phone into his pocket. He looked as if he could kill someone with one hand, but it was the first time Wade had seen the man look so pissed.

"Hey, Trunk." Wade held out his hand.

"Nice to see you again, Wade." Trunk shook hands with Wade.

"What's up your ass?" Keith asked, obviously seeing the anger on Trunk's face.

"One word, fucking women," Trunk grumbled.

"That's actually two words, Trunk." Sandy laughed. "Abbie giving you blue balls again?"

"Shut it, Sandy. Nothing's going on with me and that woman." Trunk narrowed his eyes and glared at Sandy.

"Maybe not but it doesn't mean you don't want a piece of it." Sandy laughed as she packed her laptop into a bag.

"Sandy, leave the man alone." Keith laughed.

"I'm gonna do a round outside." Trunk turned and stomped out of the office.

"What was that about?" Josie raised an eyebrow as she linked into Harry's arm.

"Two people who are madly in love with each other but neither of them will get their heads out of their asses," Sandy said in a matter-of-fact tone.

"At least this one finally woke up and went after what he wanted." Josie nodded toward Wade.

"Yes, I did, and if everyone is done with me, I'm about to take a beautiful lady out to supper." Wade backed out of the office.

"I'll make sure everything is in place before I go," Harry shouted.

Wade waved and made his way out to the front of the building. Smash and Rex sat on the leather chairs watching the television mounted on the wall over the front counter.

"Did Jess go outside?" Wade asked as he walked toward the exit.

"Jess didn't come out this way," Smash said.

Wade furrowed his brow as he walked back toward the office. He checked the door on the parts room, but it was locked. Wade pushed open the door to the garage and his heart rate started to pick up when he didn't see her.

The hair on the back of his neck prickled as he ambled to the end of the garage. He stepped next to one of the large doors and glanced out back. Again, Jess was nowhere to be seen. Wade started back toward the door leading to the front. He stopped when he noticed the wall next to the last lift was moved.

"What the fuck?" Wade made his way toward the opening.

He'd been in the building for almost six months and it was the first time Wade noticed that part of the wall opened. He was about to step inside when someone slammed into him.

"Oh my God." Jess gasped.

"Jess?" Wade caught her before she fell back.

"You scared the shit out of me." She placed her hands against his chest.

"How did you know that wall moved?" Wade glanced inside the opening.

"I saw a small crack in the corner and when I pushed it, I found a room. You didn't know it was there?" Jess tugged him into the room.

"No, what's in here?" Wade followed her.

He couldn't believe that he didn't know about the room. It smelled musty and looked as if it had been closed up for a while. He saw the mini-fridge and started toward it, but Jess stopped him.

"You don't want to open that." She wrinkled her nose and pinched it.

"Is that a mattress?" Wade stepped closer to the object.

"Do you think someone was living here before you bought the building?" Jess asked.

Wade took Jess' hand and tugged her out of the room. He pulled the wall closed, and practically dragged Jess behind him. Was it possible a squatter was screwing with his business because Wade took his home?

"I've got to talk to Harry." Wade exited the garage.

He entered his office and immediately went to Harry. His foreman turned to look at him. Harry's smile faded when he saw Wade's expression.

"What's wrong now?" Harry asked.

"Do you know if homeless people were living around this building?" Wade asked.

"Not that I know of. Why?" Harry asked.

"Jess just found a room on the back of the counter in the shop. We've been in this building six fucking months and nobody noticed a room hidden in there." Wade was pissed.

He started to wonder if the reason he got the building for such a reasonable price was that the owner couldn't deal with the squatters or homeless.

"Are you fucking kidding me?" Harry looked as stunned as Wade felt.

"I only noticed it because it was opened a little. Maybe one of the inspectors leaned against it or something," Jess said almost apologetically.

Wade had everyone follow him back to the hidden area of his garage. Harry, Josie, Sandy, Keith, and James each checked out the room and Jess warned them not to open the fridge before they went inside.

James spent the most time looking around. Wade figured he was checking for some kind of clue. It was creepy that someone could possibly live in the dusty area, but it was sad as well. The homeless population wasn't significant in St. John's, but the city did have them.

"It doesn't seem as if anyone has been there in a while, but I'm going to have a cam set up in that room. I also want to leave it the way it is, just in case." James tapped frantically into his phone.

A few seconds later, Smash walked in with another camera in his hand. While James explained what he wanted to be done, Smash quickly installed the tiny wireless device in an area that it wouldn't be seen easily.

"Since these have night vision, it won't matter how dark this room is. If anyone comes in here. They'll be recorded," Smash explained as Sandy hastily tapped the keys on the laptop Smash handed to her.

"Good." Wade blew out a breath.

"You go ahead and take Jess out. We'll deal with this." Harry nodded toward the exit.

"You sure?" Wade hated to leave everything on Harry's shoulders.

"I'm positive." Harry winked.

Wade was reluctant to leave, but when his gaze fell on Jess, she smiled. Wade took her hand and after a quick glance toward the people in his garage, he left the building.

"Where are we going?" Jess asked as she headed toward her sister's car.

"To supper, but not in that car." Wade tugged her toward his truck.

"Aw, come on. I want to see you try to get into it." Jess snickered.

"Not a chance, Blue Eyes." He pulled the passenger door of his truck open and waited for her to climb inside.

Wade thought about taking her to his favorite fish and chips place, but Jess was a little bit of a health nut. He didn't want to take her someplace where she wouldn't eat anything.

"I'm in the mood for something greasy and unhealthy," Jess said as if she read his mind.

"Really?" Wade asked as they made their way out of the city toward the little place he loved.

"Yeah." Jess laughed.

"I thought you only ate kale and that funny stuff that people try to replace with rice." Wade chuckled.

"You mean Quinoa?" Jess snorted.

"Yeah, Carla tries to trick us with that shit all the time." Wade shuddered.

"It's not that bad, and to answer your question, yes, I do eat mostly healthy, but I do fall off the wagon now and then." Jess smiled and he reached across the seat to take her hand.

"I doubt you do it very often." Wade turned into the parking lot of the small restaurant just outside of town.

*By the Beach* was exactly that. It was located across from Logy Bay Beach and had a breathtaking view of the ocean. The food was also some of the best in the province.

"Wow, this reminds me of Hopedale." Jess scanned the area as he helped her out of the truck.

"I've only been to Hopedale a few times, but it seems like a great place to live." Wade wished he'd gone there more often because maybe he would've met Jess sooner.

"It's a great place to grow up. I'm hoping to buy a house soon," Jess said shyly.

"Is that the reason you refuse to buy a new car?" Wade smiled as they sat across the table from each other.

"Yeah." Jess linked their hands together. "I never expected to meet anyone, and I wanted a home of my own."

"It's the same reason I bought a house big enough for my parents and sister to live with me." Wade ran his thumb across his knuckles. "It's not conducive to dating when you tell someone you live with your parents, sister, and daughter."

"I think it's wonderful." Jess' smile made his heart feel as if it was going to burst.

"I think you're wonderful, beautiful, sweet, smart, and the sexiest damn woman I've ever met," he whispered as he brought her hand up to his lips.

"What can I get ya?" A young girl stepped up to the table, chewing gum and looking really bored.

"We'll have two specials with gravy." Wade didn't look up at the girl because his eyes were locked on Jess.

"Drinks?" the girl asked.

"I'll have water," Jess answered.

"I'll have water as well." Wade smiled when Jess tried to pull her hands back from where he had them pressed against his lips.

"Order should be up in a few minutes," the waitress said and walked away from the table.

"Stay at my house tonight." Wade didn't actually ask, but he was hoping she wouldn't slap him.

"Wade, I don't sleep with a guy on the first date." She winked.

"That's not why I'm asking you to stay at the house. We have a guest room. I just don't like you driving back to Hopedale on your own." Wade sighed when she ran her thumb across his lower lip.

"I've been driving that road since I was seventeen." Jess chuckled.

"How often did your father follow you before he allowed you to do it on your own?" Wade raised an eyebrow, knowing it was the type of father Kurt was.

"Probably for a year." Jess rolled her eyes.

"He's a bit protective." Wade chuckled.

The food arrived and as usual, it was delicious. The fish was fresh, and the batter was crispy. It was paired with thick homemade fries and smothered in gravy. However, Jess made it difficult for him to enjoy the meal because the soft moans she continued to emit had him rock hard.

Of course, she was just enjoying the meal, but it made his oversexed brain think of how he could make her moan like that in bed.

"I've never had anything so good in my mouth," Jess said, making Wade almost choke on his food.

When his eyes met hers, he could see she knew where his mind went. Thankfully, she didn't toss her fork at him. She smirked and pulled the fork slowly out of her mouth, making sure her lips were pressed tightly against it. It was Wade's turn to moan.

"Mr. Rivers, where exactly did your mind go a second ago?" Jess narrowed her eyes and pointed her fork at him.

"Ms. O'Connor, I have no idea what you mean." Wade feigned innocence and pushed back his almost empty plate.

"Sure, you don't." She stared at him for a moment then went back to her food.

Wade watched her as she took her time savoring every bite she took. He noticed she ate slowly, almost deliberately and took small bites. It made him wonder if she really liked the food. As if she sensed him staring at her, she glanced up and then at his plate. She let out a huge sigh and put her fork down.

"I know, I eat really slow." She rolled her eyes.

"Nothing wrong with that." Wade smiled.

"Tell that to my parents, my sisters, and anyone else who has ever sat down to eat with me," Jess grumbled.

"I don't care if it takes two hours for you to eat. As long as you enjoy it and I get to spend time with you." Wade picked up her fork and held it out to her.

Jess stared at him for a moment before she hesitantly took the fork and began to eat again. He really didn't care if it took her all night to eat her meal.

The waitress returned several times to see if they wanted anything else. She almost seemed annoyed when she saw Jess still eating. Wade asked for a coffee and told her he'd let her know when they were done.

"This is why I hate going out to restaurants. At least ones that are not owned by my family." Jess smiled as she put her fork on her almost empty plate.

"Did you enjoy the meal?" Wade reached across and grasped her hand in his.

"Yes, it was so good." Jess smiled.

"Well, that's all that matters to me." Wade brought her hand to his lips and placed a kiss on each knuckle.

After they'd shared dessert, Wade paid for the meal and they left the restaurant. There was a chill in the air but considering it was

September, that wasn't unusual. Jess wrapped her arm around his waist and tugged him toward the beach.

"I love the smell of the salt water. It always calms me. I know you do yoga, but have you ever gone to the beach to meditate or actually practice yoga?" Jess asked as they found a large rock to sit on.

"Blue Eyes, you are probably the only person who knows I practice yoga. Well, besides my physical therapist who was the first one to tell me about it. He was pretty stubborn about the whole thing and convinced it would help." Wade wrapped his arm around her shoulder, and she snuggled into his side.

"Does it?" Jess asked.

Wade didn't know how to answer the question because he'd been doing it for so long, he wasn't sure how bad his leg would be if he didn't do it. He was convinced he'd be in worse shape if he didn't practice it regularly.

"I think it does," Wade admitted.

"Then why do you keep it a secret?" Jess snickered.

"I don't really. I just started to do it in my room where it was quiet." He really didn't care who knew.

They were quiet for a few minutes as they watched the waves crash on the rocks and roll out again. Jess was right, it was calming, and being there with the woman who'd stolen his heart made it that much better. All the stress of the last week started to fade away.

Wade had always loved the ocean. When he was a little boy, he'd go on his father's fishing boat whenever he could. As much as he liked to fish, it wasn't what he wanted to do with his life. Wade was surprised his father hadn't been upset when Wade told him he didn't want to spend his life on the water.

His father had said fishing was his life, but it was hard and could be very dangerous around the Newfoundland coast. Wade's dad had lost a lot of friends to the Atlantic Ocean, but he never regretted becoming a fisherman. Wade's father worked hard to support the family.

It suddenly hit Wade that maybe moving to Hopedale would be suitable for his whole family. His father would be near the water, Ocean would've good friends close by. She'd really clicked with Sandy's daughters and it was much like the town where Wade grew up. He wanted that for his daughter.

It was definitely something to consider, especially if he wanted to spend his life with Jess. Hopefully, they'd figure out what was going on at his shop before someone put him out of business or worse, killed someone.

# Chapter 11

Jess watched him as they drove back to the garage to get her sister's car. It took almost an hour for her to convince him he didn't have to drive her home. She had to admit she was tempted to stay at his house, but she didn't want to stay in the guest room.

They pulled into the parking lot as Trunk appeared around the corner of the building. He seemed relaxed and grinned when he sauntered toward them.

"Hey, what are you doing back here? Rivers, a garage is no place to end a date." Trunk chuckled.

"How would you know?" Rex called out as he came from the other side of the building.

"Don't you have something to do inside, fucker?" Trunk grumbled.

"When you two are finished with your lover's spat could you tell me where Kristy's car is?" Jess scanned around the lot.

"James had it brought back to Kristy because he thought Wade would be driving you home." Trunk leaned his large arms on the window of the truck.

"Damn it." Jess sighed.

"I guess I'm driving you home, after all." Wade winked at Trunk.

"Did you tell James to bring the car home?" Jess narrowed her eyes and glared at him.

"Nope." Wade smiled.

Jess sat back in the truck and crossed her arms over her chest. She had a feeling Wade did call her cousin. She was happy to spend a little more time with him, but she wasn't about to let him know that.

While Wade chatted with Trunk for several minutes, Jess' mind went back to the hidden area inside the building. Torbay Road wasn't an area where the homeless of the city usually hung out. She doubted it had anything to do with that community. Not that there were as many homeless as in the larger cities like Toronto, but it was a problem.

Whoever owned the building before Wade may know something about the room. Jess heard Wade say that the building had been a garage in the past, which was why he jumped at the chance to get it. Knowing James, he'd probably already contacted the old owner.

Maybe the previous owner had issues and it was why he sold the building. Her police instincts were on high alert and she knew the answer to what was happening with Wade's business was right in front of them. She just couldn't put her finger on it.

"Ready, to go, Blue Eyes?" Wade's voice brought her out of her thoughts.

"Yeah, although I still think this was a setup." Jess smirked.

"Are you getting tired of spending time with me?" Wade ran his finger under her chin.

"No, I just don't like the thought of you driving home alone." Jess lay back on the headrest and gazed at the man she was quickly falling in love with.

"I'll be fine." Wade pulled out of the lot and headed toward the highway.

When Wade drove into her father's driveway and shut off his truck. As he picked up her hand, he turned to face her and brought it to his lips.

He seemed to have a thing for kissing her hand, but she thought it was romantic and sweet. Wade tucked a piece of her hair behind her ear and smiled.

"You're so beautiful," Wade whispered. "You take my breath away every time I look at you."

Jess slid closer to him and brushed her lips against his. He hadn't kissed her since earlier that day and she ached to feel his lips against hers.

Wade cupped her cheek and she moaned when his warm mouth covered hers. The feel of his strong, calloused hand against her cheek was sensual, and as their lips moved against each other, Jess wondered how his hands would feel on her naked skin.

As she slid her hand behind his neck, she opened her mouth to his tongue. Their tongues swirled together in an erotic dance that had her heart pounding and her sex throbbing.

"Jesus, Jess." Wade gasped as he pulled his lips from hers.

"Don't stop." Jess panted as she pulled him to her again.

Wade plowed his hands into her hair and tilted her head as he covered her mouth. She didn't care that it was after midnight or that her parents' house was less than ten feet away. Jess wanted to lose herself in Wade.

"Jess, if your father comes out here and sees us like this, he'll shoot me." Wade breathed against her neck.

"Come inside." The words were out of her mouth before she could stop it.

"Blue Eyes, as much as I'd love to go inside and continue this, I think we need to cool down a little. Fuck, it's not going to be easy because I want to strip you naked and bury myself deep inside you." Wade's voice was strained, and he pressed his forehead against hers.

"Wade," she moaned because she was on fire.

"Jess, I want you. More than I've ever wanted anyone in my life, but you're special to me. The first time I take you, I'm going to take my time and not worry about your family or my family barging in." Wade gazed into her eyes, and she fell for him a little more.

"As much as I hate this, I know my family. If they see your truck in the driveway, they'll all be banging down the door." Jess sighed.

"Yeah, it's not the way I want to tell your parents how I feel about you." Wade ran his thumb across her lower lip and smiled.

"How do you feel about me, Wade?" Jess bit her lip.

"If I tell you that, you might run away." Wade held her face between his hands and she could see the apprehension in his eyes.

"What about if I tell you how I feel?" She covered his hands with hers.

"Okay," he whispered and gazed into her eyes.

"I'm in love with you, and I can say with one hundred percent truth that I've never felt this way about anyone in my entire life. I know it hasn't been that long, but I know without a doubt that I love you, Wade." Her eyes filled with tears when she saw one run down his cheek.

"Jesus, you just made me the happiest man on the face of this earth, Blue Eyes. I never thought I could fall in love so damn fast, but I swear the first time you got snarky about that piece-of-shit

Honda, I knew it then. I just never thought I had a chance in hell with you." Wade pulled her closer and stared into her eyes.

"My car is not a piece of shit. I'm starting to wonder if I brought it to the right garage." She smirked.

"Jesus, I love you, Jess. Don't ever lose that smart mouth." With those words, he slammed his lips against hers and she fisted his shirt as they devoured each other's mouths.

Wade pulled away first and pressed his forehead against hers. They stayed like that for several minutes until their heavy breathing returned to normal.

"I need to go," he whispered as he kissed her temple.

"Okay." Jess closed her eyes and took a deep breath.

"It's not that I want to." He groaned.

"I know, but the last thing I want is Dad, Mom, or even Nan busting into my apartment because your truck is here." She kissed his cheek.

"I love you, Jess," Wade whispered once more as she reached for the door handle.

"I love you too, Wade. Very much." Jess gave him another quick kiss and jumped out of the truck.

He waited until she was inside the apartment before he pulled out of the driveway. Jess rolled her eyes when he motioned for her to go in before he left. It wasn't like she couldn't protect herself, but it gave her a warm feeling to know he worried about her.

Before she went to bed, she checked the living room to see if her cousin was there. Pam had texted her earlier and said she wasn't sure if she would be staying at her own place or if she would be back to Jess' apartment.

Since Pam wasn't in the living room, she assumed she now had her apartment to herself again. She knew she had a long day at the flower shop the next day because it was her payroll day. She also had a meeting with Jason's niece to give her a schedule of what shifts she'd be working.

Jess did feel less stressed even though it had been less than a week since her last shift with the NPD. She was also in her element when she was in the back of her shop putting flower arrangements together.

*The Rose Garden* was all hers and had been for over ten years. Jess took over the business when her old boss retired. Edith Buckley had opened the shop when she was in her early twenties. Jess started working there when she was in high school and continued through university. Even when she was going through the police academy, she worked there part-time.

The day she graduated from university with a Bachelor of Business, Edith called her into her office and offered Jess the opportunity of a lifetime. Jess would pay Edith a percentage of the profits until she'd paid off the business. Jess had talked to her parents about it and after several meetings with lawyers, Jess owned the flower shop.

Two years later, Edith passed away suddenly. To Jess' surprise, the debt was cleared and she owned the shop free and clear. It was tough to lose Edith because she'd been such a big part of Jess' life, but she would forever be thankful to the sweet lady.

Now she was the boss and treated her employees the same way Edith treated her. It was why she hadn't had a huge turnover in staff over the years. Janelle Holden worked at the shop when Edith owned it and Jess kept her on staff. Jess hired Monica Fleet after she'd started with the NPD. It helped free up some time for Jess having two employees, but she did need more help.

That was why she hired Melina as well. Jason's niece would only work part-time, but she was glad to be able to help someone the way Edith helped her.

Jess woke up still smiling from the night before. As much as she wished Wade had stayed, the fact that he felt the same way she did made her giddy with joy.

She laughed when she realized she'd been singing to herself the whole time she got ready to go to the shop. She was on the bottom of the steps from her apartment when she realized Kristy's car wasn't in her driveway. Trunk said the vehicle was brought back to Hopedale, but they probably brought it to Kristy's place.

She was almost at the end of the driveway when Isabelle pulled in next to her. Her sister looked flustered and obviously needed to talk.

"Get in," Isabelle snapped.

"I've got to go get Kristy's car," Jess told her sister.

"Yeah, I'm driving you to the shop. I need to vent and Kristy is on a double-shift at the hospital, Pam's hiding from her mother, and I know I vented to you already, but please let me do it again." Isabelle held her hands together as Jess pulled open the door.

"I'm assuming the venting is about a certain sexy chef." Jess chuckled.

"Yes, but stop calling him sexy." Isabelle playfully slapped Jess on the leg.

"I call it like I see it." Jess slapped her sister back on the arm.

"I'm addicted," Isabelle whined.

"To …" Jess circled her hand in the air, indicating that her sister should elaborate.

"Roman," Isabelle sighed.

"You're addicted to Roman?" Jess tried not to laugh, but she didn't see the problem.

"I keep sleeping with him." Isabelle groaned.

"And that's a bad thing, why?" Jess furrowed her brow.

"Because he works for me," Isabelle continued.

"Is it just sex or is it more?" Jess knew Isabelle hadn't been in a relationship in a long time.

"No. Yes. Shit, I don't know," Isabelle shouted.

"Okay, look. The first thing you need to do is find out if this is more than sex or not." Jess could see the turmoil in her sister's expression.

One thing Isabelle hated was not being in control and if she didn't know how she felt about Roman, she was out of control. If she was falling for Roman, her sister's little controlled world was about to tip on its axis.

"That's the same thing that Kristy said," Isabelle groaned.

"Our little sister is a smart cookie." Jess snorted.

"I can't be falling for him." Isabelle sighed.

"Has he met Cora yet?" Jess snorted when Isabelle glared at her.

"No," her sister snapped.

"Maybe he should. At least then you'd know if there is something there." Cora had never been wrong about any couple Jess could remember.

"Since when do you believe in Cora the Cupid?" Isabelle laughed.

Jess didn't answer and Isabelle's head snapped to the side as she stopped in front of the shop. Jess met her sister's blue eyes and smiled.

"Oh. My. God. You and the mechanic?" Isabelle grinned.

"He's so great, Isabelle." Jess sighed.

"Why are my little sisters falling in love before me?" Isabelle pulled Jess into her arms and hugged her.

"If you'd let yourself lose control for a minute maybe you'd figure out what's going on with you and the chef," Jess teased her sister.

"That the problem. I lose control around him. He smiles and that fucking dimple shows and I swear my clothes just vanish." Isabelle pulled back and shook her head. "I'm helpless around him."

"Well, keep your clothes on and try a date or two." Jess giggled as Isabelle narrowed her eyes.

"Go pick some flowers." Isabelle pointed at the shop.

"Thanks for driving me to work. Have no idea how I'm getting home, but I'll get someone to pick me up. Love you." Jess waved as Isabelle drove off.

Jess unlocked the door to her shop, and the intense floral aroma instantly made her smile. She loved it when she walked into her shop first thing because she could really smell the array of different flowers. Once she was in the shop for a while, the scent wasn't as noticeable. So that first sniff in the morning was probably how people felt when they got the whiff of coffee first thing in the morning.

The store didn't open until ten in the morning and she asked Melina to come in at nine so Jess could show her around. Since Janelle opened the store in the morning, she also usually arrived around nine.

Jess made her way to the greenhouse at the back of the shop. Most of the flowers she sold were grown there. Jess special ordered some flowers if a customer requested plants they didn't grow themselves or if she didn't have any left in the store. For the most part, most people ordered simple flowers like roses, carnations, sunflowers, tulips, and orchids. She also carried a small selection of house plants, but most of her inventory was flowers.

Jess made her rounds in the greenhouse. She watered what needed water and pruned what needed pruning. She was on her way back to the front of the shop to wait for Melina when her phone vibrated in her pocket.

Jess pulled it out and smiled. The text from Wade was sweet, and sappy all at the same time. He even included two heart emojis at the end of his text.

*Wade: How is the most beautiful woman in the world today?*

*Jess: You should text her and ask.*

*Wade: I did, Blue Eyes. You're the most beautiful woman in the world.*

*Jess: If you say so.*

*Wade: I do. Now, you didn't answer my question.*

*Jess: I'm good. Just at the shop waiting for the new girl I hired. What about you?*

*Wade: I'm trying to get used to having so much security around here. I thought they'd only be here after we close, but according to James, one of them will be here during the day as well.*

*Jess: He just wants to be careful.*

*Wade: I know.*

Jess was about to text him back, but her phone rang. She laughed as his number appeared on her screen.

"Why didn't you just call in the first place?" Jess climbed on the stool behind the counter.

"I don't know. I don't mind short texts, but I'd rather hear your sexy voice." Wade's voice rumbled in her ear.

"I like hearing your voice too." Jess smiled.

"I know it's only Thursday, but can I see you tonight?" Wade asked.

"Sure, I'll be done here around four." Jess wiggled in the seat with excitement.

"We don't close until five but fuck it, I'm leaving early."
Wade chuckled.

"Won't you get in trouble with the boss? I heard he could be
a real hard ass," Jess teased.

"Nah, he's a pushover." Wade laughed.

"He might fire you." Jess laughed.

"I'd never fire myself." Wade's sexy laugh tickled her ear
even through the phone.

"That would be kind of weird." Jess saw Melina wave at her
from the front door.

"True. So, will I meet you at home?" Wade asked.

"If it's not too much trouble, would you pick me up here?
Isabelle dropped me off this morning." Jess hurried to the door to let
Melina in.

"I'll be there at four, but we'll have to run to my house so I
can clean up," Wade said. "Maybe you could wash my back for me."

"Only if you do mine too." Jess burst out laughing when he
groaned.

"You're trying to kill me, Blue Eyes." Wade growled. "I'll
see you later."

When she hung up, she turned to Melina. She hadn't seen
much of the young girl over the last several years but seeing her
standing head and shoulders above her made Jess feel short and old.

"I see you've inherited your dad's height." Jess hugged the pretty brunette.

"Yeah." Melina smiled.

"Let's start in the greenhouse and work our way out front." Jess motioned for Melina to follow her.

They were about to walk to the back when Janelle entered into the shop. She grinned as she locked the door behind her and hurried toward Jess.

"You must be the new girl. I'm Janelle." She held out her hand and shook Melina's hand.

"Nice to meet you." Melina smiled shyly.

"So, one question. Do you know that man in the car?" Janelle asked Jess.

"If you're talking about the white mustang, that's my dad." Melina laughed.

"Your dad?" Janelle looked completely shocked.

Jess knew exactly what her friend was thinking. Jason's brother was an incredibly handsome man. Jess always joked with Jason and Noel that they should have been models. They reminded Jess of the actors Jerry and Charlie O'Connell.

"Yes." Melina laughed.

"Is he single?" Janelle asked not so innocently.

"Today, yes, but that could change by tomorrow." Melina rolled her eyes.

"I see he hasn't changed." Jess rolled her eyes.

Noel was a great father, but he was a player and lived in a bachelor apartment in downtown St. John's. Although he always put Melina first in his life, he still had his share of ladies, even at nearly forty years old.

"Oh, he's another A.J. and Nick." Janelle rolled her eyes.

"Not sure what that means, but if you mean he changes girlfriends like underwear, then yes. I love him, but it's gross the way he shuffles women." Melina shuddered.

"By the way, Janelle, A.J. and Nick are not like that anymore." Jess felt the need to defend her happily married cousins.

By three-forty-five, Jess had everything done she needed to get done. The schedule for two weeks, the payroll, and she even managed to pay some bills.

She was killing time adjusting things that didn't need to be fixed out front while she waited for Wade to pick her up. She had just checked through the door for the third time when she heard a snicker behind her.

"She's got it so bad." Janelle nudged Monica with her elbow.

"That's the understatement of the year. She's arse over kettle." Monica snorted as she prepared a flower arrangement in a vase.

Arse over kettle was a Newfoundland way of saying a person was head over heels. It could mean they were head over heels in love or they tripped and tumbled over.

"I wonder when we get to meet the man that put that rosy color in her cheeks." Janelle placed her elbow on the counter and rested her chin on her fist.

"Will you please stop talking like I'm not here." Jess rolled her eyes.

"When do we meet him?" Monica asked as the bell over the front door chimed.

"If it's me you're talking about, how about we meet right now?" Jess turned as Wade stepped behind her.

"Oh my." Janelle fanned herself.

"You can say that again." Monica tilted her head as she blatantly eyed Wade from head to toe.

"Wade, Janelle is the one fanning herself and Monica is the one undressing you with her eyes." Jess laughed.

"Who wouldn't want to undress him? Damn." Monica winked.

"Okay, so we're going now." Jess turned and pushed Wade back toward the door.

"Nice meeting you ladies," Wade shouted over her head as they stepped outside.

Before the door closed, Wade pulled her against him and covered her mouth with his before she could utter a word of protest. She vaguely heard Janelle and Monica hoot from inside the store, but it was hard to say for sure because she was completely lost in Wade's kiss.

# *Chapter 12*

Wade ended the kiss before he pushed Jess against the side of the building and finished what he'd wanted to do since the previous night.

"Hi," Jess panted when he pulled back.

"Hi." Wade tucked a piece of hair behind her ear.

"How was your day?" Jess cleared her throat as he linked his fingers with hers.

"Much better now." He brought her hand to his lips as they walked toward his truck.

He opened the door of the truck and Jess smiled as she climbed inside. Wade couldn't help himself as he gave her a quick kiss before he closed the door and walked around the truck to get in.

"I need to make a quick stop at the house to get cleaned up and help Ocean with something for school. Is that okay?" Wade asked.

Ocean had called him just before he left the garage to ask for his help with a project for school. For some reason, his parents told his daughter that Wade was the only one that could help with that particular homework. Before he could ask what it was, he got interrupted by one of the mechanics. He told Ocean he'd help when he got home.

"Of course not. She's your daughter, Ocean should be your first priority." Jess touched his cheek.

Wade smiled as he pulled away from the flower shop and headed home. He was excited about what he had planned for Jess that evening. He wanted her to have a great time.

Wade arrived home and Jess was out of the truck before he could get around to open her door. She looked at him sheepishly when he told her he was supposed to open her door. Apparently, she hadn't been shown by previous boyfriends how she should be treated.

Before they made it to the front steps the front door of his house opened. Wade's mother met Jess at the top of the steps and hugged her tightly.

"There's the beautiful woman that saved my son's life." When he heard the way his mother's voice cracked he felt terrible for worrying her.

"Mom, let Jess go before you smother her." Carla laughed from the door.

"I'm sorry, I haven't had a chance to thank you for what you did." His mom cupped Jess' face in her hands.

"I didn't do anything, Renee." Jess looked uncomfortable.

"If you hadn't gone when you did, God knows what would've happened. That terrible person might have gone back and done more damage to Wade and that poor officer." His mother pulled Jess into a hug again.

"Mom, can we go inside before Jess decides my family is crazy and runs away?" Wade pulled his mother back from Jess and turned her toward the door.

"You've met my family, right?" Jess raised an eyebrow.

Wade reluctantly left Jess in the kitchen with his mother and sister while he went to help Ocean with her project. It wasn't unusual for her to ask for help, but it was a little odd for his parents or Carla to tell him he was the only one who could help.

"Come in," Ocean shouted from inside her room after he'd knocked.

"Hey, baby." Wade made his way to where Ocean sat at her desk.

"Hi, Dad." Ocean seemed sad somehow.

"What's wrong?" Wade crouched next to her and his daddy instincts went on high alert when he saw the tears in his daughter's eyes.

"Nothing." She sniffed and wiped away the tears.

Wade grabbed the arm of her chair and turned her to face him. Ocean didn't cry for no reason and the tears running down her cheeks broke his heart.

"Baby, I can't fix it if you don't tell me what's causing those tears." Wade used his knuckle to wipe a tear running down her cheek.

"You can't fix this, Dad." She sighed.

"I'd like to be the judge of that." Wade hated to move away from her, but crouching didn't feel good on his leg.

He dragged her chair next to the bed and sat down. He pulled Ocean in front of him and took her small hands in his. He'd do anything to take away her pain.

"I don't know anything about my mother." He barely heard her, but the words were clear.

"I see." Wade squeezed her hand gently.

"I'm doing a family tree for social studies and I know everything about your side, but the only thing I know about my mother's side is her name." Ocean wouldn't look at him.

"And if you don't get that information, you'll fail the project." Wade knew that wasn't the reason she was so upset.

"No, my teacher said to just put in the family members I know." She sighed.

"Ocean, come here." Wade tugged her out of the chair and she sat on his lap.

She hadn't done that in a long time. She was growing up so fast she didn't need his cuddles as much as she used to, but the last thing he wanted was for her to be upset.

"Do you remember when you were five, you asked why you didn't have a mommy?" He kissed her temple.

"Yeah, all my friends had their moms taking them to school, but I didn't." She rested her head on his shoulder.

"Do you remember what I told you?" He wrapped his arms tightly around her.

"That I did have a mommy, but she knew she could never be the kind of mom I needed. It's why she left me with you, nana, pop, and Aunt Carla. She knew I'd have all the love and care I needed," Ocean repeated almost verbatim what he'd told her back then.

"That's right," Wade said.

"Dad, that explanation was okay for a five-year-old, but I know that isn't the real reason. She didn't want me." Ocean sniffed.

"Ocean, that's not true." Wade pulled her back so he could look in her eyes.

"Dad, I've heard you and Nana talk about her over the years." Ocean sighed.

"Baby, your mother didn't know how to be a mom. She didn't have a great childhood and you were a surprise when we weren't exactly careful." Wade cringed at the way Ocean gagged.

"God, Dad, I don't want to hear about how you had unprotected sex." She shuddered.

"Okay, but don't ever think or believe you were never wanted." Wade held her face in his hands.

"I was an accident, Dad." Tears started to stream down her cheeks again.

"No, you were a surprise." Wade insisted.

"What's the difference, Dad?" Ocean rolled her eyes.

"The difference is an accident is not something you would want to happen again. A surprise is something you would do over because it was something you never knew you wanted or needed until you had it." Wade stared straight into her grey eyes.

"I…" She stopped and bit her lip.

"You want to meet her." Wade finished the sentence that he knew would come one day.

"Yes." She sounded so apologetic for what she wanted.

"Then I'll see what I can do about that." He smiled and kissed her forehead.

Ocean wrapped her arms around his neck, and he hugged her tightly. He'd do anything to keep a smile on his daughter's face. If he had to track down Sky and force her to meet with Ocean, he'd move heaven and earth to do it.

"It doesn't mean I don't love you, Dad. I'd like to meet her just once." She sobbed against his shoulder.

"I'll make sure you do," Wade promised.

After he'd settled Ocean into her bed to watch a movie, he showered and changed. As he walked into the kitchen, his thoughts were distracted with how he'd find Sky. He didn't have a clue on how to go about it.

"Did you work everything out?" His mother glanced at him.

"Yeah, I just don't know how to give her what she wants." Wade glanced at Jess and forced a smile.

"I know." Jess pulled out her phone. "If you don't mind me helping."

"I knew what Ocean wanted, but I told her she needed to talk to you about that." His mother smoothed her hand over the top of his head.

"How can you help me find Sky?" Wade asked Jess.

"You've met Sandy and Slash right?" She smiled when he nodded. "If someone exists, they'll find them."

Jess put the phone to her ear after she tapped in a number. Wade waited patiently as Jess discussed his issue with Sandy. He didn't like the thought of bringing Sky back into Ocean's life because if she was still the same way as she was when he'd first met her, he knew she'd probably not want to talk to her daughter. He prayed the woman had some maternal instinct and she'd agree to meet with Ocean.

"Yeah, Carla said she's seen her in the city, but we don't know where she lives or works. All Wade knows is her name, the year she graduated from Memorial University, and her age." Jess gave Sandy all the information Wade remembered.

It didn't seem like much to go on to find a person in more than half a million people in the province of Newfoundland. It would be like finding a needle in a haystack.

"Sandy said she could find Sky with her eyes closed and we should give her something more challenging next time." Jess smirked after she hung up the phone.

"You mean like who the hell is trying to put me out of business?" Wade snorted.

"Damn, I should have said that to her." Jess slapped her hand on the table.

Wade and Jess snuggled together in one of the lawn chairs on the back deck after supper. It was a little nippy outside and his mother brought them a blanket as well as hot chocolate before she called it a night.

"It's so nice out here," Jess said as she sipped on her drink.

"I love this area. It's far enough out of town that it's peaceful. It's not exactly like the town I grew up in, but for being close to the city, it's as good as I'm going to get," Wade said as he stared up at the starlit sky.

"That's what I love about Hopedale," Jess said.

Wade was born and raised in an outport town. When he was younger, he itched to get away from small-town life. As he got older, he realized how great it was to live outside the city. It was why he jumped at the house where he currently lived.

"You're quiet." Jess brought him out of his thoughts.

"I'm sorry our date got ruined." He kissed the top of her head.

Jess shifted around so she was looking at him straight in the face. She put her drink on the ground and ran her hand over the top of his head.

"This date isn't ruined. As a matter of fact, this is probably one of the best dates we've ever had." She brushed her lips against his. "I wouldn't change a thing."

"You're so damn beautiful." He cupped her cheek and ran his thumb across her lower lip.

"I love you, Wade," Jess whispered as he lost himself in her blue eyes.

He loved her, but it didn't hit him until that moment that Jess was his and Ocean's future. Wade didn't know if Jess would be ready to become an instant parent. He knew Ocean liked her because she'd told him a couple of nights earlier.

"I love you, too, Jess, but are you ready to be with me and all my baggage?" Wade needed to know before he could take another step with her.

"What baggage?" Jess furrowed her brow.

"I'm a single dad with a permanent limp. I'll never be more than a broken mechanic." He saw her eyes widen.

"Is that what you think of yourself?" Jess looked pissed.

"It's what I am," he returned.

"You're so much more than that. You're an amazing father, to a wonderful young lady. You risked your life eight years ago to save the life of another little girl. Your mom and dad told me you take care of them every day and your sister idolizes you." Jess smiled. "I think you're pretty great too."

"Oh, you do, do you?" Wade wrapped his arms around her.

"I do, so stop calling yourself a broken-down mechanic because you're so much more than that to me and a lot of others." Jess placed a soft kiss on his lips and pulled back. "Got it?"

"Got it. How did you get so bossy?" Wade chuckled.

"My grandmother taught me." Jess snickered.

"I've heard she's everyone's boss." Wade tucked his face into the crook of her neck and breathed in her scent. "Jesus, you always smell so good."

Wade ran his lips up and down the side of her neck. His dick hardened instantly when she melted into him and moaned. With her warm body basically on top of him, it made him want to forget where they were and take her right there.

Jess grazed her lips against his ear and her hot breath sent shivers of desire through his body. It had been so long since he'd been intimate with anyone except himself. It seemed since he first saw Jess that happened more often.

She shifted so she straddled his hips and he tucked the blanket around them. He could feel her heat through their clothes and knowing she was as turned on as he was made his cock throb.

Wade grasped her hips as she pressed herself against his aching dick. Wade's lips found hers and he plunged his tongue into her mouth. Jess met his kiss with equal enthusiasm, and he moaned as she swiveled her hips in circles, making his dick rock-hard.

"Wade, I want you," Jess murmured against his lips.

"I want you too. So fucking bad." He cupped her ass and pressed her against his cock.

"We probably should stop before this goes too far." Jess panted as she lay her forehead against his.

"Everyone should be gone to bed by now," Wade whispered.

"Wade," she gasped his name.

"What? Carla is probably in her apartment with her headphones on." Wade knew his family's schedule better than his own. "Dad went to bed before we came out here, and Mom said she was heading to bed when she brought out the blanket." He kissed along her jaw.

"What about Ocean?" Jess slid her hands under his shirt and made him gasp.

"Fuck, your hands are cold." Wade sighed as she slowly caressed his chest.

"Wade, will Ocean get upset if I stay?" Jess sat up and gazed into his eyes.

"Ocean doesn't come into my room. Her room is on the other side of the house, but I understand if you don't feel comfortable staying." Wade did understand.

"Take me to your room," Jess whispered.

Wade lifted her off his lap and got to his feet. For the first time in a long time, he wished he could run because he would've picked her up and ran into the house.

Wade tugged her with him as they headed inside the house. When they stepped inside the kitchen from the back yard, she stopped.

"Are you sure?" She gripped his hand tightly.

"I'm positive, but if you're not ready, I'll take you home." Wade pulled her into his arms.

"Wade, I want you." She breathed against his lips.

Wade took her hand as they walked upstairs and down the hall to his bedroom. He couldn't believe how nervous he was. It wasn't as if he was a virgin, but it had been so long since he'd had a woman in his bed, he felt that way.

He closed the bedroom door behind them and leaned against it. Jess turned to face him and he tugged her into his arms. He didn't want to rush, but his body ached for her.

Wade slid his hands around to the back of her neck and lowered his lips to meet hers. Her arms wrapped around his waist as he kissed her slowly enjoying how her warm, soft lips felt against his.

Her tongue flicked across his lower lip. Wade caught it and sucked it inside his mouth. Jess moaned and Wade backed her toward the bed. His cock pressed painfully against the zipper of his jeans, but he wasn't about to set it free yet.

Jess eased the bottom of his shirt up over his body and he pulled his lips away from hers until he could pull it over his head. As soon as it fell to the floor, Wade consumed her lips again. Thankfully, her shirt had buttons and he opened them one by one as he moved his tongue across her jaw and down the side of her neck.

"Wade," she breathed against his cheek.

He slid her blouse down her arms as he kissed across her shoulder. Her skin was soft and silky against his hands and her floral scent intoxicated him. Wade stepped back to put some space between them before he spoke.

"You're so fucking beautiful." He glided his finger down her shoulder and followed the edge of her bra where it covered her plump breasts.

Wade sat on the bed. He pulled her between his knees as he placed soft kisses across her chest and slipped his tongue inside the edge of her cotton sports bra. Her nipples poked hard against the fabric and begged for his tongue.

Wade cupped one breast while he sucked the hard nipple through the soft fabric. Jess held his head between her hands as he worshipped her breasts with his hands and mouth.

"Oh, God. Wade," she breathed when he scraped his teeth against her nipple.

"Tell me what you want, Blue Eyes." He growled against her skin.

"Take off my bra and suck my nipples." She reached behind her.

Wade pulled her hands away to remove the garment. The sight of her naked tits begging to be touched had him ready to go off in his jeans.

"Touch me, Wade." Jess picked up one of his hands and brought it to her mouth.

Jess sucked his index finger into her mouth and Wade could swear he felt it in his dick. Her tongue swirled around the tip of his finger, making him groan with pleasure.

"Fuck." He cupped the back of her head and pulled her down to watch his finger slip from between her pink lips.

He pulled his finger out of her mouth and lowered his gaze to her nipple. Wade ran the finger slowly around her areola and her nipple pebbled hard and pink. Wade covered her breast with his hand and sucked her nipple hard into his mouth.

"Ah," Jess groaned.

Wade moved from one breast to the other and ran his hand down to the waistband of her jeans. Without a second thought, he popped the button on her jeans and unzipped them. He tugged them down over the curve of her hips.

She wore a pair of white cotton panties that he wanted to rip from her body. He slid his hand up her flat stomach and wasn't surprised to feel the muscle definition. Jess kept herself in top-notch shape and it was sexy as hell to him.

"Wade, touch me," she begged as he slipped her panties down her sexy legs.

He could smell her arousal and it only made him want to bury his cock deep inside her wetness. He could see her moisture glisten on her folds. What drove him crazy was she was bare except for a tiny patch of hair above her pussy.

Wade stood up and moved her until her knees hit the edge of the bed. Before he could lay her back on the bed, she grabbed the waistband of his jeans and tugged him toward her.

"These need to go." She purred as she released the top button. The head of his dick peeked out from the band of his boxers and she ran her finger over the pre-cum oozing out.

Wade shuddered when she put her finger into her mouth and sucked his essence from her finger. She tugged down his zipper and it was both painful and pleasurable to relieve the pressure against his dick.

"Jess, I'm about to go off like Old Faithful if you keep doing that." Wade groaned as she ran her tongue around the tip of his swollen member.

She pulled his jeans down along with his boxers, and his cock sprang forward, pointing right to her. Wade stepped out of his clothes and held her hands. If she touched his dick again, he wouldn't be able to hold back.

Jess moved up on the bed, and he crawled over her. He wanted to taste her so bad. Wade started at her ankles and kissed up each leg, slowly stopping short of where he wanted to kiss the most. He grinned when her hips raised off the bed and begged for him to taste her.

"You want my mouth there, Blue Eyes? You want my tongue to lick every sweet inch of you?" Wade whispered against her inner thigh.

"Fuck, yes." She groaned and fisted the hair at the back of his head.

Wade pushed her legs further apart and positioned himself so he wasn't putting any weight on her or his bad leg. Wade rested his weight on his elbows and lowered his head until his lips were a hair away from her wet folds.

"Look at me, Jess. Watch me while I taste you for the first time." Wade growled the words and knew she could feel the warmth of his breath against her because she shivered.

He looked up as he gently blew against her moisture. Jess opened her eyes and his gaze locked with hers as he licked his lips before he allowed his tongue to finally slide between her wet folds. She was soaked and tasted so much better than he could've ever imagined.

Wade slowly slid his tongue up and down, never breaking eye contact with her. He could tell she was struggling to keep her eyes from rolling back in her head when he licked slowly around her swollen clitoris. He grinned when she pressed her heels into the bed and slapped her hands against the mattress.

"Wade, please," she begged.

"What do you want, Jess?" Wade blew against her swollen nub.

"I need you to suck on it." She groaned.

"Gladly." Wade used one hand to open her folds and covered her clitoris with his lips.

Wade sucked it hard as he inserted two fingers into her hot opening. Her body started to convulse, and Wade sucked harder as he curled his fingers and pressed them against the inner wall of her pussy.

"Oh. My. God. Wade, yes," Jess moaned and shook as her orgasm slammed through her body.

Wade continued his ministrations until she grabbed the back of his head and pulled him away. He loved the way she tasted and didn't want to miss a drop of her release.

"Wade. God. I need to breathe," she panted.

Wade pulled his finger slowly from inside her, and she shivered once more. He slid his fingers inside his mouth and licked every drop of her essence off them.

She smiled as he slowly moved up until his mouth hovered over hers. His cock grazed her inner thigh and it was his turn to tremble. He couldn't remember ever being so hard and still not wanting it to be over.

"Wade, lay on your back," Jess whispered.

"Why?" He raised an eyebrow in confusion.

"I know this position can't be comfortable on your leg." She ran her hands across his chest.

"It's okay." He smiled.

She stopped him by pressing her lips against his and rolling them both over until she was on top. It was probably the best position in the world

"Can't you take a hint. I want to be on top." She sat up and winked.

"You'll get no argument from me." He cupped her breasts in his hands.

Jess straddled his legs and ran her hands lightly down his chest. The moonlight shining through the window glistened against her skin and made her look angelic. She continued to lightly caress his body and stopped at his hip.

Wade tensed. He knew she saw the scar and his first thought was it turned her off. He was about to say something when she leaned down over him and kissed her way down the entire length of the scar.

"Jess." Wade could barely say her name as she gently massaged his thigh where it always ached the most.

"Shhh," she whispered as she continued to work her way down to his knee.

He relaxed when he didn't see any disgust or any sign she was turned off by his scars. In fact, she seemed to be hypnotized by them.

"These have to be the sexiest scars I've ever seen," she whispered.

"There's nothing sexy about my leg, Jess." Wade chuckled.

Jess kissed the scars once more and moved until her wet heat rubbed against his balls. Jess leaned down and kissed across his chest as she continued to circle her hips.

"Your scars are sexy because you got them saving a little girl's life. It makes you who you are, and I love who you are." She lifted her head, and he cupped her face between his hands.

"I love you, Jess," he said through the lump that had formed in his throat.

"Make love to me, Wade," Jess whispered against his lips.

Wade had been smart earlier in the week and made the good decision of picking up a box of condoms. He yanked out the drawer of his side table and pulled out a strip of the foil packets. He tore one off and tossed the rest back in the drawer.

"I bought these recently." He told her because he didn't want her to think he had them there all the time.

"See, even your brain is sexy." Jess giggled as she took the condom from his hand.

Wade clenched his teeth as she slowly rolled the latex over his aching dick. He squeezed his eyes shut to keep from going off in her hand.

"I need to be inside you, Jess." Wade grabbed her hips and lifted her until she hovered over his swollen cock.

Jess rested her hands on his chest as she lowered herself onto him. It felt so good to be inside her, even if it was only the tip. Not only had it been a long time for him, but Jess told him she hadn't been with anyone in a long time.

Wade gripped her hips and kept her from moving down any further on his cock. It was like torture, but he was a large man and he needed to make sure he didn't do anything to make it painful for her. She looked at him and he could see the confusion in her expression.

"I don't want to hurt you. Are you okay?" He strangled on the words as she squirmed to take more of him inside.

"God, yes," Jess whispered.

Wade blew out a breath as he relaxed his grip and she slipped down over his hard length. He shivered at the pleasure that shot through him from just being inside her.

"Don't move yet, Jess. I need a minute." Wade took several deep breaths to calm himself before he went off.

Jess wasn't helping, she leaned over and began to circle each of his nipples with her tongue. When she sucked one into her hot mouth, Wade flipped her over and pinned her arms above her head.

"Baby, you keep doing that and this will be over in less than two seconds." Wade growled.

"I want to make you come," Jess whispered as she lifted her hips off the bed.

That was it for him. Wade covered her mouth with his and began to thrust in and out of her. The feel of her clenched around him was almost enough to make him want to shout out in pleasure.

Jess' hands grabbed his ass and squeezed as he pounded into her. He loved the fact that she wasn't afraid to show what she wanted, and she obviously wanted him to go faster.

"Oh. Wade. I'm gonna…" Jess arched off the bed and her pussy gripped tightly around his cock.

That was all he needed and after one more thrust, Wade exploded inside her. He squeezed his eyes shut as his body vibrated with pleasure. Every muscle in his body contracted and seemed like it wouldn't stop.

"Fuck, Jess." Wade groaned into her ear as his cock jerked inside her.

Wade collapsed and tried to keep from dropping his entire weight on top of her. He just didn't have the strength to flip them over at that moment.

The only sound in the room was the heavy breathing from both of them as they tried to catch their breath. Wade was about to move when he felt something cold hit the bottom of his foot.

Wade jumped off Jess and sat straight up in the bed. He had no idea what touched his foot, but when he turned to Jess, she was laughing and his dog's head rested on the edge of the mattress.

"Fuck, Rufus. How the hell did you get in the room?" Wade glanced up to see the door slightly ajar.

"Is he the reason you jumped off me?" Jess giggled.

"I felt something cold against the bottom of my foot. Guess it was that asshole's nose." Wade glared at the dog who didn't seem to care in the least as Jess scratched his ear.

"He probably thought we were in pain." Jess sounded completely serious.

"What?" Wade stared at her in confusion.

"Your mom said that when you have bad dreams, Rufus goes crazy trying to get into your room." Jess smiled at the dog.

"I wasn't in pain." Wade got down eye to eye with the dog. "In fact, quite the opposite."

"In the dog's defense, you were doing a lot of moaning and groaning. Probably sounded like pain to him." Jess smirked.

"I wasn't the only one moaning." Wade lay down next to Jess and whispered into her ear.

Jess giggled and it was the best thing he'd ever heard in his life. After several minutes of watching Rufus enjoy Jess' attention, Wade felt the condom wet against his leg.

"I need to get rid of the condom and put nosey out of the room." Wade got out of bed and headed to the bathroom.

When he returned, Jess had the blankets pulled over her and Rufus lay curled up next to her. Wade shook his head.

"Not a chance, Rufus." Wade pointed to the door.

Rufus lifted his head and looked at the door, then back at Jess. When the dog's eyes went back to Wade and he dropped his head back on the bed, Wade knew he wasn't about to win the argument with his dog. It looked like Jess had stolen Rufus's heart as well.

# *Chapter 13*

Jess was so warm. It was almost stifling but when she tried to move, it was as if she was trapped. Her eyes flew open when she heard what sounded like a whimper.

Jess blew out a breath of relief when she looked into the dark brown eyes of Rufus. He seemed concerned that Jess was squirming. When she turned her head she realized why she was so warm.

Wade had her practically under him with his arm wrapped around her chest, and his leg lay across hers. His hot breath blew against the side of her head, as he snored softly.

"I think he's trying to smother me, Rufus," Jess whispered as she ruffled the dog's ear.

Rufus sat up and wagged his tail frantically as he started to lick Wade's face. At first, Wade pushed the dog away and grumbled something under his breath. When Rufus refused to stop, Wade groaned and rolled over away from the dog.

"Rufus, get the hell off the bed." Wade draped his arm over his face as his dog refused to be ignored.

"I think he was trying to save me from smothering." Jess rolled onto her side and propped her chin up on her fist.

"He tends to try to lay on top of you." Wade playfully pushed the dog down.

"He wasn't the one with his arm and leg draped over me." Jess kissed his cheek.

"Oh, sorry. I was afraid you'd run out in the middle of the night." Wade smiled.

"That would never happen, but we'll have to talk about that snoring." Jess poked him in the chest, and he rolled over her, pinning her to the bed.

"I don't snore." He nipped the side of her neck.

Before she could respond, Rufus jumped on Wade and growled. Wade pushed the dog back but continued to tease, lick, and nip up and down Jess' neck.

Rufus wouldn't be ignored. Wade lifted his head to glare at his dog. When Jess turned to look at the sweet retriever, she started to laugh. Rufus sat on the bed with his head tilted, and tongue out.

"You're screwing with my mojo here, Rufus." Wade narrowed his eyes at the dog.

"You do realize you're glaring at a dog, right?" Jess snorted.

"Rufus, Pop got bacon." Wade pointed to the slightly opened bedroom door.

The dog obviously understood the word *bacon* because he jumped off the bed and ran out of the room. Wade practically tripped over his own feet as he hurried after the dog to close and lock the door.

"That was so cruel. It's only six in the morning." Jess felt bad for the poor little pooch who was happily bounding down the stairs in the hopes of having a feed of bacon.

"Trust me. That dog won't be disappointed. Dad gets up at five." Wade grinned as he crawled back under the covers and pulled her into his arms.

"What time do you have to be to work?" Jess sighed against his body.

"We open at eight but I'm pretty close to the owner. He said it was okay to go in late today." Wade cupped her ass and pulled her against him.

When she felt his hard length against her stomach, Jess reached between them and wrapped her hand around his shaft. Wade took a quick intake of air and moaned.

"Damn, I love your hand on me." Wade's hand glided up her back and around to cup her bare breast.

Wade lowered his head and ran his tongue around her nipple. She always had sensitive nipples, and her body shuddered as he sucked her hard bud into his warm mouth.

Jess stroked his thick length, and he moaned against her chest. She pushed him onto his back and got up on her knees. He tucked his hands behind his head.

"What time do you have to be at work?" Wade asked.

"Not until ten, but I have to go home to get changed before I go in. I can't exactly wear the same clothes I had on at work yesterday." Jess leaned down and ran her tongue around one of his flat nipples.

"I guess I'll have to drive you to your apartment to get changed." Wade closed his eyes as she placed soft kisses across his chest and down over his abdominals.

"I have at least an hour to enjoy this hard body." Jess smirked as she lowered her head and ran her tongue around the head of his cock.

"Fuck, take as much time as you want." Wade moaned.

It took a little more than an hour to get her fill of him, but they finally got dressed and were on the road to Hopedale. Jess couldn't wipe the smile off her face if she tried.

She was a little embarrassed when she walked into Wade's kitchen and his parents were at the table. They didn't say anything, but Renee winked at her when they were leaving.

Wade pulled into the driveway a little before eight, and she hoped to get dressed and back to the truck before someone saw her.

She was out of luck because as Jess hopped out of the truck, her mother came out of the house.

"Jess, thanks for letting me know you would be gone all night. I think your father would've had a search party out for you if I hadn't told him I got your text." Her mom said a little louder than normal, but when Jess looked toward the door, she saw her dad brooding on the step.

"It's why I texted you." Jess kissed her mother's cheek. "Thanks for the heads up, Mom," she whispered next to her mother's ear.

"If you couldn't get home last night, you could've called me." Her father grumbled as he opened the car door for her mother.

"I spent the evening with Wade's parents and daughter." Jess met her father's suspicious gaze.

"Where did you sleep?" her father asked.

"Kurt, that's none of your business. She's almost thirty-five years old. Now stop your sulking and drive me to work or I'll walk." Her mother shoved open the car door and glared at her dad.

"Fucking Cora needs to stay away from my girls." Her dad grumbled as he gave Wade a glare before he got in the car with her mother.

"You should drop over for breakfast before you go to town again," her mother shouted through the car window.

Jess turned as Wade stepped behind her and chuckled. He seemed amused by her father's grumpy mood. She'd expected it the minute he found out she was dating Wade. Not because he didn't like him but because her father had an issue with any man who looked at either of his daughters. He still didn't like Bull kissing Kristy in front of him and they'd been married for almost four years.

"Breakfast with your dad. I think he'd be praying I choke on the food." Wade laughed.

"Maybe, but we have time if you're hungry." Jess stood on her toes and kissed his chin.

"Sure, I always like to give Kurt a hard time. Dating his daughter is going to be fun." Wade winked as he followed her up the steps to her apartment.

"You must have a death wish." Jess snorted as she made her way to her bedroom to change.

Jess walked into the diner, and as usual, the place was packed with the breakfast crowd. She sometimes wondered why Hopedale had a grocery store because it seemed like half the population ate at *Jack's Place* or Isabelle's restaurant, *A Taste of Hopedale*.

She scanned the tables looking for family and didn't have to look very far when she spotted Sandy and Ian sitting at a corner booth. When Sandy spotted her, she motioned for Jess to sit with them.

"Hey, I was just about to call you. I found Sky." Sandy grinned.

"That was fast," Wade said as he slid into the booth next to Jess.

"I actually found her ten minutes after I hung up from Jess, but Ian came home and distracted me." Sandy wiggled her eyebrows.

"Lies." Ian gasped. "She jumped my bones as soon as I walked into the house."

"Where exactly were the kids?" Jess laughed.

"In bed. He was out with John and Keith. Kids were out like a light by the time he came home primed and ready to go." Sandy winked.

"Sandy, could you give this to your friend? He left it on the table just before he ran out of here." The pretty waitress handed a wallet to Sandy.

"That's because you make him nervous, Sabrina." Sandy winked at the waitress.

"Umm… I… can I take your order, Jess?" Sabrina completely ignored Sandy's statement.

Sabrina Burke had been working at the diner for over a year. Jess didn't know a lot about her except that she worked mornings at *Jack's Place*, afternoons at Pam's store cleaning, and evenings she cleaned Emily's beauty salon after it closed. She was a private person who worked really hard, but Hunter "Crunch" Crawford ate almost every breakfast and lunch at the diner since Sabrina started to work there. Lora told Jess she was sure Crunch had it bad for Sabrina but was too shy to ask her out.

"I'll have Mom's famous oatmeal with blueberries," Jess told the blushing girl.

"I'll have the same and a cup of black coffee." Wade smiled up at Sabrina.

"Tea for me, Sabrina," Jess smiled as Sabrina left the table

"Seriously, do you ever put anything in your mouth that's not good for you?" Ian asked making Sandy spew coffee across the table.

"I'm sure she did last night." Sandy snickered.

"Shut up." Jess tossed a napkin at her.

"You did have some of mom's chocolate cake." Wade turned to Jess and smirked.

"So, you had two desserts last night." Sandy laughed and slapped her hand on the table.

"Ian, shut her up." Jess glared at her cousin who sat across from her, grinning.

"He can only shut me up one way, and I don't think it's appropriate to do that here." Sandy winked.

"I knew we should have sat at another table." Jess sighed.

Jess wished she'd just gone straight to her shop when her mother arrived with their breakfast, instead of Sabrina. She glanced at Sandy when she heard her stifle a laugh.

"I don't think we have ever been introduced properly." Her mother held out her hand. "I'm, Alice O'Connor."

"Wade Rivers, it's nice to meet you, Mrs. O'Connor." Wade held out his hand.

Her mother grabbed Wade's hand and held it between her own two hands. Jess knew what was coming and closed her eyes. It probably wouldn't be a great idea to crawl under the table.

"Don't you go calling me Mrs. O'Connor. You call me Alice or if you're comfortable enough, call me Mom." Jess heard her mother walk away after the statement and opened her eyes.

Sandy had her lips pressed together, obviously trying to keep from laughing, and Ian had a huge smirk on his face. When she turned to look at Wade, instead of looking scared to death, he smiled.

"Does everyone call her mom, or should I consider myself special?" Wade laughed.

"Oh, you're special, Wade." Sandy laughed.

"Yeah, you're the chosen one." Ian chuckled.

"Shut. Up." Jess glared at her cousin.

"The chosen one?" Wade glanced around the table.

"Jess hasn't told you about her Aunt Cora, has she?" Sandy laughed.

"No, is that the woman I met the day the car caught on fire?" Wade glanced at Jess.

"Yes, they call her Cora the Cupid." Ian leaned back in the seat.

"Dear God." Jess dropped her head in her hand.

"I'm assuming there's a reason for that." Wade laughed.

"Aunt Cora has a special gift," Ian began.

"What kind of gift?" Wade seemed genuinely interested in what Ian was telling him.

"Since Aunt Cora was a little girl, she'd been able to tell people who they are meant to be with." Ian's face was completely serious.

Jess looked at Wade, who seemed to be waiting for a punchline of a joke. He kept glancing from Ian to her and obviously thought they were pulling his leg.

"She describes it as feeling warm and seeing flashes of the person in front of her or something like that. I usually don't listen because even though she's never been wrong, I still find it hard to believe." Ian wrapped his arm around Sandy.

"You're serious?" Wade narrowed his eyes at Ian.

"Completely, hence the name, Cora the Cupid," Ian said.

Wade sat back in the chair as if he was still waiting for everyone to laugh, but when they didn't, he looked down at Jess. She held her breath as she waited for him to run out of the diner screaming, but instead, a huge smile came across his face, and he kissed the top of her head as he draped his arm around her shoulders.

"Well, if Cora the Cupid says it's true, then who are we to doubt her?" Wade winked.

Jess blew out the breath she'd been holding and relaxed against his side. If that freaky story didn't make him run for the hills, then maybe Cora was right.

# Chapter 14

Monday morning came way too soon for Wade. He'd spent the entire weekend with Jess and it would be the first day they'd spent apart since Friday. Wade missed her the minute she left that morning.

He sat behind his desk and turned on his laptop. He went through his usual paperwork, sending appointment emails to Josie, sending invoices, and paying bills. It was almost lunchtime by the time he headed out of his office to see if he was needed in the garage.

He was also putting off making the dreaded call to Sky. Sandy gave him all of Ocean's mother's contact information, and he debated whether he should actually use it or not.

"Harry, need any extra help or is everything on schedule?" Wade shouted as he entered the garage.

"We're actually ahead of schedule," Harry replied.

"Great." Wade tried not to sound disappointed.

"Stop stalling and call her mother." Josie poked Wade in the side as she handed him a cup of coffee.

"I'm not stalling," Wade grumbled.

"Yes, you are. Look, I know you're scared, but Ocean wants to meet her mother, and you need to give her that." Josie was right.

The problem was Wade was terrified that Sky would say something to hurt Ocean. Sky wasn't exactly the maternal type from what he saw all those years ago. He didn't want his daughter to feel like she was never wanted.

"I know." Wade gave Josie a side hug and headed back to his office.

He pulled out his phone and brought up the phone number that Sandy gave him. He was about to tap it when a call came in. He wasn't about to ignore the only person that could make him feel calm.

"Hey, Blue Eyes," Wade answered.

"Hi, I just finished lunch and wanted to hear your voice before I get back to work." Jess' soft voice instantly calmed his frayed nerves.

"Hearing from you makes my day a whole lot brighter," Wade told her.

"That's nice to hear," she said.

"I've been putting off making a call today," Wade admitted.

"You've been putting it off all weekend, Wade. Ocean wants to talk to her mom," Jess replied.

"I'm concerned Ocean's going to get hurt, and it's going to kill me." Wade blew out a breath.

"Is it that, or are you worried Ocean will want to spend more time with Sky?" Jess hit the nail right on the head.

Wade was scared he'd lose his daughter if Sky decided she wanted to be a mother. She might have signed away her parental rights when Ocean was born, but if his daughter wanted to be with her mother, he couldn't deny that to her.

"That's part of it too." Wade sighed.

"Babe, your daughter loves you, and you'll always be her father. If she wants a relationship with her mom, you've got to give her that choice. She'll always be your little girl." He knew Jess was right.

"I know, but hearing you say it makes me believe it," Wade told her.

"Glad I can help." He could hear the smile in her voice.

"I love you, Jess," Wade whispered.

"I love you too. Go make your call, and I'll call you after work." She ended the call, and Sky's number showed on his phone again.

"Fuck it." Wade tapped the number and put the phone to his ear.

The phone rang several times before it went to voicemail, and he hung up. He didn't want to leave a message, but then he figured she might be one of those people who didn't answer for numbers she didn't know.

He was about to call back when his phone rang. It came up with a blocked caller, but he answered, hoping it wasn't some telemarketer.

"Hello?" Wade answered.

"Umm… Hi, you just called my number," a female voice said.

"Is this Sky Pushman?" For a second, he hoped it was a wrong number.

"Yes, who's this?" She didn't recognize his voice.

"Sky, this is Wade Rivers." There was silence for a moment.

"I'm sorry, Wade who?" She didn't remember him.

"Rivers," he repeated his last name.

"Oh, Wade. Talk about a blast from the past." She chuckled.

"Sky, I need to speak with you about Ocean." Wade figured the best way to start the conversation was get to the point.

"Who's Ocean?" Sky asked.

Wade clenched his teeth together. She didn't even remember her own daughter's name. It angered him, but he had to keep calm for Ocean's sake.

"My daughter," Wade snapped.

"Oh, what about her?" The more he talked to Sky, the more he wanted to lie to Ocean and say he couldn't find her.

"She's doing a project in school and needs information about her mother's family. She asked me to get in touch with you and to see if you can meet with her to fill in the missing areas of her project." Wade pressed his lips together as he waited for her to respond.

"There isn't much to tell. I don't have any family," she responded.

"Sky, I know your family life wasn't the best growing up, but my daughter needs to meet you. Can you please take an hour out of your life to meet with her? Did you think she was never going to want to meet you?" Wade tried to remain calm, but it was difficult.

"I figured you would've told her I died or something. I mean, it wasn't like I was involved in anything with her. I gave birth and handed her to you. I don't want to be a mother. I never did." She sounded so cold.

"I know that. Believe me, I remember that. Just give her an hour and then you can go on with your life. You owe her that much," Wade snapped.

Sky didn't speak for several minutes, and Wade was doing everything he could not to hang up on her. He did understand her aversion to parenting. Sky's mother was abusive, and her father wasn't in the picture.

"Sky?" Wade needed an answer so he could figure out what he needed to tell Ocean.

"Okay," she said, and for a moment Wade thought she was crying.

"When can you meet with us?" Wade's heart pounded with the thought of his daughter meeting Sky.

"I'm free tomorrow evening. Where can I meet you?" She seemed apprehensive but he expected that.

Wade gave her the address to his house. If she was going to meet with Ocean, Wade wanted his daughter to have support around her in case it didn't go well.

"Thanks, Sky. I know you aren't comfortable with this, but for what it's worth, Ocean needs this," Wade said.

"I understand. I hope this isn't a mistake." She hung up before Wade could answer.

Wade tossed his phone on the desk and ran his hand down over his face. Sky's words echoed in his brain. *I hope this isn't a mistake.* Wade hoped the same thing.

The rest of the day dragged on, but the little texts from Jess made the day easier. At a little past five, he walked out to the front reception area as Harry was impatiently arguing with a man Wade didn't recognize.

"I'm telling you, the car does not have a flat tire, the rear axle is broken, and we ordered the part," Harry snapped.

"My son wouldn't lie to me. He said he brought the car here, and you told him you'd fix the flat tire," the man shouted.

"Harry, what's the problem?" Wade dropped his hand on Harry's shoulder.

"Mr. Duggan says his son dropped off his vehicle with a flat tire." Harry turned to Wade. "It's the car with the cracked rear axle."

"Mr. Duggan, I was the one who checked the vehicle. Your son, is Lee Duggan, is that correct?" Wade took the work order from Harry.

"Yes, I just established that with this idiot." The man pointed at Harry.

"Mr. Duggan, I'd appreciate if you didn't disrespect the staff." Wade kept his demeanor calm.

"I call it like I see it. My son wouldn't lie to me about something so serious." The man had to be delusional.

"The car is still on the ramp. I can bring you back and show you the damage." Wade motioned for Mr. Duggan to follow.

"I'm sure you could show me the damage, but it wasn't damaged when it got here. I'm not paying for that damage. I'll be calling my lawyer." He pulled out his phone.

"You can do that, Mr. Duggan but I'm afraid it would be a waste of your time. We have time-coded photos of the vehicle when it came into the shop." Wade didn't know if that would hold water, but he took the chance.

He glared at Wade for several minutes before he shoved his phone into his pocket again. Wade waited for the man to start another rant.

"Fix my car by the end of the day, or you'll be sorry you ever heard the name Miles Duggan." He turned and started for the exit.

"Are you related to Kaylee Duggan?" Wade shouted and Miles spun around.

"She's my daughter," he snapped at Wade. "How would you know her?"

"She goes to school with my daughter, Ocean," Wade answered.

"Oh, the little shoplifter. Kaylee told me about her. Guess it figures her father would own a garage that rips off its customers." Miles gave him a sly grin.

"Mr. Duggan, I'll be towing your vehicle to the address on the work order. We do not want or need your business. Just so you know, it will cost a lot more at the dealer." Wade handed the paper to Harry. "Call Curtis to tow that Lexus to the dealership."

"You can't do that." Miles started toward Wade.

"I can, and I am. I don't like the way you've spoken to me or my staff. Not to mention how you referred to my daughter. I'd appreciate it if you never stepped foot in my garage again. Oh, and a word of advice, you might want to buy a cheaper vehicle if your son is going to go off-roading." Wade stepped outside the counter.

"You'll be sorry for this." Miles took a step toward Wade.

"I'm already sorry I brought the car into my shop." Wade crossed his arms over his chest.

"Mr. Duggan, I think it's time for you to leave." Wade hadn't seen Trunk walk out from the back of the garage.

"Who's this, the fucking muscle?" Miles shouted.

"I'm security, and if you don't leave on your own, I'll help you make the right decision." Trunk's voice was calm, but his tone practically shouted, *don't fuck with me*.

It looked like Miles was about to challenge Trunk when another of Keith's security team stepped next to Trunk. Bruce "Hulk" Steel was not as tall as Trunk but just as wide. At the sight of the two large men, Miles spun on his heel and stomped through the door.

"Fucking asshole." Hulk shook his head.

"There's always one that reminds us not all Newfie's are happy-go-lucky." Harry laughed.

"Yeah, we've seen our fair share of them." Trunk rested his elbow on the counter.

"Lock the fucking door before any more find their way in here." Harry tossed Hulk the keys.

Wade pulled into the driveway of his house and sat in his truck. He still wasn't sure it was a good idea to have Sky and Ocean meet, but it was too late to change it now. He prayed Sky would show up, for Ocean's sake, but he wouldn't be disappointed if she bailed.

Wade stepped out of his truck and turned as a vehicle pulled into his driveway. He didn't recognize it, but it was new. He waited until the driver got out to approach the car.

Jess stepped out of the car with a massive grin on her face. It was a new Honda Civic, and he laughed as she waved her arm along the front of the car.

"Didn't you hear me when I said those cars are a piece of shit?" Wade leaned against the side of his truck and laughed.

"My other baby lasted me almost ten years so I figure if I can get ten years out of this, that's great." Jess walked right into his arms.

"I guess they are good cars, but I won't drive one." Wade tugged her against his body and wrapped his arms around her.

"I decided to bite the bullet and take your advice. I picked her up an hour ago." She seemed so proud of herself.

"Good. At least I know you have a somewhat decent car under your butt." Wade chuckled when she slapped his arm.

"Stop picking on my baby." She wrapped her arms around his neck. "Or you may not get a kiss from me."

Wade cupped the back of her head and covered her mouth with his. She resisted for about two seconds then melted into his arms. He plunged his tongue into her mouth, and she pressed against him.

His dick hardened, and he cupped her ass to pull her hard against him. Jess moaned into his mouth and fisted the hair at the back of his head.

"Fuck, Blue Eyes." Wade panted as he pulled his lips from hers.

"Sorry, I forget where I am when you kiss me." She smiled sheepishly.

"You're not the only one." Wade squeezed her ass and pulled away from the truck, keeping her in his arms.

"I hate to do this, but I can't stay tonight." Jess sighed and stepped back.

"Is everything okay?" Wade asked.

"Yeah, I've got to do the books for the Karate school. I do it on Mondays usually, but I missed last week. I also promised Sandy I'd work out with her in the morning before work." She linked her fingers with his.

"That's okay. I can't say I won't miss you, but I understand. Besides, I've got to talk to Ocean about her mother's visit tomorrow evening." Wade rested his forehead against hers.

"It will be okay." Jess cupped his cheek.

"I don't want my baby girl to get hurt. The last time I saw Sky, she was telling me to get the baby away from her." Wade remembered the day Ocean was born.

"Hopefully, she's matured a little in twelve years or at least can fake some compassion." Jess tilted her head up and kissed his lips. "I do have to get going."

"Okay." He walked her to the driver's side of her car.

"I wanted to show you my new car and get a kiss before I headed home." Jess grinned at him.

"Congrats on the car but if I kiss you again right now, I'll be dragging you in the back seat to baptize the new car." Wade growled as she gave him a quick kiss on the lips and hopped into her car.

"I'll take a rain check on that baptism." Jess winked as she slowly backed out of his driveway.

Wade sat at the kitchen table, trying to figure out a way to talk to Ocean and prepare her for Sky's visit. His daughter wanted it, but was she ready for it?

He was about to head to her room when his phone buzzed in his pocket. He glanced at the screen and saw a call from Trunk. The hair on the back of Wade's neck stood up as he answered the phone.

"Trunk, what's wrong?" Nothing had happened at the shop since he'd gotten the extra security, but that didn't mean the assholes wouldn't try again.

"We had a situation in that hidden room. It looks like the mattress on the floor covers a hatch that runs under the building." Trunk told him.

"That's how they were getting into the building. Fuck." Wade made a fist and pounded it on the counter.

"Yeah," Trunk answered.

"Did you catch them?" Wade hoped so because he'd like five minutes with the assholes.

"Unfortunately, by the time we got to the room they'd disappeared in the tunnel under the building. It comes up on the other side of the building next door. Hulk got it secured now, and James is sending someone over to look at the tunnel in the morning." Trunk sounded pissed.

"Did you want me to come in?" Wade asked.

"Nah, we got this. Little fuckers are going to get a surprise if they try to come in that way again. Hulk nailed a couple of two-by-fours over the door." Trunk chuckled.

Wade thanked him and hung up the phone. He still didn't know why or who was fucking with his business, but he'd have to put that on the back burner for the evening. Ocean needed to be prepared for Sky's arrival the next day.

Wade knocked on Ocean's bedroom door. When she didn't answer, he pushed open the door and smiled. She lay on the bed with earbuds in her ears, and her nose in a book. Ocean loved to read.

Wade walked toward the bed, and she glanced up. She pulled out the earbuds and grinned up at him. His daughter reminded him so much of his sister when she was younger. The only thing she seemed to have of her mother was the light hair.

"Hey, Dad." Ocean smiled at him

"Hi, baby." Wade bent over and kissed the top of her head.

"You just getting home?" She glanced at the time on her phone.

"No, I showered, ate, and then came up to see you." He sat on the edge of her bed. "I need to talk to you for a few minutes."

"Dad, if it's about you and Jess, I'm great with it. She's awesome." Ocean sat up and crossed her legs. "She said if it's okay with you, I can join her beginner's Karate classes after Christmas."

"If it's something you want to do, it's fine with me, but, sweetheart, this isn't about Jess, although I'm glad you like her." Wade knew nothing would work with Jess if his daughter weren't comfortable with it.

"I think you kinda like her too." Ocean smirked.

"Yeah, I do, but this is about that school project." Wade hated that her face went suddenly serious.

"What about it?" Ocean asked and he could see the hopeful look in her eyes.

"I talked to Sky today." Wade waited for her to digest that information.

"You found her?" Ocean placed her book on the bed and stared at Wade.

"Actually, a friend found her for me and I called her today." Wade reached over and took his daughter's hand.

"Did she say she'd meet me?" The hopeful sound in her voice concerned him.

"She'll be here tomorrow after supper, but Ocean, I don't want you to have any expectations. She's coming to help with the project. I can't guarantee that she's going to want anything else." Wade wanted to prepare her before Sky arrived.

He'd always been honest with Ocean. He didn't want her to someday find out that everything he'd told her was a lie. He was honest and expected her to do the same.

"I've got no expectations, Dad. Promise. I'd just like to meet her once and get the information I need for my project." She smiled.

"You know you're loved very much by me, Nana, Pop, and Aunt Carla, right?" He cupped her face in his hands.

"I know, Dad. I love you too." She wrapped her arms around his neck as he hugged her.

Ocean didn't hug him often since she was on the precipice of becoming a teenager, but when she did he treasured it.

"Will Jess be here when Sky comes?" Ocean pulled back and sat back on the bed.

"Not if you don't want her to be here," Wade responded.

"I'd rather she be here." Ocean's request surprised him.

It seemed that Ocean had fallen for Jess as much as he did. He couldn't be certain Jess would want to be there for the awkward meeting, but he'd certainly feel better if she was.

"I'll ask her, but I can't promise she'll be able to make it." Wade kissed the top of her head. "Now, get some sleep."

"Good-night, Dad. I love you." As he expected she grabbed her book and put her earbuds back in.

"I love you too, baby," Wade said even though she couldn't hear him at that point.

He made his way to his bedroom and flopped down on his bed. Wade knew he probably wouldn't sleep much, but he stripped down and crawled into the bed. He grabbed the pillow that Jess slept on the night before and buried his face into it. Her floral scent was still there. Wade closed his eyes, letting the smell of her relax him until he drifted off to sleep.

# *Chapter 15*

Jess sat in the living room next to Wade's sister as they waited for Sky to arrive. Ocean looked about ready to jump out of her skin, and Wade seemed like his head was ready to explode.

He kept glancing at his watch because Sky was thirty minutes late. He'd called her, but it went straight to voicemail, which only pissed Wade off more. Jess was impressed that he seemed to hide it for Ocean's sake. The way he clenched his jaw and rubbed the back of his neck, it was obvious to Jess he was angry.

"Maybe she couldn't find the house." Renee sat next to Ocean and wrapped her arm around the girl.

"It is kind of out of the way. The first time I came here if Ocean hadn't given me directions, I wouldn't have found it." Jess tried to make Ocean feel better.

"Most people would call if they were lost," Carla grumbled under her breath.

"Shut up, Carla," Wade snapped.

"Wade, that wasn't necessary." His father spoke for the first time since they'd all gathered in the room.

Before Wade responded, there was a light knock on the door. Ocean shot to her feet. Wade took a deep breath before he slowly made his way to the door as if he was on his way to the gallows.

When he returned, he was followed by an attractive blonde woman. She looked as if she was a businesswoman with her blue pantsuit. Her hair and makeup were impeccable, and Jess squirmed at the sight of the very put-together woman.

"I'm so sorry I'm late. My phone died and I couldn't find my charger. Without my GPS, I get lost easy. I'm kind of directionally challenged." The woman smiled, but it was evident the woman was anxious.

"Ocean, this is Sky." Wade stepped next to his daughter and wrapped his arm around her.

"It's nice to meet you, Ocean." Sky held out her hand and Jess noticed how the woman's hand shook.

"It's nice to meet you too." Ocean shook Sky's hand.

"Well, we're glad you got here safely." Renee smiled. "Would you like something to drink?"

"I'd like a coffee if it's not too much trouble." Sky hadn't moved into the room.

"No trouble at all. Carla, Seamus would you come help me get coffee for everyone?" Renee didn't give them a choice as she dragged Carla into the kitchen.

"Sky, this is Dad's girlfriend, Jess." Ocean walked over and sat down next to Jess.

"It's so nice to meet you." Sky nodded.

"You can come in and sit, Sky." Wade's tone didn't sound inviting.

Sky walked into the room and sat on the chair closest to the door. She looked about ready to run at the slightest sign of trouble. Wade sat next to Ocean and rested his elbows on his knees. The silence was uncomfortable and after several minutes, Jess couldn't take it anymore.

"Sky, what is it you do?" Jess asked.

"I'm a real estate lawyer," Sky responded with a thankful smile.

"Figures," Carla muttered from the doorway.

"Carla, get in here," Renee shouted from the kitchen.

"Ocean, what grade are you in?" Sky asked with a slight tremor in her voice.

"I'm in grade seven," Ocean answered.

"Junior High. Yikes. They weren't my favorite years in school." Sky rubbed her hands on the top of her thighs.

"Mine either," Jess admitted.

"I know, right? Girls acting older than they are, and boys acting like pre-schoolers." Sky chuckled.

"Sounds about right." Jess laughed.

"I've got a project to do." Ocean finally spoke and stood up.

Sky mouthed the words *thank you* to Jess, and Jess nodded. When she felt Wade's hand on her shoulder, Jess turned to see him smile at her.

Ocean disappeared from the room and returned a few minutes later with a clipboard and pen. She glanced at Wade as she slowly eased down next to Sky.

"I have these questions, but Dad didn't know anything about your family." Ocean held out the clipboard to Sky.

To her credit, Sky didn't hesitate and took the clipboard. Jess noticed her tense as she read through the questions. When she finally raised her head, Jess saw the slight hint of tears in her eyes.

"Ocean, I'll tell you what I can, but my family wasn't exactly traditional." Sky glimpsed at Wade and when he nodded she turned her attention back to Ocean.

"I... I just want to be able to say I know something about my mother." Ocean's voice was barely above a whisper.

Wade sat up straight. For a moment, Jess thought he would tell Sky to leave. His body was tense, but when Sky put her finger under Ocean's chin, Wade relaxed a little.

"I'll tell you everything I know." Sky stared into Ocean's eyes and smiled.

Jess had no idea how the woman felt. She also didn't know how a woman could walk away from her child.

"I was born in Labrador, but my mom moved us to St. John's when I was a baby. She was an orphan and had no siblings or extended family that she knew of." Sky folded her hands together in her lap.

"You had no grandparents?" Ocean seemed completely stunned.

"No. My mother wasn't a nice person. When I was little, she would get mad because she couldn't go party with her friends. When I was sixteen, she kicked me out, and I ended up in a group home until I turned eighteen." Sky didn't seem emotionally connected to her story.

"What about your dad?" Ocean placed her hand on top of Sky's shaking hands.

"My mother didn't know who he was. He was a man she went home with one night and never saw again," Sky said.

"I'm sorry," Ocean said.

"It's okay, Ocean. It made me want to work hard and get a good education. I didn't want to be anything like her." Sky smiled.

Jess glanced at Wade. He met her eyes and she could see the apprehension in his grey-blue eyes. He'd taken her hand when Sky started to talk to Ocean, and the more Sky spoke, the more he squeezed Jess' hand.

"Ocean, I wasn't meant to be a parent. Your dad was the best place for you to be. You have your grandparents, Carla, and Jess. I'll always be your mother, but I know I'd never be the parent your dad is." Sky's voice cracked.

"I understand. You weren't taught how, and I'm glad you let my dad take care of me. I've got a great life." Ocean smiled and glanced toward Wade.

"I can see that." Sky looked at Wade.

"I'd like to be able to tell your story in my project. If that's okay?" Ocean held up the clipboard.

"It's fine. I'll give you my email so if you have any other questions, you can email me. If that's okay with your dad?" Sky glanced at Wade.

"It's fine." Wade had stopped squeezing Jess' hand and started to run his thumb along the side of her hand.

"Thank you, Sky. It was really great to meet you, but I'd like to get started on this." Ocean shot to her feet.

"It was great to meet you too." Sky tensed when Ocean hugged her quickly and ran out of the room.

Again, there was an awkward silence. Sky reached for her purse and after digging inside for a few seconds, she pulled out a card. She held it in her hand for several seconds before she spoke.

"Wade, this is my card. It has my email on it." Sky stood up and held out the card.

"I'll make sure Ocean gets it." Wade took the card and shoved it into his shirt pocket.

"I know it seems weird that I don't want to be a mom, but the smartest thing I ever did was have that girl, and hand her over to you, Wade. You should be proud of the job you're doing." Sky held out her hand.

"That means a lot, Sky." Wade shook her hand.

"Jess, it was nice to meet you. I can see by the way Ocean kept glancing to you that she thinks a lot of you. It's good she has you in her life." Sky shook Jess' hand.

"She's a wonderful young lady." Jess smiled.

"I'm going to go. Thank you for giving me the chance to meet her. I never thought I would want to, but I'm glad I did. Wade, if you ever need anything for her, let me know," Sky said.

Sky turned and started to head out of the room. She turned back, and Jess saw a tear run down her cheek.

"Tell your mom and dad thank you for accepting her into their lives. I wasn't kind to them back then. I just didn't know what family was until I met yours. I was jealous of what you had. Tell Ocean bye for me." Sky turned away, and a few seconds later, Jess heard the front door shut.

Wade wrapped Jess in his arms and tucked his head into the crook of her neck. Jess held his shaking body until he calmed. She could feel the tension slowly ease after a few minutes.

"Thank you," Wade said after several minutes.

"For what?" Jess ran her hand down his cheek.

"For being here and keeping me calm." Wade kissed her cheek.

"I didn't exactly do anything." Jess smiled.

"You were here. That was enough." Wade kissed her lips softly and stared into her eyes.

"I was happy to be here for you and Ocean." Jess was honored when he'd asked her to be there.

"I'm going to check to make sure Ocean is okay." Wade kissed her again before he stood up and left her alone in the living room.

Jess made her way to the kitchen while Wade went to talk to his daughter. Carla and Renee were seated at the table, talking quietly. When Wade's sister saw Jess, she motioned for her to join them.

"Seamus headed to bed." Renee picked up the teapot and filled a cup for Jess.

"Dad, can't seem to stay up past nine at night." Carla laughed.

"My dad is up until midnight and up again at six in the morning. I don't know how he functions." Jess wrapped her hand around the cup.

"Seamus has always been early to bed and up before the birds. It's the fisherman in him." Renee smiled.

They chatted for a while until Wade made his way into the kitchen. He looked relaxed and had the hint of a smile as he sat next to her.

"Is Ocean okay?" Renee asked.

"Surprisingly, she's great. She's working on her project and said she wasn't sure she wanted to see Sky again, but she's glad she had the chance to meet her. She also said it's sad that she had such a horrible mother." Wade shook his head.

"She's not wrong there," Jess said.

As a former police officer, Jess knew how bad some parents could be. It made her skin crawl when she saw a sweet little child be neglected or hurt.

"At least she's done well for herself, and she's not using her terrible childhood as an excuse." Renee was right because Sky could have turned out a whole lot worse.

"Just an excuse not to be a mother," Carla grumbled.

"Carla," Wade and Renee said together.

"Sorry." Carla held up her hands and stood up. "I'm going to take a hot bath and crawl in bed with a good book.

"I think I'll do the same." Renee kissed Wade's cheek then did the same to Jess. "Goodnight, you two."

Jess glanced at Wade when she heard him laugh. He seemed amused by something, but she didn't have any idea what he'd be laughing at.

"Want to share the joke?" Jess chuckled.

"I just feel relieved. I never expected to feel that way. I've always dreaded the thought of Ocean meeting her mother." Wade tugged on Jess' ponytail. "Of course, having you here made it that much easier."

"I'm glad I could be here for you." Jess leaned closer to kiss his cheek.

Wade yanked her out of the chair and positioned her so that she straddled his lap. He held her hair in his hand as he pressed his lips to hers. Jess cupped the back of his head with both her hands and when he plunged his tongue into her mouth, she sucked it hard. Wade groaned and hardened beneath her.

Jess ground her core against him as they devoured each other. Wade groaned every time she nipped or sucked his tongue. He slid his hand under her shirt and cupped her breast through her bra.

"Jess, if we don't get upstairs, I'm going to toss you on that table and bury myself inside you," Wade murmured into her ear.

"If there weren't so many people in this house, I'd say go for it, but I'd rather not have one of your family walk in on us." Jess nipped the side of his neck.

Wade stood up and started to head toward the stairs with Jess in his arms. She protested, knowing that his leg probably ached from his day at work, but Wade stopped at the bottom of the stairs and pressed her against the wall.

"I can carry you upstairs like this. I lift car parts heavier than you," Wade whispered then kissed her hard on the mouth.

By the time they made it to his room, Jess was ready to scream with need. Her shirt got tossed on his bedroom floor the minute they entered the room. Wade put her on her feet as he closed and locked the bedroom door.

"Get the clothes off, Blue Eyes." Wade growled as he yanked his shirt over his head.

"Bossy much?" Jess removed her jeans and backed toward the bed.

"You love when I'm bossy." Wade stripped naked.

"Only when you're naked." Jess crawled on the bed and kneeled in the middle of the bed.

Wade climbed on the bed and pulled her against him. He was a little dominant in bed, but she didn't mind. He wasn't rough or harsh with her. It was just the opposite. The way he touched her, kissed her, and held her made her feel cherished, wanted, and loved.

He told her one night the previous weekend that he didn't like the idea of bondage. Wade wanted to have her hands on him but if she were tied up, she wouldn't be able to touch him.

"Fuck, baby. You have me so damn hard." Wade groaned against her neck.

"I guess I better help you with that." Jess wrapped her hand around his thick cock.

Wade moaned and flopped back on the bed. Jess grinned as she gave him exactly what he needed.

# Chapter 16

It was the first week of November and the garage was crazy busy. Especially when the weatherman predicted there would be a major snowstorm early the next week. It seemed as if everyone in St. John's and the surrounding towns wanted their winter tires on right away.

"Curtis and Cody said they can stay late to catch up some jobs." Harry stuck his head into Wade's office.

"I'll stay too." With three of them, they could get the rest of the jobs completed.

"I'm gonna stay too. We've got a full house again tomorrow. If all the jobs are straight forward, we should get out of here on time tomorrow," Harry told him.

"When have you ever seen a day go by with at least one job causing a fuck up?" Wade scoffed.

"True." Harry laughed.

"If we can get them all done by six tomorrow, that would be good with me. I'm taking Jess out to supper for her birthday." Wade couldn't stop the smile just at the mention of her name.

"You should take off early tomorrow then. Can't take that beautiful lady out without scrubbing this place off ya." Harry grinned.

"I'll have time to get cleaned up." Wade laughed.

"So whatcha doin' for her birthday?" Harry rested his shoulder against the door.

"Taking her to her sister's restaurant for supper, and then we're going to a bed and breakfast in Cupids. George Crocker told me about." Wade grinned.

"Sounds good. You deserve to get away." Harry nodded his head.

"The way I look at it, we deserve to get away. She's been working day and night too. I want to give her a nice relaxing weekend. Ocean is spending the weekend with Jess' cousin's kids." Wade wanted to give her the romantic night she deserved.

Over the last month, Ocean had become close to Ian's daughters, and James' older boys. Sandy planned a girl's weekend for her daughters and invited Ocean to join them.

"She's good for you. Love looks good on you." Harry smiled.

"Feels good too." Wade winked as he stood up and pulled on his overalls before he headed back to the garage.

By eight that evening, all the vehicles were finished and Wade was waiting for the last three customers to pick up their cars. Crash and Crunch were the security for that day and sat in the front area chatting with Wade.

"Is it always this busy during this time of year?" Crash asked.

"Every November and May people want tires changed and changed right away." Wade chuckled.

"You couldn't pay me enough to work in customer service again." Crunch snickered.

"It's not fun sometimes, but I love this business. The assholes just make it interesting." Wade laughed.

After the last of the customers picked up their cars, it was almost nine. Wade ran off the sales for the day and dropped the deposit bag in the safe in his office. He was on the way out of the parking lot when his phone rang.

"Hello?" Wade tapped his Bluetooth as he pulled his truck out of the lot.

"Hi, sexy." Jess purred and his dick instantly hardened.

"Well, hello, beautiful lady." Wade couldn't stop the smile.

"I wanted to give you a call since I won't see you until tomorrow. What are you doing?" Jess asked.

"I just left the shop. Busy day today," he admitted.

"How's your leg?" She inquired.

He smiled at her concern because in the short couple of months they'd been dating, Jess knew without asking if he hadn't rested his leg during the day. It was nice to have her concerned about him, and he loved her for it.

"It's not bad," he lied.

"Wade." She dragged out his name as a warning.

"Okay, it's sore, but I'll be okay," he said.

As they talked, he eased onto the brake to make the turn onto the off-ramp. Wade's brake pedal went straight to the floor. Wade pumped the brake several times, but nothing happened.

"Fuck," Wade cursed as he kept tried to keep the truck on the highway.

He couldn't turn onto the ramp because of the steep incline. With no brakes, he'd be screwed. Wade glanced to his right and left, and thankfully traffic was light because it was later in the evening.

"Wade, what's wrong?" Jess asked.

"I… I don't have any brakes," Wade replied.

"What?" Jess gasped.

"I had to stay on the highway because I couldn't slow down to get onto the ramp," Wade told her.

"Turn on your emergency lights, and I'll call nine-one-one," Jess shouted to her father without giving Wade a chance to respond.

Wade knew he had at least ten minutes before there was an area where he could turn off into a field, but he was headed for a section of the highway with a steep incline.

He flicked on his emergency blinkers and hit the brake again. The truck didn't slow and he yanked up on the hand brake. Still nothing.

"Wade?" Jess sounded panicked.

"I'm here." Wade tried to sound calm for her sake, but he was nervous.

"There are a couple of cruisers up ahead of you. They're going to keep other traffic out of the way," Jess said.

"Okay." Wade swallowed as he started to descend the hill.

Wade grabbed the gear stick and tried to shove it into neutral, but it wouldn't move. His heart thundered in his chest as the truck picked up speed. He didn't want to say anything to worry Jess further but he didn't see a way out of this.

"Wade, stay calm." She obviously could hear the tension in his voice.

"I'm okay, Jess," Wade said.

"I'm not," she squeaked.

"Damn it." He bit down on his lip as he struggled to keep the truck from going out of control as he careened down the hill.

"Wade," Jess shouted.

"I'm here," Wade replied.

By the time he was more than halfway down the hill, his speedometer hit one hundred and eighty kilometers and continued to climb.

When Wade hit the bottom of the hill, his front tire hit a divot in the side of the road. Wade tried to swerve back onto the road, but the truck tipped. As the truck slid closer to the edge of the road, it slipped off the edge and began to roll down the embankment toward the large pond below.

"Fuck," Wade shouted.

The truck stopped when it landed on the passenger side in the water. Wade could see the water rise slowly on the passenger side and he released his seatbelt. He looked up to the top of the embankment to see a huge boulder slowly roll down toward him. The last thing he heard was her shouting his name over, and over.

"Wade?" Jess screamed.

"I love you, Jess," he whispered.

# *Chapter 17*

When she heard the loud clunking, and his panicked curses, Jess was about to drive to St. John's herself, but Ian followed her to the car and tugged her to his truck. Her dad jumped into the back of Ian's SUV and they were on their way. She still had the phone to her ear, but Wade's line had gone dead before she left the house.

"Try calling again," her father demanded.

Jess didn't speak because she was afraid she'd burst into tears. She tapped Wade's number, but it went straight to voicemail. The pleasant sound of his greeting didn't make her feel any better because it meant his phone was dead. Wade never let his cell phone run out of battery power.

"Jess, don't think the worst." Ian reached for her hand.

"I'm trying, but it was so loud," Jess choked out.

"I know." Ian squeezed her hand, and her father's hand landed on her shoulder.

"He'll be okay, Pumpkin," her father whispered.

They had an idea of where Wade might be. They figured out the time where he'd missed his turnoff and where she lost his call. Her father called the St. John's division of the NPD and the RCMP office while they were on the way to have them be on the lookout for an accident.

Jess saw the lights of the emergency vehicles as they crested the hill. Ian didn't seem to care if there were cops on the road because he crossed the median and spun the truck next to one of the police cruisers.

Her father was out of the car before Ian turned off the engine. Jess jumped out and sprang into a full run toward the edge of the embankment.

"Jess," she heard the voices behind her, but she didn't stop until she could look to where the truck lay.

It was on its side, almost entirely submerged in the water, and a huge rock sat on top of the driver's side. Jess couldn't see inside the vehicle and was about to climb down. The idiots were standing around doing nothing, and Wade was probably drowning.

"Jess, stop," someone shouted behind her.

She ignored the shouts and pulled off her coat, but before she could start down the bank, someone grabbed her arm.

"I've got to help him." Jess tugged her arm away from the firm grip.

"Jess, look." Nick pointed down the road toward the ambulance.

Jess didn't have time to play games with Nick, and she was about to say so as she glanced in the direction of the emergency vehicles. She held her breath as she slowly started to walk toward them, but when he lifted his head, Jess took off running.

The ambulance doors were open, and Wade sat in the back, wrapped in a blanket. He had an oxygen mask over his mouth and nose but it was the most beautiful sight she'd ever seen.

"Wade," she roared as she ran toward him.

He stood when he saw her, but she couldn't stop and lunged into his arms. She probably should have seen if he was okay, but he was there, and she needed to hold him.

"I'm fine, Blue Eyes." Wade pulled her tightly into his arms.

"I couldn't get ahold of you. Your phone went to voicemail. I heard the crash, I thought…" She squeezed her eyes closed and started to tremble as tears spilled down her cheeks.

"Shhh… I'm okay." He cupped the back of her head and whispered into her ear. "I'm fine."

"I want that fucking truck brought right to the garage at the RCMP. I want it checked with a fine-tooth comb. That wasn't an accident," her father shouted behind her.

"I was so scared." Jess sniffed.

"Me too." Wade kissed the side of her head.

"Wade, we should get you to the hospital, and check you out," Ian said from behind Jess.

"I'm okay," Wade said.

"You might feel okay, but that was a pretty rough ride. I'd feel better if we get some x-rays," Ian pushed.

"Please, Wade. Get checked out." Jess pulled back and gazed up at him.

He had mud all over his face, and his hair was wet, but he looked perfect to her. He was alive. Still, she knew he could have internal injuries after such an accident.

"Okay." Wade kissed her forehead.

Two hours later, Wade was cleared with only a few bumps and bruises. He'd asked her not to call his family because they'd worry. Somehow, they found out and called Jess.

Wade told them he was fine and they should stay at home. Once he was cleared, Ian drove him home. Her father wasn't happy about it, but Jess stayed with Wade.

"I'll get your car brought out here in the morning," her father said as she and Wade got out of Ian's SUV.

"Thanks, Dad. You too, Ian." Jess hugged them both.

After Wade assured his mother, father, sister, and daughter he was perfectly fine, he took Jess' hand, and they made their way to his room. He was quiet as he stripped off his clothes.

"I'm going to take a quick shower." Wade walked naked into his bathroom.

Jess heard him turn on the water, and after a few seconds, walked into the bathroom to join him. She needed to be near him, and she shivered as the fear finally started to dissipate.

After she stripped out of her clothes, she walked into the large shower and stepped behind him. Jess slipped her hands around his body and rested her head against his back as the water ran over both of them. Neither of them moved for several minutes.

Jess pressed her lips to the center of his back, and he turned in her arms. He pulled her body against him and buried his face in the nape of her neck. When Wade started to tremble, Jess knew he'd finally realized how lucky he was to walk away from the accident.

"I wanted the last thing you heard from me to be, I love you," Wade whispered into her neck.

"Wade." A lump formed in her throat at the thought of the fear he must've felt at that moment.

"Jess, I saw that rock rolling down the bank and I thought that was it." Wade squeezed her against him.

"How did you get out?" Jess smoothed her hands up and down his back.

"It stuck on something for a few minutes. I kicked out the windshield and climbed out over the front of the truck. The rock cracked whatever it got caught on, then rolled down on top of the truck as I got out. It made the truck sink deeper into the water. It was so fucking cold." Wade shivered.

"Someone was watching over you." Jess choked on the words as she tried to keep from bursting into tears.

Jess looked up at him when he lifted his head. His eyes were filled with tears and her heart broke for him. Wade smoothed her now soaked hair back and pressed his lips to her forehead.

"I love you, Jess," Wade whispered as he kissed down the side of her face.

"I love you too," she breathed the words into his ear.

Wade turned his head and his lips met hers in a slow, tender kiss. His arms slipped around her as he made love to her mouth with a kiss that took her breath away.

Wade cupped the back of her head and tilted her head as he deepened the kiss. He slipped his tongue inside her mouth, swirling it around hers as he pulled her body tighter against his.

The kiss was different, almost as if he was afraid it would be his last. It scared her, and she pulled back. Wade had a tear rolling down his cheek and she wiped it away.

"I don't know what the fuck is wrong with me." Wade blew out a shaky breath.

"You had a near-death experience and the adrenalin is wearing off. Wade, your truck rolled over twenty feet down a cliff into a freezing cold lake. I feel like bursting into tears because I was terrified. I heard the loud crunching, and I thought I lost you." As if saying the words brought them on, tears slipped from the corners of her eyes.

"I've had a lot of them lately." Wade turned off the water and stepped out of the shower.

He wrapped a towel around his waist and grabbed another towel from the shelf next to the tub. He tugged Jess out of the shower and wrapped the large blue towel around her.

"Someone's out to get me. I don't know who they are or why." Wade stared into her eyes. "I've never done anything that would make someone want to kill me."

"Wade, I know that, and whoever's doing this will be caught." Jess held his face between her hands.

"I don't know if you and I are a good idea right now." Wade pulled away and stalked out of the bathroom, leaving her alone.

Jess shook her head and spun around. She followed him into his bedroom and found him holding her clothes in his hand. He held them out to her as if telling her to put them on.

"I think you should go home and stay away from me." Wade lay the clothes on the foot of the bed when she didn't take them from him.

He turned away and stared out the window. Jess glanced at her clothes on the bed then back to Wade. His shoulders were tense, and she could see the muscles in his biceps flexing as he crossed his arms over his chest.

"Wade Rivers, there isn't a snowball's chance in hell of me leaving right now. You're not going to push me away." Jess kept her voice calm, but she did raise it to make sure he heard her. "Do you hear me?"

Jess stomped over behind him and grabbed his arm, forcing him to turn to face her. His eyes were closed, and she could see his Adam's apple bob up and down several times.

"Wade, look at me." Jess lowered her voice as she held his face between her hands.

Wade opened his eyes. She wasn't about to lose him, no matter how much he tried to push her away. Jess loved him, and if someone was out to get him, she'd be damned if she let them take away the first man to make her look forward to her future.

"I love you, and I'm not leaving." Jess pulled his face down and pressed her lips to his.

For a second, he didn't move, but Jess stepped back yanked off his towel and dropped her own. Wade reached for her and slammed his lips against hers.

Wade lifted her into his arms, and she wrapped her legs around his waist as he spun around and pressed her up against the wall while he devoured her mouth.

# *Chapter 18*

Wade couldn't stop himself if he wanted to. He loved her. The only thing he wanted at that moment was to make love to her. It took every ounce of strength he had to step away from her in the bathroom, but when she looked at him with such determination, he was finished.

Jess was the first woman he'd ever loved. She was the woman he wanted to have with him for the rest of his life, but he was terrified whoever wanted to hurt him would come after her or one of his family.

"Wade, I love you." Jess moaned as he lifted her up and drove his cock inside her.

"I love you too, Jess. So damn much." Wade growled as he felt her hot pussy suck him inside.

"Yes, you feel so good." Jess gasped as Wade slammed into her over and over.

"You feel so fucking good around me." Wade clenched his teeth as he tried to keep control.

"Harder, Wade. Harder." Jess fisted his hair in her hands.

How could he ever let her go when she was the one who made him feel whole again? Jess made him happy, and he could see a future with her. His family adored her, but he was worried about putting all of them in danger.

Jess groaned as she squirmed against his body. Wade squeezed her ass as he pushed deep inside her. He held her with one arm as he slipped his hand between them and pressed his thumb against her swollen clit. He didn't know if he could hold on any longer, and he urged her to come. When she finally clenched around him, he pounded into her until he couldn't hold back anymore.

"Wade, oh yes." Jess tipped her head back against the wall.

"Fuck, I'm gonna…" Wade groaned and pushed deep inside her as he exploded.

His legs shook as he spilled inside her. He eased down to the floor and cradled her in his arms with his dick jerking inside her.

Jess wrapped her arms around his neck, and they stayed that way for a long time before one of them moved. Wade could feel the wetness between them slipping from inside her, and he stiffened.

"Fuck, we didn't use a condom." Wade pulled back and held her head in his hands. "I'm so sorry."

"It's okay, I've got an IUD, and I'm clean." Jess smiled.

"Me too. You're the first woman I've been with in more than nine years." The last time he'd had sex with anyone besides his own hand was before he'd been hit by the car.

"It's been more than eleven for me." Jess smirked.

Wade's smile slipped as he blew out a breath. If Jess had taken what he said to heart, he could have lost her. It would've killed him to watch her walk away.

"Don't ever try to push me away again." Jess ran a finger down his cheek and stared into his eyes. "I can protect myself, and I've got a big overbearing family that will keep you, Ocean, your parents, and sister safe as well."

"I can't drag your family into this. Hell, I don't even know what this is." Wade shifted so his back was against the wall and Jess straddled on his legs.

"That's what James and the police are doing. I'm just trying to figure out how someone managed to get to your truck with everyone at the shop today." Jess narrowed her eyes as if she was trying to come up with an answer.

"My truck was on the side of the building because it was busy today. We needed the parking for the customers. We all park our vehicles back there." Wade always made sure the area was clear during the busy times.

"So anyone could have gotten to your truck without anyone seeing them." Jess sighed.

"The cameras should've caught them." Wade struggled to get to his feet with Jess still in his arms.

"Where are you going?" Jess asked as she moved out of his way.

"My phone." Wade searched the room.

"Wade, it fell in the water, remember?" Jess reminded him.

"Fuck." Wade plowed his hands through his hair.

"Look, it's too late to call anyone right now, and knowing my dad, he has someone looking at the video as we speak. You need to rest." Jess wrapped her arms around his waist.

Wade knew she was right because he felt completely drained. He allowed her to tug him to the bathroom where they both cleaned up. He couldn't help but laugh when she grumbled about how the woman was always left with the biggest mess.

An hour later, he lay in his bed with her wrapped in his arms. He couldn't believe that he'd been stupid enough to try and push her away. He thanked his lucky stars that she was stubborn as a mule and loved him as much as she did.

The next morning was a series of arguments with Jess, his mother, his sister, and Harry. None of them wanted him to go to work, and Jess even threatened to handcuff him to his bed.

He could understand their concern but the appointments for that day were crazy. He wasn't leaving the garage shorthanded because of what happened the previous day no matter how stiff and sore he felt.

Even as he drove Jess to her shop in his father's car, he could see how concerned she was. He hated to see her or his parents so worried, but he wasn't letting some asshole ruin his business.

"I'll be careful, I promise." Wade took her hand when he stopped in front of her flower shop.

She didn't answer him and wouldn't look at him either. He smiled because it was her stubborn streak showing, and he loved that part of her. Wade cupped her cheek and turned her face toward him.

"I. Will. Be. Careful." He kissed her on the lips one time for each word.

"If you get hurt again, I will nurse you back to health so I can kick your ass." Jess poked him in the chest then practically lunged into his arms.

"I love you, Blue Eyes." He kissed her temple and hugged her tightly to him.

"I love you too. Ya big oaf." Jess pulled back and looked into his eyes. "Call me when you get to work, please."

"I promise." He gave her a soft kiss on the lips.

He waited for her to get inside her shop before he backed out and headed to work. Wade hated to tie up his dad's vehicle, but until he could get another one, he was stuck.

"Two fucking new vehicles in less than six months," Wade grumbled to himself.

Wade walked into the shop and met Josie's angry glare. She stepped in front of him and crossed her arms over her chest. He didn't know what he did to piss her off, but he was sure he was about to hear it.

"Josie, can you move so I can get to work?" Wade sighed.

"You shouldn't even be here. You were almost killed yesterday. What's wrong with you?" Josie was as bad as his mother.

"I wasn't killed, and I'm needed here." Wade stepped to the side, but she moved in front of him.

"When Harry told me what happened, I couldn't stop shaking. You're like a son to me. I never had any children of my own, Wade Rivers, but if you get yourself killed, I'll be…" Josie stopped and pressed her lips together as a tear slipped out of the corner of her eye.

"Aw, Josie." Wade wrapped his arms around her and gave her a hug.

"All of you boys are like my kids. Coming in here makes me feel like a mother. Then you almost get killed." Josie sobbed into his shirt.

"I'm sorry for worrying you, but I'm fine, and we'll find out who fucked with my truck, okay?" Wade kissed the top of her head and looked down at the woman who was definitely like a second mother.

"Okay, but don't overdo it. You've got to be sore from that accident. Harry showed me pictures of the truck…" Josie pressed her lips together and inhaled through her nose. "You had an angel on your shoulder yesterday."

"I'm a little sore but sitting around will make it worse." Wade kissed her forehead.

Wade didn't disagree with her because he knew exactly how close he came to losing his life. He'd thought about it all night as he held a sleeping Jess in his arms. He hoped something showed up on the security video.

Once he was sure Josie had calmed and wasn't going to worry about him all day, Wade made his way into the garage. The deafening clicking sound of the impact drivers used for removing lug nuts echoed through the area.

He strolled down through the garage and checked out each of the ramps as Everett, Logan, Curtis, Dwayne, and Cody worked on the first vehicles of the morning.

"I see you wrote off another vehicle. You know you can trade them in for a new one instead of destroying them," Everett teased.

"Yeah, I was gonna borrow your car today. You don't care if I break it up, do you?" Wade laughed.

"You stay the fuck away from my baby." Everett tossed a rag at Wade.

"I swear he'd fuck that car if it had a pussy," Dwayne shouted from the next ramp.

"I think he does. I've seen a few stains on the back seat." Curtis laughed.

"You two should be comedians." Everett pulled a tire off the car and dropped it to the ground.

"Where's Harry?" Wade asked.

"He's in that new room. Said when the cops clear it, he's turning it into his own office." Everett pointed toward the room they referred to as the hidden room.

"Good idea. He needs his own space." Wade made his way back to find Harry.

The wall that had once hidden the room had been removed, and the hatch in the floor had been completely secured. Harry got rid of the old fridge and mattress, mostly because they smelled terrible, and in a garage, that was saying something.

"I hear this is gonna be my new office." Wade smirked as he stepped into the room.

"Not a fucking chance." Harry laughed.

"Why don't you talk to Keith to see if he can put in a couple of windows and redo the walls and floor? This room looks like it's been closed off for a long time. We didn't even know it was here." Wade walked around the room.

The old sheetrock on the walls was practically crumbling. Wade pressed against the outer wall and his hand went through it. It was all going to have to be replaced.

"Yeah, I wouldn't trust that heater over there either." Harry nodded toward the old rusty wall heater hanging off the wall.

"Nope, that has fire hazard written all over it." Wade kicked it, and it fell to the floor.

Harry deserved to have his own space at the shop, and since he was the shop foreman, Wade would make sure that he got the office he earned. He'd call Keith when he finished for the day and get him to give an estimate of what it would cost to renovate the room.

"Do you have a job for me?" Wade asked as he and Harry walked out of the room.

"Yep, but don't you think you should take it easy?" Harry raised an eyebrow.

"Don't start." Wade snatched the work order out of Harry's hand and grabbed the keys from the peg wall.

"If you get hurt, I'm telling your mother and girlfriend you didn't listen to me," Harry shouted as Wade headed outside to grab the vehicle.

Wade shook his head and made his way outside. It had started snowing, and he cursed as he pulled his coat collar up around his neck. He was about to get in the car when he saw James and Kurt walk toward him.

"Wade, we need to talk." James looked serious.

"What's up?" Wade asked.

"I think we should go inside." Kurt's posture told Wade something was wrong.

"What is it? Did something happen to my daughter? My parents? Fuck, is Jess okay?" Wade's body trembled as it hit him that someone could've gone after the people, he loved to get to him.

"They are all fine, but we need to talk about what happened yesterday," James said.

"What do you need to know?" Wade calmed, knowing that everyone was fine.

"We had forensics check your truck. It looks like a hole was poked in your brake lines and the handbrake cable was cut." Kurt held out a folder.

"Let's go inside." Wade took the file and headed inside the building.

He gave the work order and keys to Josie as he stalked to his office. He told her to get another tech on the job because his hands shook at the thought of someone tampering with his truck.

Wade wasn't sure he wanted to know anything else they had to tell him, but all this shit had to end. Wade shrugged out of his coat and opened the first picture as he eased into his chair. There were several pictures of the brake lines and handbrake of his truck. The hole in the line was circled in red ink as was the section where the cable was cut.

"A.J.'s going through the video with Cory, but the only thing they saw so far was a dark shadow. That side of the building doesn't have the best lighting," James explained.

What was he supposed to say to all of it? He'd hoped in the back of his mind that it had really been an accident, but the proof was in front of him. Someone wanted to kill him. He just didn't know why.

"Wade, with all this, we should put a security detail on you." Kurt lay a hand on Wade's shoulder.

"I'm sure that's not necessary." Wade shook his head.

"It's necessary. I saw my daughter when she thought you were… Well, let's say, I never want to see that look on her face again." Kurt glanced at James.

"Your family has been moved to Hopedale as a precaution. We wanted to move you with them, but you already left to come here." James seemed almost apologetic.

"I can't leave now. We've got a ton of jobs that have to be done by the end of the day." Wade motioned toward the garage.

"I thought you might not want to leave, so I've got Hulk outside." James turned to leave and then stopped. "I probably should warn you, Nanny Betty is in emergency mode."

"I don't know what that means." Wade shrugged.

"Trust me, you will." Kurt snorted and followed James out of the office.

Wade sat in his chair and leaned his head back. His family was in Hopedale and probably worried to death and a fucking bodyguard following him. Getting his head around that was difficult.

"We brought your dog to my place. The boys will love him, and our dog seems to like having a new friend." James stuck his head into his office and then left again.

Rufus was probably in his glee having another dog to play with, but Wade wasn't sure he'd feel good about not having his dog in the house with him. He was used to Rufus worming his way into the bed most nights. Wade was about to have way too many changes in his life and it made him uneasy.

Hulk was a great guy to have around. He knew his way around a car and told Wade that he was a mechanic before he got into security. He helped clear out some of the jobs and entertained the guys with stories about Jess' grandmother.

"The woman hears emergency, she starts a menu and makes enough food to feed a small army." Hulk chuckled as he helped Wade with an engine repair.

"Hey, a woman that makes me food any day is a woman I would marry." Curtis chuckled.

"Sorry, man. She's taken by one of the wealthiest men in Newfoundland. Have you heard of Tom Roberts?" Hulk asked.

"Yeah, he has a ton of businesses," Dwayne shouted across the garage.

"They were sweethearts when they were young but didn't find each other again until a few years back," Hulk yelled back.

Wade didn't say much to join in the conversation, but he thought it was pretty great that Jess' grandmother could rekindle an old romance after so many years. Although, Wade wouldn't want to be in his late seventies before he found the love of his life. He was so glad Jess came into his life when she did.

Hulk wouldn't allow Wade to drive his father's car when they left for the day. Wade had to drive home with Hulk in the monstrous SUV that looked like it should be driving the Prime Minister of Canada around the country.

Hulk explained that Keith had several vehicles decked out for security jobs. The vehicles had saved some of their clients' lives. Wade wondered how much it was going to cost for all the security he'd had to hire recently.

Financially, he'd been smart with the money he received from the accident and invested it well. He still had a healthy savings account, but he'd hoped to keep that for Ocean's education.

"I should ask Keith when he sends out his invoices," Wade said mostly to himself.

"That should be interesting." Hulk chuckled.

"Yeah, I'll probably have to take out a mortgage to pay for all you guys." Wade knew the cost would put a major dent in his savings, and profits at the garage.

"Wade, the O'Connors think of you as family," Hulk said as they turned off the highway.

"Okay?" Wade was happy that Jess' family liked him, but what that had to do with his security bill, Wade had no idea.

"Trust me, your bill will be very affordable, that's if you get one at all." Hulk opened the window of the SUV and punched a code into a panel.

Two large iron gates opened, and Hulk drove through them. He stopped on the other side and waited for the gates to close before continuing further.

"Where are we?" Wade asked.

"This is Keith's place. You'll be staying in the safe house at the back of the property." Hulk nodded toward a house as they passed by. "That's Keith's house."

Wade was surprised by the house Hulk called a safe house. It looked like a cute little cottage in the middle of the woods but since there were two large men stood outside the door, it kind of killed that illusion.

"That's Rex and Damon." Hulk pointed to the two men. "They'll be here for the night, then I'll be back in the morning. Since today is Friday, I'm assuming your garage is closed tomorrow."

"Yeah, if we hadn't gotten all the work done, we would've gone in to finish it tomorrow but thanks to you, we had an extra hand today," Wade said as they walked toward the house.

"Wade, this is Caden Dixon, but we call him Rex, and that's Damon Blackwood." Each of the men shook Wade's hand.

"What no nickname for Damon?" Wade smirked.

"Pam calls him asshole." Rex laughed.

"Shut it." Damon snapped.

"Isn't Pam Jess' cousin?" Wade asked as he stepped inside the house with Hulk.

"Yeah, that's a long story that none of us know but Pam's mother says Damon and Pam are meant to be. With the O'Connors, that's as good as a marriage proposal." Hulk pulled off his gloves and stepped into the living room.

Wade had the air whoosh out of him as Ocean ran into his arms. Since she'd hit her preteens, she wasn't as affectionate with him, so the fact that she ran into his arms meant she was scared.

"Dad, I was so worried about you," Ocean whispered.

"I'm fine, baby. This is just a precaution." Wade glared at his mother and sister.

He knew by the expressions on their faces that they hadn't exactly been secretive about what they discussed in front of his daughter. For some reason, the women in his family didn't consider Ocean a little girl anymore.

"I told them to keep quiet," his father grumbled from an armchair next to the window.

"Seamus, if it was up to you and Wade, that girl would be still in diapers and a crib." His mother glared at Wade.

Wade rolled his eyes and walked further into the room. It wasn't what he'd picture as a safe house and actually looked like a regular home. It was an open concept with an island separating the kitchen from the other part of the room. Stools lined the counter that separated the kitchen from the rest of the area. The living room was decked out with a large television, fireplace, dark-blue sofa, and two armchairs.

"Let me show you around." Hulk nodded toward the hallway.

Wade followed as Hulk showed him several bedrooms. One had a bathroom and another adjoining room. There was a bathroom at the end of the hall as well. Hulk explained the main room was usually for the client, and the security stayed in the other room in case they needed to get to the client quickly.

"Your parents will be going to stay with Kurt and Alice. Your sister is staying with them as well, but Sandy and Ian are taking Ocean with them. Mostly to give Ocean something to distract her from all this," Hulk explained as Wade looked around the main bedroom.

"Why can't we all stay here?" Wade turned to look at Hulk.

"You can if you want them here, but I think it would be better if they were all separated," Hulk said. "Trust me, it's better this way, and they'll be just as safe as you are."

"What about Jess?" Wade figured if he were separated from his family, Kurt would want his daughter out of danger as well.

"Kurt and James lost the argument with Jess, Alice, and Nanny Betty." Hulk laughed.

"Why does that not surprise me?" Wade snorted.

"Because you know how stubborn I am, and Nan is ten times worse." Jess grinned from the doorway.

"Kurt never wins arguments with his wife. I should probably warn you, none of the men win arguments in that family." Hulk laughed as he walked out of the room, leaving Jess and Wade alone.

For a moment, he gazed at her, then Wade plopped down on the foot of the bed. He was overwhelmed and wasn't sure how to deal with everything.

Jess walked into the room and sat next to him on the bed. She linked her arm into his elbow and rested her head on his shoulder. They sat in silence for several minutes before he spoke again.

"You're safe here," Jess whispered.

"That's not what I'm worried about." Wade kissed the top of her head.

"What then?" Jess lifted her head and rested her chin on his shoulder.

"I feel like I'm hiding, but I don't know why I have to hide. Nobody knows who's trying to kill me or if they really are trying to kill me." Wade sighed.

"James is working through the list of customers with an ax to grind that Harry gave him, and they are also looking into the man who almost hit the little girl," Jess said.

"Why would you be looking into Mr. Pippy?" Wade had no issues with the man who hit him all those years ago.

Timothy Pippy had a drinking problem, and Wade didn't blame him for that. Sure, he definitely shouldn't have gotten behind the wheel that day, but the man was devastated with what he'd done.

He'd come to the hospital to apologize to Wade, and he always called to see if Wade needed anything. Timothy changed his life back then and got help for his drinking. He also helped other people with addiction issues and became an advocate against drunk drivers.

Not only did he help Wade, but he also started an education fund for Addison Fry. She was the girl he'd almost hit and one of Ocean's friends. Wade's family had become close to the little girl's family after what happened.

Unfortunately, Timothy died from cancer a year earlier. Timothy had nothing to do with the situation and even if he was still alive, Wade knew with certainty that the man wouldn't be involved.

"It's not Timothy." Wade verbalized his thoughts.

"I know. Sandy found out he passed away." Jess smiled.

"Is there anything that woman can't find on the computer?" Wade shook his head and flopped back on the bed, pulling her with him.

"Not that I know of." Jess rested her head on his chest and curled into his side.

Wade lay holding her for a while and tried to clear all the clutter in his head. He couldn't remember ever doing anything in his life that would make someone want to kill him.

"Wade?" Jess' voice was quiet.

"Yeah?" He kissed the top of her head.

"You don't think… What about Sky?" Jess almost sounded ashamed of saying the name.

"I don't remember a lot about the person who attacked me at the garage, but it was definitely not a woman." Wade knew that for a fact.

"She could have hired someone," Jess said.

"Good point, but I doubt it." Wade couldn't think of a reason why Sky would want him dead.

"I'm sure they are checking her out too." Jess yawned.

"I feel terrible that I haven't gone to see Officer Simms." Wade hated that the man nearly lost his leg because of all the shit going down.

"He's actually doing well. He's home and his family is taking care of him. He was actually worried about you." Jess snuggled into his side.

"Will he get back to work?" He worried that Neil's injury would end his career.

"Yes, it will be a few months, but there wasn't as much damage as they initially thought." Jess wrapped her arm across his chest and yawned again.

"Am I boring you, Blue Eyes?" Wade chuckled.

"No, it was just a long freaking day," Jess grumbled sleepily.

Wade smiled as he hugged her against his side. He tucked his other arm under his head and closed his eyes. He knew how she felt because he was exhausted. He hadn't eaten supper, but he was too tired to care. All he wanted was to wake up and know the whole situation was a bad dream.

Wade didn't know how long he'd been asleep, but he woke up to a lot of commotion in the living room. He looked at Jess, and she rolled her eyes.

"You're about to find out what happens with my family when there's danger." Jess snorted and sat up.

"I'm feeling a little scared." Wade laughed.

"You should be." Jess took his hand and dragged him out of the room.

Wade rounded the corner to a house full of people. It was a little after nine, and he was a little groggy from being woken suddenly. Jess looked up at him and laughed.

"What are they doing?" Wade whispered.

"The thing they always do when there's drama. They feed everyone." Jess tugged him into the kitchen.

"Dere ya are. Yer mudder and fadder are all settled into Kurt's place. Da little one is havin' a time wit da girls. Yer sister is wit da little one." Jess' grandmother chatted as she filled a plate full of food and handed it to Wade.

"That's good." Wade nodded and took the plate.

"Doncha worry about anyting else. Jus' fill yer belly and get a good night's rest." The tiny woman scurried around the kitchen, ordering Hulk and Bull around as if they were little boys.

"Thank you, Mrs. O'Connor." Wade smiled at her.

"Uh oh." Bull laughed and backed out of the kitchen.

"You're about to get the speech," Hulk whispered as he snatched his plate off the counter and stepped behind Wade.

"Mrs. O'Connor was me mudder-in-law and let me tell ya, dat woman was a witch. Ya call me Nan like all me udder lads. You got dat?" Nanny Betty pointed her finger at him, and although it was the funniest thing he'd ever seen, he was a little scared of her.

"Yes, Nan," Wade said and shoved a spoonful of potatoes into his mouth to keep Nanny Betty from seeing his smirk.

Jess sat next to him at the counter and hid her smile behind her fork. He had no idea why Nanny Betty didn't like her mother-in-law, but Wade wouldn't make the mistake of calling her Mrs. O'Connor again.

"Just for future reference. Do I call your mom Mrs. O'Connor or something else?" Wade whispered to Jess when Nanny Betty stepped away.

"Bull calls her Alice but she told you that at the diner, remember?" Jess smiled.

"Right. Okay." Wade grinned as he proceeded to dig into the delicious food piled on his plate.

Wade hoped the whole situation was over soon. He could get back to his life and finally take Jess out for her birthday. He'd had it all planned for the evening, but he'd been told that his plans were put on the back burner. He wondered if there was any way to do something even if it had to be in the seclusion of the small house.

# Chapter 19

Jess sat across the desk from James at the police station, but she had no idea why. Wade was still at the safe house and seemed to be going stir crazy. It was why when James called and asked her to come help him with something, she'd refused. It wasn't until Wade told her he wanted to take a nap that she went to find out what her cousin wanted.

"I don't know what I could help you with. I'm not a cop anymore." Jess leaned back in the chair and crossed her legs.

"I wanted to know how well you know the guys who work for Wade." There was something odd in James expression, but she couldn't put her finger on it.

"I know they've either worked for him from the beginning or they went through the mechanic program with him." Wade had told her about all the guys one night when they were laying in bed earlier that week.

"I see." James didn't look at her as he shuffled through some papers on his desk.

"Okay. What's going on?" Jess slapped her hand on his desk and was happy when he jumped.

"What are you talking about?" James' eyes grew wide.

He was hiding something, and she didn't have the patience to deal with his bullshit. Jess shot to her feet and leaned over the desk. Jess narrowed her eyes as she scrutinized him because she knew James well enough to know there was no way he called her into the station to ask about Wade's employees.

"Spill it," Jess ordered.

"I don't know what you're talking about. I wanted to ask you about the guys." James leaned toward her and narrowed his eyes. "Is there something you're hiding, little cousin?"

"Yeah, my temper. James, you didn't call me in here just for that. Now, what gives?" Jess dropped into the chair.

"I needed to get you here so I could ask about the guys at the garage. I didn't want Wade getting pissed off when I asked about them." James looked at her, but Jess didn't believe him.

"You know those guys better than I do. You've been going there longer than I have. Even A.J. would be a better person to ask about it," Jess pushed.

"Who's using my name in vain?" Aaron's voice floated in from the hallway.

"You're not God, A.J." Jess rolled her eyes.

"Bethany called me it several times last night." Aaron grinned.

"You're such a pig. You think with a wife and a baby on the way you'd grow up a little." Jess rolled her eyes.

"You wanted to see me, James?" Aaron rested his hands on Jess' shoulders as he stood behind her chair.

"Yeah, I need you to check into all the guys that work for Wade." James held out a thick folder.

"James, those guys wouldn't do anything to hurt Wade. He gave all of them a place to work when they needed it. You know that as well as I do." Aaron stood up straight and took the folder.

"I know, but we need to rule them out. You know that." James nodded toward the folder. "Slash is waiting for you at Keith's office."

"Well, if you're done with me, I'll get A.J. to drop me back to the compound." Jess stood up.

They always referred to Keith's property as The Compound because it was surrounded by a high-security fence and nobody could get on the property without a code.

"No," James and Aaron said together.

"What's going on?" Jess pointed her finger back and forth between her cousins.

"Nothing." Aaron backed out of the office.

"James." Jess dragged out his name in a warning tone.

"I told him he should've gotten Nan to distract you." James blew out a breath.

"Who?" Jess asked.

Before James answered, his phone beeped and he glanced down at it. A huge grin spread across his face as he looked back up at her.

"If you want A.J. to drive you back, you better catch up with him before he leaves." James grinned and sat back in his chair.

Jess stared at him for a minute, then turned and practically ran right into Aaron. He had the same sneaky grin that James had. Jess wanted to smack it off his face.

"Did you want a ride or not?" Aaron asked.

"When I find out what you two are up to, I'm going to kick both your asses." Jess stomped out of the office and purposely stepped on Aaron's foot.

He cursed and mumbled something about it being the last time he helped out one of his cousins. Jess didn't know what it meant, but she'd find out.

By the time Aaron dropped her off in front of the safe house, Jess wanted to smack him. He had a stupid grin on his face the entire way back to the safe house. Whenever she'd ask why he was smiling, he'd shrug and give her some lame reason about being happy.

Jess walked the four steps up to the front door and turned when she saw Hulk sitting on one of the deck chairs with his feet propped up on the rail. He was smiling as he tapped something into his phone.

"Is that the girl Sandy says you're secretly seeing?" Jess teased.

"I'm not seeing anyone and you need to get inside." Hulk didn't look up at her as he pulled his hood up.

"Shouldn't you go inside? It's freezing out here." Jess tucked her hands into her coat pocket.

"I'll be fine. I'm spending the night in the van when Bull gets back." Hulk looked up and with a similar sly smile as Aaron had when he'd dropped her off.

"Why?" There were two other rooms in the house, and he'd stayed in one the previous night.

"Just want to rough it for a night." Hulk waved his hand in the air. "Now go inside before you freeze."

Jess looked at him suspiciously for a few seconds, but the cold wind lessened her curiosity, and she pushed open the door. The aroma of something cooking hit her as soon as she entered, and she chuckled. Nanny Betty had been by again.

"Wade?" Jess shouted as she shrugged out of her jacket and hung it up.

"Close your eyes," Wade whispered behind her.

"What? Why?" Jess tried to turn, but he kept her turned away from him.

"Close your eyes, or I'll have to blindfold you," Wade whispered into her ear.

Jess huffed and closed her eyes. Wade placed his hands on her shoulders and turned her around. He warned her to keep her eyes closed, then took her hands and guided her to where he wanted her.

"Just a couple of more steps," Wade said as he pulled her with him.

When they stopped, he stepped behind her and wrapped his arms around her waist. Jess wasn't sure what was happening, but she played by his rules and kept her eyes closed.

"Happy Birthday, Jess," Wade whispered in her ear. "Open your eyes."

Jess slowly opened her eyes and gasped. The entire living room was glowing in candlelight and flames flickered in the fireplace. In the middle of the living room, a small table had been set with roses and two domes that she recognized from Isabelle's restaurant.

"Wade, what did you do?" Jess swallowed the lump in her throat because it was the most romantic thing a man had ever done for her.

"Since I couldn't take you out for your birthday last night like I'd planned, I had to make some little changes to our plans and enlist some of your family to help," Wade whispered into her ear.

"James and A.J. knew what you were doing." Jess sighed.

"Yeah, it was the only way to get you out of here for a little while so I could do all this. You know, your family can certainly put things together pretty fast." Wade chuckled.

"So I see." Jess turned into his arms and snaked her arms around his neck.

"I'm sorry it has to be here, but I couldn't let your birthday go by without doing something." Wade rested his forehead against hers.

"It's perfect," Jess whispered.

"You're perfect." Wade kissed her nose.

"Come on. The smell of that food is making my stomach growl." Wade backed her toward the table and helped her down to the floor.

"The roses are beautiful." Jess pulled one from the vase and smelled it.

"Hulk picked them up for me at your shop." Wade grinned.

"Is this the reason he's sleeping in the van?" Jess smirked.

"His idea." Wade lifted the domes off the table, and Jess's mouth watered.

Her plate contained pan-fried cod with mashed potatoes, spinach, and sliced carrots. It was her favorite meal at Isabelle's restaurant. It was somewhat healthy but mouthwatering.

"Isabelle picked the meal." Wade eased down next to her.

"We can sit at the table if it's easier for you." Jess figured it wouldn't be comfortable on the floor for him.

"This is perfect." Wade lifted the remote.

Soft country music started to play, and she smiled. He loved the country, and although she wasn't a fan, it had begun to grow on her.

"Eat. Dessert is in the fridge." Wade picked up his fork and started to eat.

"Here I thought I was going to be dessert." Jess grinned as she picked up a forkful of the flaky fish.

"Oh, you will be." Wade winked and dug into his food.

The food was delicious, as usual. She and Wade talked the whole time they ate. They talked about their childhood and how it was growing up outside the city. Wade never liked living in the city, but it was the best place to run his business.

Jess knew the feeling. Hopedale was a great place, but the population was small. It was surprising that her family had so many businesses that were thriving. Although, since they were so well known outside the town, people came to them.

Wade stood up and took the plates from the table. Jess offered, but he hushed her with his finger to her lips. When he returned, he had a small plate with a strawberry shortcake on it. She knew it was from Isabelle's restaurant as well.

He placed the cake in front of her and she grinned as he lit the candle. He sang happy birthday a little off key, but to her it was beautiful. Jess closed her eyes for a second and when she opened them again, she blew out the candle. Jess tipped her head back and grinned up at Wade when she saw him hold two forks as he eased down next to her.

"You want me to share?" Jess feigned shock.

"Damn right. This looks incredible." Wade dug his fork into the cake and picked up a huge chunk.

Jess laughed when he moaned as he put it into his mouth. He picked up a smaller forkful and held it out to her. She allowed him to feed her and she giggled when he smeared some of the cream across her lower lip.

Wade leaned forward and ran his thumb across her lip. He wiped off the cream and sucked it off his thumb. Before he pulled back, Jess grabbed his hand and sucked his thumb into her mouth. She swirled her tongue around it, then released it with a pop.

"Are you trying to make me come right now?" Wade growled.

"I know you have better restraint than that, Wade." Jess licked some cream off her fork.

"Yeah, but Jesus, Blue Eyes. When you look at me like that, and I feel your lips on me, it drives me fucking crazy. Even if it's just my thumb." Wade cupped the back of her head and brushed his lips against hers.

"I like when you get crazy." Jess gently nipped his lower lip.

"Fuck, okay. Before I jump you right here on the floor. I have something for you." Wade reached behind him under the couch and pulled out a square box. "Happy Birthday, Jess."

"Wade, this is too much." Jess shook her head as he put the pink box in her hand.

"Open it," Wade urged her.

Jess opened the box and looked inside. There was another pink box, but it looked like a ring box. For a moment she froze, then with a shaky hand, she pulled it out of the other box.

Jess slowly opened the box and gasped. Inside was a gold pendant with two hearts on the front of it. She touched it and saw it had something engraved on the front of the hearts.

"It's the date I first met you," Wade said.

"You remembered the date?" Jess looked up at him with tears in her eyes.

"Of course. It's the day my heart came alive." Wade cupped her cheek. "Turn it over."

Jess lifted the hearts and flipped it over. On the other side, engraved on one heart, were the words I love you, and an infinity symbol on the other heart.

"I'll love you forever," Wade whispered.

"It's so beautiful." Jess sniffed and lifted her eyes to meet his.

"It seems like such a small thing to show you how I feel. Jess, if I gave a pendant to show you how much I love you, you'd need a crane to carry it." Wade smiled.

"How did I get lucky enough to find you?" Jess whispered.

"You were driving a piece of shit." Wade chuckled.

"Stop picking on my old baby." Jess playfully pushed him.

Jess pulled the necklace out of the box and handed it to Wade. He fumbled with the clasp but managed to get it on with his large hands. Jess touched the beautiful pendant that lay against her chest and smiled.

Jess knew the man in front of her was the love of her life. It made her stomach clench when she thought about someone wanting to hurt him. She lunged at him and wrapped her arms around his neck as she buried her face in the crook of his neck.

"Jess, baby. I didn't want to upset you. I wanted to show you how much you mean to me." Wade hugged her tightly as she straddled his legs and sobbed into his neck.

"I don't want to lose you." Jess sniffed and kissed his neck.

"I'm not going anywhere." He rubbed his hands up and down her back.

"I have to find out who's trying to hurt you." Jess sat up and held his face between her hands.

"You don't have to do anything. Let your cousins deal with this." Wade covered her hands.

"I need to help somehow." Jess stared into his eyes.

"You help by being here. It's the best help I could ever have," Wade whispered.

"I love you so much." Jess choked out the words because she knew if anything happened to him, it would kill her.

"I love you too, sweetheart. Forever." With those words, Wade covered her mouth with his, kissing her with every ounce of love he felt for her.

Wade lowered her to the floor in front of the fireplace and slid his tongue into her mouth. He tasted like wine, chocolate, and Wade.

Wade's hand slid under her shirt and the heat of his palm against her skin was heaven. Jess lifted the bottom of his shirt and he pulled away long enough to rip the shirt over his head.

Wade was sexy and handsome, but that wasn't the reason she loved him. That was a perk. Wade was a kind, hardworking man with a huge heart. He made Jess feel treasured and loved in the way she'd always wanted.

He glided his hand over her stomach until he could cup her breast. His thumb circled her nipple through her bra and it pebbled against his touch. His lips trailed a line of soft kisses down her neck and across her shoulder.

"Wade, make love to me." Jess moaned.

Their clothes vanished with those words When Jess wrapped her hand around his hard length, Wade groaned. He trembled at her slow strokes, and his sounds were erotic.

"Jess, baby. If you keep doing that I'm going to come before I get inside you." Wade panted.

"As much as I'd love to make you explode all over your stomach, I need you deep inside me." He gripped her hips as she straddled him.

"Ride me, baby." Wade practically begged.

Jess lowered herself onto his thick length. Wade moaned her name as he sat up and gripped onto her hips and guided her the rest of the way down on his cock.

"You feel so good inside me." Jess panted as he filled her.

"We fit together perfectly," Wade whispered into her ear as Jess slowly raised up and dropped back down over him.

"Wade, I love you." Jess moaned against his cheek.

"I love you too, Jess. Forever," Wade whispered as he flipped her onto her back and showed her exactly what that meant.

# *Chapter 20*

Wade sat at a large table in a room at the Hopedale Police Station. James handed him a file folder, but Wade shook his head. There was no way he could believe the file contained information about the person trying to kill him and destroy his business.

He'd been followed around by security for two weeks, his family could only go back to their house if someone were with them. Wade could go to work but only if one of Keith's security team was with him.

Now James told him one of the people he trusted completely could be involved in all the shit that had gone down over the last few months. Wade opened the folder and cursed under his breath at the mugshot.

"How the fuck did I not know about this?" Wade shook his head as he looked through the charges listed on the paper.

"In his defense, it was before you guys met. I'm assuming you never did a background check when you hired him." James sat across from Wade.

"No, I guess, I should have, but I've known all these guys for a long time." Wade picked up the mugshot and stared at it.

"From what Sandy dug up, Dwayne used to hang with a hard crowd when he was younger. I mean, those charges were when he was from eighteen to twenty-two. For what it's worth, he hasn't been in trouble since." James rested his arms on the table.

"So why do you think he could be involved in this?" Wade asked.

"The building next to your shop was one of the ones he and his buddies broke into. Actually, most of the B and E's he did were buildings in that area," James explained.

"I want to talk to him." Wade closed the folder.

"Nick is questioning him now," James said.

"I want to talk to him. Please." Wade pushed the folder back to James.

Wade didn't know if he'd be able to talk to his friend, considering it was a police investigation, but he needed to hear it from Dwayne. He wanted to know if his buddy was involved before he would ever believe it. James stared at him for a minute before he stood up and walked to the door. He stopped and turned.

"Okay, but I'll be watching through the window, and Nick will stay in there with you." James motioned for Wade to follow.

James opened a door a few feet down from the room Wade had been. He stepped back for Wade to enter, and as soon as Wade walked into the room, Dwayne glanced up. Wade could only see the fear in his friend's eyes as he made his way to the chair across from Dwayne. Nick stood and motioned for Wade to sit.

"I had nothing to do with this, Wade. I swear," Dwayne choked out the words.

"Why didn't you tell me about your record?" Wade asked.

"It was ancient history. I was young and hung around with a bunch of assholes who liked to break into buildings. We never stole anything. They'd get a rush out of it, and I guess I did too, but Wade, I swear on my life, I would never do anything to hurt you, Harry, or the shop." Dwayne didn't flinch when he looked directly into Wade's eyes.

"Do you have any idea who could be out to get me?" Wade asked.

"Jesus, no. Honestly, I can't think of anyone who dislikes you, let alone hate you enough to hurt you." Dwayne flopped back in the chair as he linked his fingers on the top of his head.

Wade stared at Dwayne for a few seconds before he dropped his head and blew out a breath. Wade knew without a doubt Dwayne wasn't involved. Not to mention Dwayne was one of his dearest friends.

"I guess I should look for another job." Dwayne almost whispered the words.

"You're not hiding anything else from me, are you?" Wade lifted his head and met Dwayne's concerned eyes.

"No, and I wasn't hiding it from you. I don't talk about those days simply because I'm not that kid anymore. I'm thirty-one years old, for Christ's sake. I work my ass off to support my son." Dwayne sounded as if he was about to burst into tears. "You know what it's like to be a single parent, Wade. My son is my life."

Wade nodded and stood up. Dwayne stared at him as he sat with his hands flat on the table. When Wade held out his hand, Dwayne shot to his feet and gripped onto Wade's hand.

"I believe you, Dwayne, and for what it's worth, I found it difficult to believe you were involved." Wade gave Dwayne's hand a tight squeeze before he released it.

"That means a lot to me." Dwayne glanced over at Nick.

The door to the room opened and James stepped inside, followed by Kurt and John. Dwayne's eyes opened wide as if he was about to face the firing squad.

"Dwayne, you're free to go. Your alibi checked out. There was no way you could be at the garage the night of the attack. You also don't match the height of the guy on the video," James informed them.

"Look, there's nobody at our shop that would hurt Wade. Everyone thinks the world of him, and they'll all tell you that." Dwayne pounded his pointer finger on the table.

"I think you're right, but we still have to make sure," John responded.

"What can we do to help find this fucker?" Dwayne asked.

"Keep your eyes open for anything strange around the shop. Make sure you check your vehicles before you leave work or home. Wade may be the target of this person, but it's not unusual for these assholes to go after others close to their victim," Kurt answered.

The word *victim* made Wade tense. He never considered himself a victim of anything. He was a grown-ass man, for Christ's sake. The whole situation was affecting his family and friends, as well as his ability to work. It was even causing havoc with his relationship. To get time alone with Jess, he basically had to get it approved with security.

He was almost at the point where he wanted to step out and let the fucker come for him. Wade knew that would be a difficult sell to the police and his family. He was pretty sure Jess would be completely against it. Plus, he wasn't sure how he would even bring the bastard out of the shadows.

"Wade, Crunch is waiting out in the lobby to bring you to the safe house," James told him.

When Wade rolled his eyes and blew out a breath, he heard Nick chuckle behind him. Wade turned around to see the amused expression on Nick's face.

"Look, we know what you're dealing with." Nick dropped his hand on Wade's shoulder.

"I doubt that," Wade complained.

"Okay, Let's see. John's wife had a crazy woman trying to kill her when John and Stephanie first met. James wife, Marina, was stalked by her ex-husband's twin brother. Sandy was held hostage by her ex-boyfriend, and her sister. Keith's wife was kidnapped by a crazy man obsessed with her. Mike's wife was almost abducted by a sex trafficking ring. Would you like me to go on?" Nick smirked.

"What the fuck?" Dwayne gasped as his jaw dropped open.

"Not to mention, Nick's wife was in the crosshairs of a serial killer a few years back, and A.J.'s wife witnessed a murder, and the killer went after her," John continued.

"Starting to think getting involved with your family is dangerous." Dwayne snorted.

"I'm starting to think that myself," Kurt grumbled.

"If getting through this means I get to spend the rest of my life with Jess, then I'd go through it a thousand times," Wade admitted.

Kurt growled as he crossed his arms over his chest. Wade smirked as John, James, and Nick burst into a fit of laughter. Kurt was the typical father of a daughter. It suddenly made Wade cringe to think about when Ocean started dating.

"Bring him out to Crunch," Kurt grumbled as he walked out of the room.

"I can't wait for him to find out that Isabelle is kind of seeing Roman Young." Nick chuckled.

"Jesus, let him get used to not being the only man in Jess' life before you spring that on him." John laughed.

"What do you mean by, *kind of seeing*?" James asked.

"Let's just say I've seen them walk to work from her house most mornings." John raised an eyebrow.

"Don't tell Uncle Kurt that. He'll have an aneurysm." James smirked.

Wade walked out to the lobby and spotted Crunch talking to Keith. Wade stepped next to them, and Keith turned. Wade didn't like the look on his face.

"Wade, I need to tell you something," Keith said.

Before Keith could say anything, James and Nick rushed out of the building. Dwayne ran behind them, looking utterly panicked.

"What's wrong?" Wade grabbed Dwayne's arm.

"Harry's been hurt," Dwayne practically shouted as he ran out through the door.

Wade didn't wait to hear what Keith said as he hurried behind Dwayne. He jumped in the truck with Dwayne, and they sped off toward the hospital. On the way, Wade tried calling Josie several times, but she didn't answer, and that made him anxious.

"What the fuck happened?" Wade asked Dwayne.

"James got a call saying Harry was being rushed to the hospital. That's all I know." Dwayne leaned on the horn as a car cut in front of him.

Wade fisted his hands as they swerved into the hospital parking lot. Thankfully, there were plenty of parking spots and they were able to get inside the building quickly.

They stepped into the emergency department and immediately saw Everett sat with his elbows on his knees and his head in his hands. Dwayne shouted to him, but when he stood up, Wade cursed. Everett's overalls were covered in blood, and his face was ghostly white. He looked devastated as he walked toward Wade and Dwayne.

"What the fuck happened?" Wade asked.

"I don't know. I went to find Harry to get another job to work on and Josie told me he'd gone out back to check something. Curtis and I went outside and we found Harry was on the ground, and …

Fuck... there was so much blood. I don't know where it was coming from." Everett plowed his hands through his hair.

"Where's Josie?" Wade asked.

"Curtis is with her in the waiting room." Everett turned and walked down the hallway.

Wade and Dwayne looked at each other as they followed Everett. This had to have something to do with whoever was after Wade. Now he was pissed.

Josie was sobbing, and Curtis looked completely devastated as he held onto Josie. Wade hurried to her and sat down as he eyed Curtis.

"We haven't heard anything yet." Curtis mouthed the words.

"Josie?" Wade spoke softly.

"Wade, he stopped breathing in the ambulance. They kept saying he was crashing." Josie cried as she wrapped her arms around Wade.

"He'll be okay, Josie," Dwayne whispered as he crouched in front of her.

Wade didn't know if his friend was right, but he prayed that Harry pulled through. Wade would never forgive himself if Harry died. He needed his friend to be okay, then Wade was going to do something to find out who the hell was fucking with his family, because Harry was family.

The waiting room filled up quickly. The men Wade and Harry worked with stayed at the garage to finish the work for the day and showed up as soon as they closed the shop.

Cody told him that the police had the rear of the shop closed off while they checked the area for evidence. Hulk had helped clear out the unfinished work, but since it had been close to four when everything happened, most of the work had been done.

Jess showed up not long after Wade had arrived at the hospital, with a lot of her family, and his own family as well. His father and Harry were like brothers, and Wade could see the strain on his dad's face as he reassured Josie while his mother held her hand.

Wade sat across the room from them with Jess next to him. It seemed as if they'd been waiting forever for news on Harry, and it worried him. He could only stare at the television on the wall, but he didn't really see it. He almost didn't notice Keith sit next to him. At least not until Keith spoke.

"You shouldn't have run off without security," Keith whispered.

"I wasn't really worried about my security detail at that moment," Wade spoke a little more harshly than he probably should have.

"I understand, but Harry could've been a distraction to throw us off," Keith continued.

"Keith, I know your job is to keep me safe, but Harry is not a distraction. He's like a second father to me. When he pulls through this, and he will pull through, I'm going to find the fucker who did this, and make him wish he was never born." With those words, Wade stomped out of the waiting room.

He forced down the lump that formed in his throat as he blinked his eyes to hold back the tears that were building. Wade would apologize to Keith later but at that moment the only thing he was concerned about was Harry.

Wade didn't know if Harry would pull through because he didn't really know what happened to his friend. The only thing he did know was the asshole who put Harry in the hospital needed to pay for what he did.

# Chapter 21

Jess glared at Keith as she stood up to follow Wade. Her cousin meant well, but considering the situation, it wasn't exactly the time to get on Wade's case about being careful. She knew what it was like to be worried about a loved one fighting for their life. After all, Keith had been one of them.

"Jess, he has to be careful. I've got a feeling whoever this is will not give up until he gets to his target." Keith grabbed her arm before she could follow Wade.

"I've got the same feeling," Jess whispered and walked out of the waiting room to find Wade.

She glanced up and down the corridor but didn't see him. Jess' heart thudded in her chest as she walked up toward the exit of the emergency department. Keith was right. The guy could've followed any one of them to the hospital and waited for them to let their guard down.

Jess turned to walk outside when she spotted Wade exit the men's room. She blew out a breath of relief at seeing him and practically ran toward him.

"Are you okay?" Jess asked as Wade leaned against the wall.

"Yeah, it's just taking so long to get news." He reached for her and wrapped his arms around her.

"I know and waiting always seems longer than it actually is." Jess lay her head against his chest.

"Harry didn't deserve this." Wade rested his chin on her head.

"Neither do you." Jess hugged him tightly.

He was quiet for several minutes before he pushed off the wall but kept his arm around her. They walked back to the waiting room in silence and stood outside listening to the quiet conversations coming from the room.

Almost two hours after the doctor had told them Harry was going into surgery, the doctor entered the waiting room looking for Harry's family. Josie shot to her feet. Wade and the guys from the shop stood behind her as they waited for the doctor to talk.

"Mrs. Saunders, your husband made it through the surgery, and we fixed the damage to the artery. He was stabbed in the chest, but thankfully, it didn't damage his heart. Things will be critical for the next forty-eight hours, but I'm very hopeful that he'll be okay." The doctor smiled as Josie grabbed his hand and thanked him over, and over. "You're most welcome. He'll be in recovery for another hour or so, then we will be moving him to ICU. You and your children can visit him then but only two at a time."

"We don't have children, but these boys are like sons to Harry." Josie sniffed.

"As long as you're okay with them visiting, I won't tell anyone they aren't your sons. One of the nurses will come to get you when you can see him, but if you want, you can make your way to the ICU waiting area." The doctor winked at her and nodded to everyone as he left the room.

"I told you he'd be fine. He's too much of a stubborn bastard to let an old stab wound get him." Seamus hugged Josie.

"Now we just have to find out who did this so we can pound the shit out of them." Logan wrapped his arm around Josie and kissed the top of her head.

"The police will handle it." Jess turned at the sound of her father's voice.

"Like they handle everything else. If they were doing something, wouldn't this fucker be behind bars instead of out running around the streets stabbing people?" Logan snapped.

"Logan, that's enough." Wade raised his voice. "This isn't the cops' fault."

"Wade's right. I know Jess' cousins are not going to stop until they find who did this, and who hurt Wade," Josie said.

Logan didn't say another word, but his expression told her he wasn't happy about the whole situation. There was also something else going on with him. Jess asked a few days earlier how June was doing, and Logan said she was doing fine, but he had issues finding her another place to live because of the lease.

At least Harry would be okay. Hopefully, none of the men who worked for Wade found the guy who did it before the police did. From the expressions on their faces, they'd probably kill the guy and then call the police. The only thing Jess was worried about was what would be this guy's next move.

# *Chapter 22*

Wade walked into the Intensive Care Unit with Josie holding tight to his hand. The couple might bicker and complain about each other, but if anything happened to Harry, Josie would be lost. Harry told Wade once that Josie was the life that kept his heart beating. Wade had thought it was a line to make Josie smile, but since Wade fell in love with Jess, he knew exactly what his friend meant.

The nurse appeared in the waiting room almost an hour after Harry came out of surgery. Although several of the guys and even his father had offered to go into the unit with Josie, she only wanted Wade. His heart pounded as he followed Josie. The last time he'd been in the Intensive Care Unit was when his father was brought in after the stroke. Wade remembered the shock of seeing his father hooked up to so many machines.

Wade and Josie turned the corner and the nurse pulled back the curtain around Harry's bed. Wade quickly wrapped his arm around Josie when he heard her gasp. It was unsettling to see Harry pale and motionless.

"He probably looks worse than he actually is," Wade whispered to Josie, but it was a reminder to himself as well.

"I've just never seen him so… helpless," Josie choked.

"He's probably going to sleep through the night. He's heavily sedated, but all his vitals are great." The nurse smiled as she checked the IV bag.

"Do you think he can hear me?" Josie asked the nurse.

"I believe they do. If you want to tell him you're here, or to hurry up and get well, go ahead." The pretty nurse nodded as she walked outside of the curtain.

"Harry, I'm here. Wade's here too. All the boys are in the waiting room, and a lot of Jess' family too." Josie held his hand between hers.

Wade stared down at Harry. It was surreal to see him so quiet and still. In all the years Wade had known the man, he'd never seen him stay still for more than five minutes. Wade didn't like it.

"You better get well, you old fart. You can't leave me yet," Josie choked.

"He's not going anywhere." Wade kept his arm around Josie's shoulder as she eased into the chair next to the bed.

"He better not. As crooked as he can be, I love the old grump." Josie kissed Harry's hand.

After he was sure Josie would be okay until one of the other guys came into the room with her, Wade made his way back to the waiting room. As he stepped out of the ICU, his phone rang.

He looked at the screen, but he didn't recognize the number and was thinking about ignoring it. He decided to answer it just in case it was something about his shop.

"Hello?" Wade said quietly.

"Wade, I need to talk to you." The female voice was familiar, but he couldn't place the voice.

"Who is this?" Wade asked.

"It's Sky." She sounded scared and Wade's heart felt like it dropped in his chest.

"What do you want?" Wade didn't mean to sound so curt, but his first thought was she wanted to take Ocean from him.

"I don't want to talk about it on the phone. Can we meet somewhere?" She sounded nervous.

"Is this important? I'm at the hospital." Wade leaned on the wall outside the ICU.

"Oh God, are you okay?" She actually sounded concerned.

Wade didn't want to go into the whole situation with her. Sky didn't know Harry, and it was really none of her concern. The last thing he wanted was to have her in the middle of everything.

"My shop foreman had a little mishap," Wade lied.

"Shit, it's true. I'm on my way. I need to talk to you, today." Sky ended the call before Wade could respond.

Confused, Wade stared at his phone. Why did she sound so panicked about Harry? His thoughts were going in circles and he couldn't understand why she'd need to talk to him so urgently.

"Are you okay?" Jess asked.

"Yeah, I just got the weirdest call." Wade shoved his phone into his pocket.

"What do you mean?" Jess asked.

"Sky called and said she had to talk to me. When I said I was here with Harry, she said she was coming and hung up." Wade shook his head.

"That is odd." Jess braced her shoulder against the wall and faced him. "It's really odd that she'd call considering what happened today. You don't think she could be involved in what's been going on, do you?"

"I can't see a connection. I also can't see her trying to kill me or stab Harry. The woman used to get upset if she spilled ketchup on her shirt." Wade rolled his eyes.

Jess didn't look as convinced that Sky wasn't the one doing all this. Wade did know she wasn't the one that attacked him because that was the one thing he was sure about.

"She's coming here?" Jess asked.

"That's what she said." Wade pushed off the wall and started toward the waiting room.

Jess hurried by him and motioned for someone inside the room to come outside. Wade waited behind her and watched as Kurt, Keith, and Hulk walked out of the room.

"Is Harry okay?" Kurt was obviously concerned.

"He's sedated, but he's doing good," Wade assured him.

"Sky called Wade and said she needed to talk to him. She's on her way here." It was the first time since he'd met Jess that he saw how she would've been as a police officer.

"Is this about Harry?" Keith asked.

"She didn't say. When I told her I was here, she sounded freaked. She said she was on the way and hung up." Wade shrugged.

"James, get over here. Now." Kurt had his phone up to his ear.

Wade was brought to another waiting area where Hulk and Damon stood outside the small room. Jess was next to him even though her father had ordered her to stay with everyone in the other waiting room. It was obvious Kurt knew better than to continue an argument with his daughter because after a quiet chat away from Wade, Jess followed him into the room.

"I need you to text her. Tell her where to meet you." James pulled down the shade on the small window of the room.

"I'm telling you, it's not her." Wade shook his head.

"Like I told you, you'd be surprised what people are capable of," Kurt said.

"I'm going to sit over here in the corner, and Uncle Kurt will sit on the other side of the room. When she comes in, it will look like we're waiting for someone. Jess, make sure you keep a close eye on her while she's close to Wade," James continued his instructions.

"Keith and Rex are in the other waiting room making sure everyone stays in there. Curtis is in the ICU with Josie and Harry." Kurt glanced up from his phone.

Wade sat back in the chair and focused on the only entrance to the room. Everything seemed over-the-top considering who was coming to see him, but he'd do as they wanted. If by some slim chance Sky was responsible for all the shit going on, Wade would be completely stunned.

Twenty minutes later, he heard voices outside the room. He recognized Sky's voice and stood up to see why there was such a commotion. Jess grasped his hand and shook her head. Wade sat down again and waited.

"Why do you need to check my purse?" Sky's voice was raised enough that they could hear her part of the conversation.

Wade glanced at James and could see a smirk. James was the only one who could look outside the room. If anyone walked in, it would look like he was reading the book in his hand, but Wade could see his focus was on the door. Kurt was identically sat on the other side of the room, but he seemed ready to jump up if anything went wrong.

"Who the hell is in there? The Prime Minister?" Sky complained, and Wade heard Jess chuckle.

"I'm sorry, Miss. It's a security check," Hulk said as he walked her into the room.

Sky glanced around the space for a few seconds. When she noticed Wade and Jess, she glanced back at Hulk. When the large man turned and left the room, Sky hurried toward Wade. Her face was pale, and Wade couldn't remember seeing her so disheveled. Her eyes shot to Jess then back to Wade as she slowly eased into the seat next to him.

She was quiet for several minutes as she seemed to check out James and Kurt. When they didn't acknowledge her, she turned to Wade. After several deep breaths, she started to speak in a low whisper.

"Wade, before I tell you all this, I want you to know I never knew any of this was happening. I only overheard their discussion by accident because I've got a client in the same building." Sky swallowed.

"Sky, tell us what you heard," Jess urged in a quiet voice.

"Are you sure it's safe here?" She nervously flicked her eyes toward James and Kurt again.

"I promise." Jess reached across Wade and grasped Sky's shaky hand.

"Okay. Ummm... okay. I had a meeting at the Delta Hotel. I was meeting with a client who's buying some property in the city. When I was leaving, I ran into an old client with another man. I chatted with them for a few minutes and then went to have a bite to eat at the restaurant in the hotel. They didn't see me when they came in and sat directly behind me." Sky took a deep breath before she continued.

"I really didn't pay attention to their conversation at first, but then I heard them say your name. The other guy said you must have a horseshoe up your ass because you walked away from the accident. I didn't know what they were talking about, but I kept listening. He said he couldn't understand why you weren't losing business with all the things that happened at your garage. Wade, what's going on at your shop?"

"We've had stuff happen to cars." Wade didn't know how much he should tell her.

"And you were in an accident?" Sky asked.

"Yeah, I lost the brakes on my truck and went over an embankment," Wade told her but only after James had given him a quick nod.

"It wasn't an accident. This guy cut your brakes." Sky pressed her lips together.

"You heard him say that?" Jess asked.

"Better than that. I started to record the conversation when I realized who they were talking about. Your friend that's in the hospital, he was stabbed, wasn't he?" Sky's eyes widened.

Wade didn't get a chance to answer the question because Kurt and James were on their feet and standing in front of them. It looked like they'd heard enough. Sky jumped back in the chair with a terrified expression.

"Sky, this is my cousin James and my father, Kurt. They're police," Jess said and Sky relaxed.

"Sorry, I thought you were part of this." Sky sighed.

"Go on, Sky," Jess urged.

"This man was pissed because the building was supposed to be his." Sky pulled out her phone and pulled up an audio file. "That's most of the conversation. When I heard the guy say he'd have the building if he had to kill everyone in it to get it, I started recording."

"Can you send that file to me?" James asked as he showed her his cell number.

Sky tapped her screen several times and then nodded to let him know that she'd sent what he wanted. Wade was thankful that she would let him know what she heard because she didn't have to. It wasn't like they were friends.

"Do they know you heard them?" James asked.

"I don't think so. They left before I did," Sky said.

"This client of yours, do you have his name?" James asked.

"I'll do you one better. I've got his phone number and address." Sky scrolled through her phone and held it up to James.

"Does the name Reginald Crocker sound familiar?" James asked.

"I know a George Crocker. He's the one who sold me the building." Wade barely had the words out of his mouth, when James had his phone up to his ear.

"Sandy, look up George and Reginald Crocker. I need everything you have on both of them." James listened for a second then hung up his phone.

"Look, George is a nice guy. He helped me get the first building I had. He's one of my most loyal customers." Wade shook his head.

"Sky, does this man look familiar?" James held up his phone with the picture of a man on it.

"Yes, that's Reg." Sky nodded.

"Wade, do you know him?" James asked, and Wade shook his head.

James tapped his phone a few times and turned the phone back to Wade. George Crocker's picture appeared on the screen, and

Wade felt suddenly ill. It was hard for him to believe that George would have anything to do with what happened.

"I know him." Wade nodded.

"Sky, was this the man with Reg?" James showed Sky the picture.

"No, but I know him. He's one of my partner's clients. He's a nice guy, and if I remember correctly, he owns a ton of commercial property. Wait, he and Reg are brothers." Sky sat up straight as if she remembered something. "There was a huge argument between them in my partner's office last year. Something about property that was left in a will. I'm not completely sure, but my partner would know. He was in the office the whole time."

"I need your partner's name, phone number, and address." James reached in his pocket and pulled out a small notepad.

"Jonah Dawson is my partner's name. This is his information." Sky handed James a business card. "He may be still at the office. Sometimes he's there until way after supper. I can call him and let him know you need to speak with him."

"I'd rather you didn't." James stopped Sky from making the phone call. "I know he's your partner, but we don't know how much he knows. Would you be willing to meet with one of our police officers to see if you can describe the other man with Reginald?"

Sky nodded, and James told her he'd call her to set up a time that would be convenient for her. He also warned her not to say anything to anyone else in her office. She seemed hesitant at first but nodded after a few seconds.

Wade glanced at Jess as if to ask her what to do next. The shop would be closed for the weekend so he would probably be shuttled off to Keith's Compound again. As spacious as the area was, he was starting to feel closed in when he was there. He also didn't want to leave Josie alone at the hospital, not that any of the guys would allow that either, but he didn't feel comfortable going until he knew Harry was out of danger.

James wanted Damon to bring Sky back to her home, but she refused the escort. She told James that she'd be fine, and if Sky felt as if she was in danger, she'd call the police. Once she was gone, the disagreement started.

# *Chapter 23*

"I'm not leaving Josie until I know Harry is going to be okay." Wade pulled his arm from her father's grasp.

"Wade, be reasonable. We know for a fact now someone is trying to get you out of the way because they want your shop." Her father's tone was calm, but Jess could see the aggravation in his expression.

"Would you leave if someone you cared about was inside that room?" Wade motioned to the doors leading to the ICU unit.

Her father didn't answer, but he looked at Jess as if to ask her for help. What was she supposed to do? Jess knew that if her father were in Wade's shoes, they would have to drag him out kicking and screaming.

"Dad, at least let him wait until he can make sure that Josie won't be alone." Jess glanced at Wade, hoping he wouldn't disagree.

Her father shook his head and walked toward where Keith, Damon, and Hulk stood, acting as if all their concentration was on the wall across from them. Jess was a little annoyed as well. Her father was the Chief of Police and didn't typically get involved in cases. At least, he didn't need to, but it seemed that when it came to his family and those involved with them, her father put himself right in the middle of the investigation.

Since James had left to follow up on some information, her father seemed to think he needed to control the situation. Even with the security there, he appeared uneasy because Wade wasn't willing to leave.

"Why do I feel like I'm about to be grounded for defying my father?" Wade whispered next to her ear.

"Because Dad likes to intimidate people," Jess grumbled.

"I'm not intimidated and I don't care what he says or does. I'm not leaving Josie." Wade turned and made his way through the door to ICU.

"Where the fuck is he going?" Her father grumbled.

"Dad, will you stop? Harry's like a second father to Wade, and until he's sure Harry is going to be okay, he doesn't really care what you think." Jess faced her father and propped her fists on her hips.

"Jesus Christ, it's like looking at mudder." Her dad shook his head.

"I'll take that as a compliment since my grandmother is an amazing person." Jess grinned and kissed her father's cheek.

"Jess, I know you love that man. I also know that man is in danger. So if you get hurt because he's careless, he'll be in bed next to Harry." Her father wrapped one arm around her and pulled her into an embrace. "I saw you when his truck went off the road. I don't want to see that look on your face again, and I told Wade that."

"Dad, I know you mean well, but he's a grown man, and you can't force him to leave someone he cares about." Jess wrapped her arms around her father and rested her cheek against his chest.

"I wish I could turn you all into little girls again and keep you from leaving me," her dad whispered, but Jess wasn't sure if he said it to himself, or if he meant her to hear it.

"I'm not leaving you, Dad." Jess smiled up at him.

"Yeah, but you're not my little girl anymore." He tapped her under the chin with his finger.

"Dad, I haven't been a little girl for a long time, but I'll always be your little girl." Jess hugged him.

Harry regained consciousness a few hours later and the doctors were optimistic about his progress. It was after midnight when Wade finally decided to leave the hospital. Logan had agreed to stay with Josie all night, which made him feel better about going back to Hopedale.

Keith and Damon drove them back to the safe house while Rex stayed at the hospital to make sure Josie, Harry, and Logan were safe. For most of the drive, everyone was quiet. The only sound was the soft rock music coming from the radio and the hard snow hitting the window.

Jess sighed when she realized Christmas was only a little over a month away and from the way things were going, she'd probably be doing her shopping the week of the holiday season. Jess hated shopping.

"So, I guess I should let you guys know, I'm leaving Newfoundland after the New Year," Damon said breaking the silence.

"What?" Keith sounded surprised.

"Why?" Jess asked.

"Nothing is keeping me here." Damon stared out through the passenger-side window.

"What about Pam?" Jess asked.

"What about her?" When he snapped at her, Jess wanted to take her question back.

"Nothing," Jess looked up to see Keith glare at her through the rearview mirror.

"I'm sorry for snapping, Jess. Your cousin and I were over a long time ago. The Trixie I knew in Ontario is not the woman she is now." Damon turned to look at Jess. "I've got things in Ontario I need to deal with. Who knows, I might show up here again one day."

"I hate to see you go," Keith said as they pulled through the gates of The Compound. "You'll always have a job here."

"Thanks, Adrian will be staying." Damon referred to another of his former military buddies who had come to Newfoundland the previous year with Damon.

They were both friends of Bethany's cousin, and when she was in trouble, they'd come running to help her. It was how they'd found out that Damon and Pam were once involved, but neither of them would talk about what happened between them nor why they ended things. There was also the question as to why Damon called her Trixie instead of Pam. Neither of them would answer that question.

Keith stopped in front of the safe house to drop off Wade and Jess. He was quiet as they walked into the house, but there was no doubt in her mind that his thoughts were going a mile a minute. Hulk arrived seconds later and plopped down on the couch as she and Wade headed to the bedroom.

"Wade, are you okay?" Jess asked.

"I miss my daughter. I miss my parents, I miss my dog, and I even miss my annoying sister. I know I've seen them every day, but I miss them being in the same house. I haven't been able to check on Ocean after she falls asleep in almost three weeks." Wade pulled his hand down over his face and blew out a breath.

"Maybe we should have Ocean stay here from now on," Jess suggested.

"No, she's having a blast with Sandy and the kids. I just want to go back to a normal life again." Wade sat on the bed and tugged her toward him. "I want to be able to take my girlfriend out to dinner or a movie. Take a walk on the beach."

"I love the beach, but I'm not taking a walk in this weather," Jess joked.

"I feel so claustrophobic that I'd walk on the beach in a tsunami." Wade snorted.

"I know, but hopefully Sky's information will end all this. James will call in the morning to let us know what he found out." Jess wrapped her arms around his neck and he rested his cheek against her breasts.

"I love you, Jess. Most women would have run away after the first thing happened," Wade whispered.

"You don't run away when you love someone, and I love you, Wade Rivers. More than I could ever tell you." Jess kissed the top of his head as they held each other.

She'd stay that way all night if it made Wade feel better. The man had been thrown so many curve balls that it was surprising he wasn't ready to snap. Wade wanted his life back and who could blame him? Although, she was getting used to sleeping next to him every night. It was the downside of going back to a normal life because she'd have to go back to her apartment to sleep alone most nights.

"Let's go to bed," Wade whispered as he kissed between her breasts through her shirt.

"Sounds like a good idea," Jess replied.

They were woken the next morning by kids shouting outside. Jess rolled over and climbed out of bed. She snatched Wade's T-shirt off the floor and pulled it on as she made her way to the window.

The ground was covered with snow and her cousin's kids were enjoying the first big snowfall of the year. John's daughter, Olivia, Ian's daughter, Grace, and Nick's step-daughter, Molly were around the same age and were always together. Equally as close were James son, Colin, and Ian's son Alexander.

Jess smiled at the giggling children as they ran from the older kids. Ocean picked up Molly and tossed her in a snow pile, making the little girl giggle hysterically. Ocean glanced toward the window and when she saw Jess, she ran back around the corner of the house.

"What's all the racket?" Wade grumbled as he flopped over on his stomach.

"Looks like the O'Conner kids have been set loose in The Compound to play in the snow." Jess laughed.

"Why would Keith have all the kids on his property?" Wade mumbled sleepily.

"It keeps all the kids in one place, I guess." Jess couldn't think of another excuse. "Ocean's out there too."

"My daughter is out playing in the snow?" Wade lifted his head.

"Yep, she's …" Jess was interrupted when Ocean burst into the room still dressed in her jacket, hat, and mittens.

"Dad, get up." She bounced on top of Wade.

"Ocean," Wade shouted when his daughter put her snow-covered mittens on his back.

"Aww, Dad. Did I get you cold?" Ocean smirked.

"You better run before I get up and get dressed, little girl." Wade flipped over and sat up.

Ocean backed away from the bed and laughed. Jess was amused because there was no way Wade was getting out of bed until his daughter left the room since he was completely naked under the blankets.

"You'll never catch me, old man." Ocean stuck out her tongue and giggled as she ran out of the room.

"Did she just call me, old man?" Wade stared at the open door dumbfounded.

"She did." Jess laughed as Wade threw back the blankets and quickly got dressed.

Jess never had so much fun in longer than she could remember. All the O'Connors were outside the safe house playing in the snow. The younger kids were being pulled around on toboggans, the older ones had fun tossing snowballs, but the adults did their share of snowball throwing.

Nanny Betty, her mom, Wade's mother, and her aunts made stews and sandwiches for when everyone was finished with the snow play. Since there were several pregnant women in the O'Connor clan, they were able to get away with a lot more than the rest.

"I figured getting all the kids over here and just having a day without worry would help Wade feel a little better," Keith said as they sipped hot chocolate on the front step.

"He's missing his family." Jess smiled as Ocean and Ian's daughter Lilly tossed snow over Wade's head.

"Do you blame him?" Keith asked.

"No. Have you heard from James today? Marina said he left early this morning to talk to some people." Jess had talked to Marina about it shortly after they'd gone outside.

"It's only noon. I'm sure James and Cory are trying to get all the info they can before they come back." Keith fixed his toque on his head.

Before she had a chance to say anything else, a blob of snow hit her in the chest. She turned in time to see Wade drop his hands and act as if he hadn't just hit her with a snowball. She narrowed her eyes and handed her empty mug to Keith.

"You better move, Rivers. She got that rutting-bull look," Keith shouted.

Jess jumped off the step and ran straight for Wade. He laughed and bent over like a football player as she headed toward him. When Jess jumped to knock him down, he grabbed her around the knees and tossed her onto her back in the snow. Before she could get up, he was on top of her, holding her hands over her head.

"You know I could flip you off me in a second, right?" Jess raised an eyebrow.

"I know, but you like me on top of you too much to do that." Wade wiggled his eyebrows and dropped his head.

"There are too many kids around here to do what I want to do right now," Jess whispered.

"Come in and get a bite ta eat," Nanny Betty shouted from the doorway of the house.

The kids and adults were like a stampede as they all stomped up the steps to the house. Jess was still pinned to the snow with Wade on top of her. He lowered his head and pressed his lips against hers.

"We better get inside before all the food is gone. That's if we can get inside. There's got to be a hundred people in there." Wade lifted off her and pulled her to her feet.

"You'd be surprised how much food Nan, Mom, Aunt Kathleen, and Aunt Cora got made in the time we were out here. Don't forget your mom is in there too. I've seen how much food she prepares for just five of you." Jess laughed as they walked to the house, holding hands.

Wade had been distracted all day, it was good to see him smile. As he sat in the living room with her cousins and the kids, he seemed relaxed for the first time in weeks. He'd spoken with Harry and was relieved to find out he would be moved out of the intensive care unit in a day or so.

It wasn't until James arrived with Cory that Wade became uneasy again. Jess immediately went to him, and he grasped her hand almost instantly. Within thirty minutes, all the kids were bundled up and brought back to their homes. Reluctantly, Wade allowed his daughter to leave with Ian's two older girls.

"Nana said we'll be having supper tomorrow at Lily and Evie's grandparents' house. I'll see you tomorrow, Dad. Love you." Ocean hugged Wade, then ran out behind the rest of the kids.

"It's the age. Trust me." Sandy smirked as she pulled out a laptop and placed it on the table.

"Danny and Mason aren't even teenagers yet, and they don't want to spend more time with us than they have to." James rolled his eyes.

"I think Ocean likes Hopedale better than she does in St. John's." Wade glanced out through the window.

"Hopedale is an addictive place," Hulk interjected.

"You got that right." Rex laughed.

"There are a few houses around here you could get for a song and lots of land if you're looking to build." Her father glanced at Jess.

"I can't think about anything like that right now. James, did you find out anything?" Wade sighed.

Jess wanted to toss something at her dad. The last thing she needed was her father hounding him about buying a house in Hopedale. As much as she wanted to stay in her hometown, if she wanted to be with Wade, they'd have to agree on where they would eventually live.

"I talked to Jonah Dawson. He remembered the argument, vividly. He told me he had to step between the brothers because they almost came to blows," James started. "He said he still isn't sure what the fight was about. The only thing he did know was that George was the executor of his father's estate, but Reginald didn't agree with the way George dictated everything."

"I don't understand what any of that has to do with me." Wade sounded as confused as Jess felt.

"Me either, but when I went to talk to George, the house looked as if nobody had been there in a while. The mail was hanging out of the mailbox." James showed them pictures he'd taken.

"When we went to see Reginald, his wife told us he went away for the weekend with his brother. She also told me Reginald didn't talk to George. Apparently, there's another brother as well. According to Mrs. Crocker, Oscar's trouble." James held out a picture.

"Who's this?" Wade asked as he held the picture in his hand.

"That would be the youngest Crocker brother. He has a record a mile long. Sandy found out he was left out of the will by Daddy." Cory jumped in.

"Have you shown this photo to Sky?" Jess asked.

"I emailed it to her, but she said she couldn't be one hundred percent sure. The guy that was with Reginald had a beard and looked bigger." James sat back on the sofa. "To be fair, this picture is from five years ago."

"Wait a second, you said it looked like George hadn't been home in a while. The last time I saw George was the day I was attacked at the shop. He said he was taking his wife away for the weekend for their anniversary. Come to think of it, he never came in to get his winter tires on." Wade sat up straight. "He has a standing appointment on November first."

"Yeah, I found a credit card charge for a bed and breakfast. When James checked on it, the manager said they showed up that Friday and left early Sunday morning." Sandy held out a piece of paper to Wade.

"Someone must know where they are. I mean, they have adult kids." Wade's hand shook as he reached for the piece of paper.

"That's just it. The oldest son said they got a text from their father three weeks ago. It said George surprised their mother with a cruise. The text said they would call when they returned," James said.

Jess didn't like what James and Sandy were saying. Parents that would go weeks without contacting their kids even if they were on vacation didn't sound right. Jess and her sister hadn't gone more than a day without talking to her parents even when they did go on vacation.

"You mean to tell me George and his wife haven't contacted their kids in wecks?" Wade seemed as shocked as Jess felt.

"His oldest son said he found it weird too," James returned.

"Can't you track their phones or bank accounts?" Wade motioned to Sandy's computer.

"We did. There hasn't been any activity on his accounts in weeks, and there were no charges for any kind of vacation except for the bed and breakfast at the end of September," Sandy replied.

"What are you thinking, James?" Jess asked.

"If George was a hurdle to someone, they might have removed it," James admitted.

"But why his wife?" Wade asked.

"I was able to get a copy of George's will from his lawyer. If anything happens to George, everything is left to his wife, but if anything happens to her, Reg is next in line," Sandy explained.

"I've filed missing person reports for the couple, and let the kids know they need to call if they hear anything. I've also put an all points bulletin out on Reg and Oscar." James stood up and pulled on his coat.

"So, what you're saying is more waiting." Wade flopped back against the back of the couch.

"I know it's frustrating, but considering what happened to Harry, it's obviously necessary." James headed toward the door. "If I get any news, I'll call."

After James left, her father, Sandy, Rex, and Hulk stayed for a while. Wade was quiet for most of the evening, and when Jess walked her father to the door, he suggested she watch her own back. If someone were out to get Wade, they would probably go after anyone he cared about, and that included her.

She could protect herself, but not all fights were fair. No matter how well she trained in self-defense, it wouldn't protect her from a bullet. Jess wasn't going to worry Wade with putting that thought in his head because he seemed about ready to explode.

Earlier that day, she'd had a conversation with his mother. Renee was concerned her son was holding everything inside to keep his family from worrying. Jess couldn't blame him since his father had a heart condition.

"I'm going to head out too," Sandy told her as Jess returned from seeing her dad out.

"Okay." Jess gave her half a smile.

"Hey, don't worry. We always find the bad guy. Remember we have the superheroes," Sandy whispered in her ear as she hugged her.

"Yeah, we do, I guess we should start calling you Wonder Woman." Jess chuckled.

"Oh honey, I'm so much better than her. I'm Super Wonder Bitch." Sandy winked as she pulled open the door.

"You're calling yourself a bitch?" Jess snorted.

"Yep, and it stands for, babe in total control of herself." Sandy walked out and closed the door as Jess burst out laughing.

"Only Sandy would come up with something like that." Rex shook his head.

"Yeah, but if we called her a bitch, she'd kick us in the balls." Hulk snorted as he poured himself a coffee.

Jess listened to Rex and Hulk chat for a few minutes, but her focus was on Wade. He was tapping frantically into his phone, but it was the look on his face that had her hurrying next to him.

"What's wrong?" Jess eased down next to him.

"Logan didn't show up at the hospital this afternoon." Wade lifted his head and met her eyes. "He told Josie he'd be there to keep her company."

"Did you call him?" Hulk asked.

"It's going right to voicemail." Wade put the phone to his ear.

"I'll have someone go to his house, and check." Hulk stepped into the kitchen with Rex.

"His sister isn't answering either." Wade took the phone from his ear.

"Is it possible he forgot?" Jess asked.

"If it was anyone else, I'd say yes, but not Logan. Harry and Josie are the closest he has to parents. He was a foster kid. Harry and Josie were foster parents to Logan and his sister until they aged out of the system." Wade sighed. "Harry was the one who got Logan interested in cars."

Jess glanced at Hulk and Rex. Both men had their phones to their ears. The expression on Hulk's face told her he didn't have good news. She'd seen that face more times than she could count.

When she turned to Wade, it was clear he'd seen the look on Hulk's face.

Jess held her breath as she saw both men lay down their phones and walk toward Wade. She didn't know if Wade would be able to handle another of his mechanics getting hurt. Plus, Logan was practically a kid at twenty-six years old. If he'd been hurt, or worse, Jess was sure Wade would snap.

Wade's blue eyes flicked back and forth between Hulk and Rex before he turned to Jess. He gripped her hand tightly as he turned back to Hulk.

"Hulk, what is it?" Jess barely heard Wade's voice.

"Logan was arrested," Hulk said.

# Chapter 24

"Wait, what?" Wade jumped to his feet.

"Hulk, what are you talking about?" He heard Jess gasp.

"He beat the shit out of someone," Hulk explained.

"Logan wouldn't do that," Wade snapped.

"Wade, the guy he put in the hospital, is the man who attacked his sister. The fucker's name is Morton Gibbons. He was waiting for Logan's sister outside of her place of employment earlier today," Hulk continued.

"Wait, that's the guy who attacked her when I was still with the department. That was my call," Jess said.

Wade remembered the incident as well. Logan called him to let him know he would need a day or so off. Logan had been furious and threatened to kick the shit out of the asshole if he ever came near June again. It took Harry, Josie, and Wade to convince Logan the asshole wasn't worth it.

"Logan heard her scream when he arrived to pick her up. Gibbons had her behind the dumpster on the side of the building," Hulk said.

"Then it's self-defense." Wade sat back on the couch.

"He put the guy in the hospital, and according to James, the guy is pretty banged up," Hulk said.

"The bastard deserved it if you ask me," Rex grumbled.

"Maybe, but until he's arraigned, they're keeping him in the lockup." Hulk eased back in the chair.

Wade wouldn't let Logan stay in jail. He'd call a lawyer in the morning and make sure Logan didn't spend another day behind bars. He couldn't blame the young man because if Wade had been in the same situation, he'd probably have done the same thing.

Before Wade could get his head around Logan being in jail, his phone rang. When he saw Josie's number on the phone, Wade's heart started to race. With everything that happened the only thing he could think about was that it was bad news.

"It's Josie." Wade swallowed hard as he tapped the screen. "Hello."

"Wade, Harry needs to talk to you." Josie sounded odd.

Wade heard Harry and Josie speak to each other, but it was muffled. It sounded as if they were in the middle of a disagreement.

"You need to tell him," he heard Josie say right before he heard Harry's gruff voice.

"Wade," Harry said.

"Harry, what's going on?" Wade asked.

"It's my fault Logan was arrested. I never should've told the kid." Harry sounded as if he was about to burst into tears.

"Harry, how is that your fault?" Wade glanced up to see Hulk giving him the sign to put the phone on speaker.

"I called the asshole's landlord. I told him what he did, and he said he'd evict Gibbons. I ran into the bastard as I was checking on June and the kid. He said I'd be sorry for fucking with him. Wade, I think he's the one who stabbed me." Harry blew out a breath.

"What happened to you has nothing to do with Wade?" Hulk asked.

"I don't think so, but when I told Logan yesterday, he was furious. I think Gibbons went after June because of what I did." Harry's words were strangled.

"Did you tell James any of this?" Rex asked.

"No, I can't remember much about the attack. Doc says I must have cracked my head when I fell to the ground." Harry went on. "Fuck, if Logan goes to jail because of all this, I'll never forgive myself."

"Don't worry about that, Harry. He was protecting his sister, and as much as I'd love to see the fucker six feet in the ground, it's better if Gibbons doesn't die," Hulk said.

"I'm going to call James. He'll probably come over and take your statement," Jess said as she stepped away from them with her phone to her ear.

"Harry, take it easy and get better. We'll take care of Logan." Wade swallowed hard.

"You fuckin' better," Harry grumbled, and the call ended.

"I guess Harry's attack has nothing to do with all the shit at the shop." Wade flopped back against the back of the couch.

"We don't know that for sure. Gibbons may not have even been the guy who attacked Harry. I'm sure Sandy and Smash are going through the security video." Hulk lowered his large body into one of the recliners.

"James is going to go talk to Harry in the morning." Jess returned and curled up next to Wade.

The sudden realization that it was possible that they had two assholes out to get them made him clench his teeth together. Harry was only trying to protect a woman he considered a daughter, and it was possible he was almost killed for it.

Wade didn't like the danger that surrounded his family and friends. The worst he'd ever dealt with over the years was the accident. Even though he'd almost died, he didn't have to worry about his family or friends being targeted.

There had to be a way to end it all, and sooner rather than later. Wade didn't have the patience to deal with it much longer. His family seemed to be dealing with it fine, but they had to be worried. It was affecting too many lives of the people he loved and cared about.

Without a word, Wade kissed Jess' temple and stood up. He walked out of the living room and grabbed his jacket from the hook next to the front door. He heard Jess and Hulk call out to him, but he wasn't letting them stop him. He needed to talk to James, and he wasn't waiting until the next day.

Wade tromped through the snow up the road toward the gate leading out of Keith's Compound. Keith had given him a code for the gate, and Wade hoped he remembered it. James didn't live far from Keith's place, and Wade was determined to get there before anyone had a chance to stop him.

"Wade, damn it, stop." He heard Jess yell to him from the truck following him down the road toward James' house.

"Jess, go back to the safe house. I'm ending this." Wade didn't turn around, but he stopped when he heard the engine rev and the vehicle pulled in front of him.

"I'm not going back. Get in that truck." Jess hopped out and blocked his path.

"Jess, I love you, but you're not changing my mind." Wade stepped around her, but she grabbed his arm.

"I'm not trying to change your mind, but if you think you're doing this alone, you've got another thing coming to you, mister. Now, I love you too, but I told you not to push me away. I'm behind you with this, but I'm not going to sit back and allow you to do this alone." Jess fisted his jacket in her hands and stared up at him.

"I wouldn't try to argue. I told you, there is no winning an argument with an O'Connor woman." Hulk chuckled.

"Jess," Wade whispered her name.

"No. Now if you want to go see James, I'm coming with you. We'll figure this out together." Jess shook him.

Wade gazed into her eyes and swallowed the lump in his throat. She was stubborn, and there was no changing her mind if it was set on something. He hated to put her in the middle, but there was no way she would back down.

"Okay." Wade pulled her into his embrace.

"Okay." Jess' voice was muffled against his heavy coat.

"Okay," Hulk repeated their confirmation.

"It's a little late to figure this out tonight. James is probably in bed or on the way there. I'll text him, and we'll start first thing in the morning. It's Sunday, and we'll have the whole day to put a plan together before Monday morning." Jess tilted her head back and gazed up at him.

"I promise you, Wade, we won't stop until we put a plan together," Hulk shouted through the window of the truck.

"Okay." Wade blew out a breath and turned to make his way back to The Compound.

"Let's get in the truck. It's freaking freezing." Jess tugged him toward where Hulk turned the SUV around and pulled in next to him.

By two in the morning, Jess was snuggled next to him sound asleep, but Wade couldn't shut his mind off. How was he supposed to bring out someone who wanted him dead when he didn't know who it was?

It was difficult to get his head around the fact that someone hated him so much they wanted him dead. Wade had never done anything in his life for someone to hate him that much. He was raised to be kind to people and help if they needed it. His parents taught him to always look for the good in people.

"Wade, you need to get some sleep," Jess whispered in the darkness of the bedroom.

"I'm trying, Blue Eyes." Wade kissed the top of her head.

"You're not doing a great job. I can practically hear your mind going in circles." Jess lifted her head and kissed his cheek.

"Read minds now, do ya?" Wade chuckled.

"I don't need to read minds to know that you're worried." The moonlight through the window illuminated her beautiful face, and her eyes sparkled.

"What do I have to worry about? I've got a great daughter, wonderful parents, terrific friends, and co-workers, and the most beautiful woman in the world loves me. Life's great." Wade tucked a piece of her hair behind her ear.

"Wade." She rolled her eyes.

"Okay, yes I'm worried, but I don't want you to be concerned about that." Wade ran his knuckle down her cheek.

"Sure, that's going to happen." Wade didn't miss her sarcasm.

"What about if I distract you?" Wade smirked as he cupped her ass and pulled her on top of him.

"Wade," Jess moaned as he nipped the side of her neck.

"Uh huh," Wade whispered against her ear.

"Distracting me with sex isn't fair." Jess sucked his earlobe into her mouth.

"I'm distracting both of us tonight," Wade growled and flipped her over on her back.

"It's actually morning, but I like the way you think." Jess arched her back as he sucked her nipple into his mouth.

Wade wanted to forget what he had to face later that morning. The best way to do that was to get lost in the love he had for the woman who'd stolen his heart. Jess made him look forward to a happy future with her and his daughter. Hopefully, he wouldn't be killed before that dream came true.

# *Chapter 25*

Jess didn't fall back to sleep after she and Wade made love. She curled up in his arms and waited until she heard the steady rhythm of his breathing. She'd noticed that when he fell asleep, his hand would start to twitch, then the soft snore would start.

It didn't bother her because it only lasted for a few minutes, then he'd fall into a deep sleep. It was why she knew she could slip out of bed without waking him. It was almost five in the morning, and there was no way she was going to go back to sleep.

"You're up early." Damon yawned as he picked up the pot of freshly brewed coffee.

"I couldn't sleep." Jess smiled as Damon handed her a full cup.

"You know your cousins will figure this out, right?" Damon was right, but it was hard to see the light at the end of the tunnel sometimes.

"I know." Jess climbed up on the stool next to the counter.

"Then what's got that little wrinkle between those brows?" Damon raised an eyebrow.

"I don't have a wrinkle." Jess immediately raised her fingers and touched between her eyebrows.

"Yeah, you do. Trixie gets the same thing when she's stressed." Damon grinned.

"I'll tell you what's on my mind if you tell me why you call her Trixie, and what happened between you two." Jess smirked.

"Sweetheart, that won't work with me." Damon chuckled. "If your family wants to know about that, you need to ask her."

"I guess we're at a stalemate then." Jess smiled as she sipped her coffee.

"I'm really gonna miss everyone here when I leave." Damon laughed as he left the kitchen.

Jess made her way to the building where Keith had added a full gym. He'd put it there for his staff and himself, but Jess and practically the entire family used it. Normally, she would go five days a week.

The gym was empty when she arrived, but it was apparent someone had been there that morning. All the lights were on, and hard rock music blared through the speakers on the wall. Since it was inside the Compound, Jess wasn't worried about a stranger coming out of the shower room.

Jess was in the middle of her second set of squats when the shower room door open and Aaron stepped out into the gym area.

"You need me to stay and spot you?" Aaron dropped his bag on the bench next to her.

"Nah, I'm just doing legs today." Jess picked up her water bottle and drank some water.

"How's Wade?" Aaron picked up his bag and hoisted it on his shoulder.

"Stressed and worried about everything." Jess dropped her bottle and started the final set of squats.

"Can't say I blame him, but we'll get this figured out. You just keep putting a smile on his face." Aaron winked.

"A.J., get the fuck out of here." Jess and Aaron spun around at the sound of her dad's voice.

"What did I do?" Aaron looked genuinely confused.

"I thought since you got married you'd keep that fucking mind out of the gutter." Her dad tossed his gym bag on the floor.

"Hey, my mind was not in the gutter. Why wouldn't Wade smile when he got to look at my beautiful cousin every day? Uncle Kurt, you really shouldn't be thinking things like that. Tsk, Tsk." Aaron shook his finger at her father who seemed about ready to explode.

"Yeah, I'm sure that's what you meant, A.J." Her father ripped off his jacket.

"Dad, in A.J.'s defense, you were the one who dived in the gutter first." Jess raised an eyebrow and smirked.

Her father glared at both her and Aaron. He stalked to the treadmill and stepped up as he grumbled under his breath. Aaron loved to yank her father's chain, but her cousin respected the hell out of him. Her dad was one of the reasons Aaron joined the NPD.

Jess finished her work out and was in the middle of stretching as her father finished his run on the treadmill. She spotted him walking toward her, and she sat cross-legged on the floor as he crouched next to her.

"Is Wade okay?" Her father looked concerned.

"I think it's just been going on too long. He wants it to end." Jess wanted it all to be over too.

"I can understand that. So, how's my baby girl dealing with all this?" Her dad smoothed his hand over the top of her head.

"She's married with a little boy and another baby on the way." Jess smirked.

"Smart ass. How's my middle baby girl?" Her father shook his head, but his lips quirked up into a smile.

Jess never understood when she was growing up why women would always talk about her father like he was some sort of sex symbol. She'd heard teachers, and women at the Karate school talk about how handsome her dad was. It made her want to throw up when she was younger. After all, he was her dad.

As an adult, she understood. For a man almost sixty years old, her father was in great shape. As a police officer and Karate instructor, he needed to be in good physical condition. With his greying hair and blue eyes her father could still turn heads, but the only woman to brighten her father's eyes was her mother.

"I'm good, Dad." Jess leaned forward and kissed his cheek.

"He better take damn good care of you." Her dad growled under his breath.

"I can take care of myself, Dad, but I'm sure if I couldn't, Wade would gladly do it." Jess smirked when he pressed his lips together.

"Thank God Isabelle is married to her restaurant. I don't think I'll ever have to worry about some guy stealing her away." Her father pulled Jess into a hug and kissed the top of her head.

Jess had to bite her tongue to keep from laughing. She didn't want to upset her father over her sister's situation. He would probably bust a blood vessel.

By the time Jess arrived back at the safe house, James, Nick, and Cory were there. Although, Wade looked ready to punch someone as he leaned over the table reading something James showed him.

"So, this guy is dead. What does that mean for Logan?" Wade sounded pained.

"Gibbons didn't die from the beating Logan gave him. His injuries from what Logan did wouldn't have killed him. A nurse found Gibbons dead with a large syringe stuck in his neck around midnight. We're having an autopsy done as we speak," James explained as Jess walked into the room.

"Logan was still locked up when it happened. Don't get pissed, but they also had to make sure Harry, Josie, and Logan's sister had alibis as well." James glanced at Jess.

"I'm guessing they were all cleared." Jess wrapped her arm around Wade.

"Yeah." James nodded.

"Of course, they were cleared. None of them would kill someone," Wade snapped.

"I know that, Wade." Jess looked up at him.

"I'm sorry. I didn't mean to snap like that, but this doesn't help my situation." Wade plopped down on the stool.

"Sandy is keeping watch on all of the bank accounts for all the Crocker brothers. Reg made a huge withdrawal the day Sky heard him talking to who we assume is Oscar." Jess could see James was doing his best to keep Wade from getting discouraged.

"What does that mean?" Wade sounded defeated.

"It means he's trying to stay off the grid, or at least that's what Sandy thinks." James shrugged.

"In this day and age, people can be tracked easily. Cell phones, bank cards, credit cards, even computers can give you a timeline of where someone has been. If you want to stay off the grid, you chuck your phone and use only cash." Nick leaned against the counter.

"That means we're still no closer. We aren't even sure Reg or George or Oscar had anything to do with this." Wade was right.

"We do have the recording that says the guy with Reg was pissed with you and had done something to screw with your business. That we know is true." James placed his phone on the counter and tapped the screen.

The sound of a conversation echoed from the speaker of the phone. As Sky had told them, the guy with Reg didn't like Wade, that was obvious in his tone. Jess watched Wade as they listened, and it wasn't hard to see he was pissed.

Sky had done a great job in recording the conversation. It was clear except for a few whispered words between the two men. Reg didn't seem angry at the situation, but he also wasn't doing anything to calm down the other man. If anything, he seemed to fuel the other man's rage.

Before the audio file ended, a call came into James phone. He apologized and excused himself while he answered the call. Wade didn't speak for several minutes, but his knuckles were white.

"They'll figure this out," Jess whispered as she covered his hands with one of hers.

"It's not that. I know that other voice," Wade said through clenched teeth.

"What?" Jess and Nick said together.

"I know that voice, and his name isn't Oscar." Wade eased to his feet.

"Who is it?" Jess asked.

"He's the father of one of Ocean's friends. He's also a big fucking asshole." Wade shot to his feet and started to pace the kitchen.

"You're sure?" Nick asked.

"I'd know that arrogant voice anywhere." Wade's face turned completely red as he slammed his hands down on the counter. "He accused me of trying to rip him off."

"Why would he think that?" Jess didn't believe for a moment that Wade would ever do that to anyone.

"His bratty son went off-roading with his brand-new Lexus and cracked the rear axle. He told his father that it was a busted tire. When Duggan came into the shop, he blamed us for the damage, but since we always take pictures of the damage, and have the customer verify they know about it before they leave, we could prove it wasn't done at our place." Wade lowered himself onto the stool.

"Wait, Duggan was the name of the girl with Ocean the day I brought her home from Piper's," Jess remembered Wade's daughter talking about the girls that had left her at the department store.

"Yeah, Kaylee is one of the kids I told Ocean to stay away from." Wade nodded.

"What's this guys name?" Nick pulled out his phone.

"Miles Duggan. His son's name is Lee." Wade seemed distracted as he watched James who was still on the phone in the living room.

"Did you hear that name, Sandy?" Nick said as he tapped the speaker on his phone.

"Yep, give me a few minutes." Sandy's voice came through the phone, and Jess could hear the clicking of the computer keys.

"Who's James talking to?" Wade asked as he stood up again.

"I'm sure he'll tell us when he's finished with the call." Jess stood behind Wade and wrapped her arms around his neck.

Wade seemed to calm a little as he leaned back into her. She hated to see him so stressed, and the fact that things only seemed to get more tangled wasn't helping. She was starting to wish she hadn't left the NPD when she did.

"Miles Duggan, thirty-nine years old, divorced, two children. He's a trust fund brat but works for his stepfather's accounting firm.

From what I can see, he doesn't really have any clients." Sandy stopped, and more clicking was heard.

Jess glanced toward James, and immediately the hair stood up on the back of her neck. The expression on her cousin's face told her he didn't like what he heard, but when he met her eyes, James turned away. That didn't make Jess worry any less.

"Okay, this guy is a piece of work. He is the highest paid at the firm, but he does nothing that I can see. According to this information, he took over when his stepfather died a couple of years ago." Sandy stopped and scoffed sarcastically. "Would you believe this guy also has a regular deposit from another trust fund that he started to receive when his biological father passed away last year. The fund is divided equally between Miles and his siblings."

"Who are his siblings?" Nick asked.

"Let's see." Sandy hummed as she looked up the information. "Well, shit. I'm on my way over."

"Sandy?" Nick leaned over the table to look down at the phone.

It seemed whatever Sandy had found was big, and she wasn't going to tell them over the phone. That didn't make Jess feel any better, and the fact that James was still on his phone only made things worse.

"What do you think she found?" Wade asked Nick.

"If she's on the way here, it's probably big." Cory hadn't spoken much since Jess arrived until that moment.

Jess had known him most of her life. He was Aaron's best friend through high school, and they both went through the police academy together. He'd also helped in a lot of the situations Jess' family had dealt with over the years.

"Wade, we got some news." James walked back into the kitchen.

From the way her cousin's jaw clenched, he had bad information. All Jess could think was things were only getting worse, and they were still no closer to ending it all.

"What is it?" Wade laid his hands against Jess' forearms where they were wrapped around his neck.

"We finally got the warrant to enter George's house." James stopped when Sandy hurried into the house.

"You've…" James held up his hand to stop Sandy.

"They found George and his wife tied up in the basement." James stopped.

"Are they okay?" Wade's voice sounded strangled.

"They're alive but barely. It looks like George was beaten pretty badly. His wife was shaken and disorientated. They're on the way to the hospital." James pulled on his jacket. "I'm heading over there now to see what I can find out."

"Does anyone care why I came all the way over here with my laptop and information?" Sandy placed her laptop on the counter and slapped her hand against the counter.

"Sorry, Sandy. Tell us what you got." James waved his hand in the air.

"Duggan's father was married three times. Miles was a result of his first marriage. His mother remarried, and Miles took his stepfather's name. The second marriage, he had three children, and she left him for another man. Her kids changed their name to her maiden name." Sandy turned the laptop around and continued. "That name is Crocker."

"Duggan and the Crockers are siblings?" James bent to look at the screen.

"Oh, Jimmy, I'm not even done yet. It seems that their daddy was a lot like my father. He liked to get his little willy wet and didn't care where. It seems like he was doing both his wives at the same time. Along with a couple of more women on the side. George and Miles only have a couple of months between them. Reg is older and was born the same year that he married wife number one." Sandy seemed way too excited about the whole sorted story.

"Sandy, is this going somewhere or are you just telling about a soap opera you watched?" James sighed.

"Have patience and Sandy will bring you home. Anyway, the third wife never had any children, but that's probably because she died of brain cancer six months after she became wife number three. That's when he fell off the deep end." Sandy turned the laptop so Wade could see what she brought up next. "Wade, do you know who this man is?"

"Holy, fuck." Wade gasped.

# *Chapter 26*

Wade stared at the picture that filled the screen in front of him. It was a picture of Timothy Pippy. The same man who had almost killed a little girl eight years earlier but ended up putting Wade in hospital.

"Wade, who is that?" Jess walked from behind him and sat next to him.

"That's Timothy Pippy." Wade pulled the laptop closer and read through the obituary.

"The man that hit you with the car?" Jess asked.

"Yes." Wade slowly shook his head.

"But he's dead. He can't be part of this." Jess was right.

"No, but I found a copy of the will. Don't ask me how because I'd have to kill you. He was worth more than twenty million dollars. He owned a ton of real estate around the province both commercial and residential. That apartment building where Logan's sister lived. He owned that, but guess who looks after it now." Sandy pushed a file folder toward James.

"Miles Duggan." James slapped the folder on the counter.

"Yep, and from what I found out on that will. George has full control of all the money that is dispersed from the trust funds to all the brothers. Wade, there's something in there about you as well." Sandy slid the folder over to him and opened it to a highlighted area of the document.

"What's this?" Wade asked.

"That's the part of Mr. Pippy's will that states the building you now own, was to go to you after his death. With the stipulation that you were not to know who left you the building. There are detailed notes on how he wanted you to have the building. George had to offer to sell it to you, and the money that you paid has been put into a trust fund for Ocean, as well as any other children that you have in the future." Sandy bowed. "And this is why you all love me."

"So, I'm not paying a mortgage. I'm paying a trust fund for my daughter and any future kids," Wade said mostly to himself.

"But for some reason, Duggan wants that building. We just don't know why." James zipped up his coat. "I've got to get to the hospital and see what I can find out about George and his wife."

"Do you want me to go bring in Duggan?" Nick asked.

"Not yet. I'm going to send a car over to keep an eye on his residence, but I don't want questions when we pull him in." James headed out of the house.

Wade stared at the picture on the screen. Timothy had made mistakes in his life, but he took care of his family and gave Wade the opportunity to fulfill his dream. He had a drinking problem, but he kicked it after he'd put Wade in hospital.

"Wade, I don't know why Duggan wants your building, but from what I can understand from the will, he's the last in line on the beneficiary list. George, Reg, Oscar, and you have to die before he can gain control of the money." Sandy pointed to the part of the will where it was all listed.

"I don't get it." Wade shook his head.

"I think he felt as if he owed you after what he did." Sandy covered his hand with hers.

"You know what's funny, he told me once I was like the son he didn't have, and he'd never forgiven himself for what he did. The money I received in the settlement was supposed to come from the insurance." Wade linked his fingers and rested his hands on top of his head.

Wade felt a cold chill run up his spine. Ocean had spent time with Kaylee and her father before Wade realized the kid was trouble. Now that he thought about it, Ocean had met the young girl shortly after Timothy passed away. It had to be all connected.

"Are you okay?" Jess asked.

"I don't know how I feel. I mean, I'm basically being marked for death because I've been named in a will." Wade shrugged. "Jesus, I hope George is okay. He's really a good guy."

Wade stood outside the safe house and watched the snow lightly fall. The wind swirled the snow as it slowly and soundlessly landed on the ground. It was cold, but Wade was numb.

If he thought his head was spinning before, it was practically like a tornado in his head with all the information he'd been given. If Duggan wanted the building so damn bad, why didn't he just ask Wade to sell it to him?

Wade was lost in thought when he felt something nudge his leg. For a moment, he was startled and stepped back, but when he looked down, he laughed. Rufus wagged his tail and whined as he lifted his front paws off the step excitedly.

"How the hell did you get here?" Wade crouched and ruffled the excited Labrador's fur.

"We brought him over." Wade looked up to see Ocean and Sandy's two daughters walking toward them.

"Did you come over here by yourselves?" Wade stood up.

"No, Dad. We came over with Sandy, but we stopped to see Emily and the little ones." Ocean stomped up the steps and wrapped her arms around him.

"We go over to Aunt Emily's all the time to play with Noah and Patrick." Evie grinned.

"She's really sick with this baby and Uncle Keith had to go somewhere. So, we entertained the kids." Lily tossed a snowball, and Rufus ran after it.

"Where are your sister and brother?" Wade asked.

"With my dad," Lily informed him.

"Is Keith back now?" Wade asked.

"Yeah." Ocean hadn't moved from where she had her arms wrapped around him.

"Is everything okay, baby?" Wade tipped her face up so he could see her eyes.

"I miss you." She smiled. "I love hanging with Lily and Evie but I miss everyone."

"I miss you too. Hopefully, we can get back home soon." Wade hugged her tightly and kissed the top of her head.

"Dad, do you think we could... I mean... Nanny Betty said there are a ton of houses in Hopedale where we could live." Ocean looked at him with such a hopeful expression that Wade couldn't help but smile.

"You like this town, huh?" Wade didn't need to ask because from what he'd heard, his entire family loved the small town, and that included himself.

Wade hadn't seen much of the town because he'd spent most of the time on Keith's Compound, but if his parents, sister, and daughter wanted to move to Hopedale, he would find a house as soon as possible.

"Aunt Billie sells houses." Evie smiled.

"Yeah, she and Abbie both sell houses." Lily leaned against the railing.

"I guess I'll have to call one of them and see what we can do." Wade chuckled.

"That would be so great." Ocean clapped her hands excitedly.

"You could even go to our school." Evie squealed as the three young girls spun around in circles.

Rufus seemed to understand their excitement and started barking excitedly. Wade shook his head as the three girls stopped and looked at him with huge knowing grins. It was at that moment he realized the three knew exactly what they were doing when they came to see him.

"What's with all the excitement?" Sandy asked as she stepped outside with Jess behind her.

"Ocean is moving to Hopedale," Lily answered.

"I didn't realize you were looking for a place." Sandy looked confused.

"I've discovered that three young girls together can be very persuasive." Wade smiled and wrapped his arm around Jess.

"I've taught them well." Sandy smiled proudly.

"That's not a good thing," Nick grumbled as he stepped out of the house.

"You better watch it, Molly spends lots of time at my house." Sandy winked as she opened the door of her SUV.

"I keep telling Lora to keep that woman away from our sweet little girl." Nick snorted.

"Sandy sure keeps things interesting." Jess laughed.

After several hugs, Ocean, Lily, Evie, Sandy, and Rufus jumped into the vehicle and headed back to Sandy's house. Wade gave Ocean the option to stay at the safe house, but she said Lily was helping her with some homework. Reluctantly, Wade let her go and went back into the house waiting for news.

# Chapter 27

Jess left for the flower shop a little before seven that morning. Monday was a hard day on the best of days but knowing that Wade was going to be at the garage, made her nervous. She had a ton of work to do, and a bunch of orders had come in for Poinsettias. Since Christmas was less than a month away, she wanted to make sure she had enough stock to fill the orders.

Jess stood at the counter counting the orders that were scheduled to be picked up that day. It was quiet in the shop, and she enjoyed the silence before the day started. Monica was due to come in at nine, which meant the peace would be over.

Monica was a chatterbox and loved to have the radio a little louder than Jess liked in the shop. It made it difficult to get paperwork done when the high-spirited girl was working. The great thing about Monica was she worked hard and made amazing arrangements.

Jess blew out a breath as she finished off the last of her paperwork when she heard the musical chime from the door. She made her way out to the front of the shop and smiled when she saw Monica standing inside the door.

Her smile disappeared when she saw the tears in Monica's eyes. She looked terrified and seemed afraid to move for some reason. Monica's body was ridged and her lip trembled.

"Monica, are you…" Before Jess could finish the question, a large figure stepped out behind one of the large flower displays next to the door.

"She'll be fine if you do as you're told." The man growled as he lifted a large gun and pressed it against Monica's temple.

"I don't have any cash on the premises except for the daily float. It's two-hundred dollars. You can have every cent of it." Jess couldn't see the man's face.

If she could get close enough to him, she wouldn't have an issue disarming him. The problem was she had to get Monica away from him, but with the grip he had on Monica's arm, that wouldn't be easy.

"I don't need your money." The man snorted and turned to lock the door.

"What do you want?" Jess asked.

"What belongs to me." He snapped and dragged Monica further into the store.

"I don't have anything belong to you." Jess recognized the man as he walked closer.

"No, but your boyfriend does, and if he cares anything about you, he'll sign the papers being delivered to him right now." Miles Duggan growled through clenched teeth.

"Miles, right?" Jess stepped back as he came closer.

He didn't respond, but Jess threw him off when she called him by name. Miles didn't do anything to hide his face. How he thought he'd get away with holding her and Monica hostage was beyond her, but until she could get Monica out of his grasp, Jess had to play along.

"Miles, why don't we head into the office? You don't want one of my customers seeing us here. They know I open at nine. If they see me and Monica, they'll know something's wrong." Jess motioned to the door of her small office.

"Fine, but you pull anything, I'll blow her pretty little head off. Understand?" Miles pressed the barrel of the gun harder against Monica's head, making her cry out.

"I understand. Don't hurt her." Jess pushed open the door of the office and motioned for him to go inside.

"Do you think I'm stupid? Get in there." He pointed the gun at Jess.

Jess walked into her small office and scanned the room as if for the first time. She didn't have any security cameras inside, and with only one window that faced the back of the store, she couldn't do anything to get someone's attention.

"Pull both of those chairs over against that wall, and sit down," Miles ordered, but he still had a death grip on Monica's arm.

When she sat down, Miles shoved Monica toward the other chair. Jess caught her before she fell and helped her ease into the other seat. Monica shook with fear, but Jess did her best to assure the girl everything would be okay.

"Miles, what exactly are we waiting for?" Jess asked.

"I'm waiting for a call. If I get the answer I want, I'll leave you both alive. If I don't, I'll let you make one call to say goodbye." Miles rested his shoulder against the closed office door.

Jess studied Miles while quietly trying to keep Monica from going into panic mode. He seemed overly calm and almost cocky. It was as if he thought he was about to get everything he ever wanted.

Miles turned his head to glance out through the window behind the desk. It was the first time Jess noticed the earpiece in his ear. She assumed that was how he kept in touch with whoever was helping him. If she hadn't left her phone on the front counter, she could've found some way to contact one of her cousins.

"Remember, do exactly what I told you," Miles said as he glanced back at Jess.

"You haven't told us anything." Jess looked at him with confusion.

"I wasn't talking to you." Miles pointed to the earpiece, verifying what Jess presumed.

Jess glanced at the clock on the top of the filing cabinet. It was nine-thirty. Unfortunately, she didn't have anyone coming to pick up an order until after lunch. There was still a chance that a customer would find the shop being closed suspicious, but she doubted it would cause anyone to call the police.

"As soon as you give him that message, he'll cave." Miles chuckled.

"You know Wade has twenty-four-hour security with him at all times." She wanted Miles to know that getting to Wade wouldn't be easy.

"Just get it done," Miles snapped and turned to Jess. "The security won't know what's going on. Trust me."

Jess wanted to smack the sly grin off Miles' face. He was too damn cocky but she had no idea why he felt so sure, his accomplice would get close to Wade. Both Hulk and Trunk were at the garage, and Cory sat at the front counter.

Wade had told Josie to take a week off, and James thought it would be a good idea to put one of the NPD in her place. It wouldn't look suspicious to have someone take Josie's place while she was off.

It seemed as if they'd been stuck in the office for a long time, but after looking at the clock for what seemed like the hundredth time, it had only been fifteen minutes. Monica had calmed a little, but she still kept a tight grip on Jess' hand.

"I can hear everything. Remember that." Miles growled.

Several more minutes passed before Miles spoke into the earpiece again. The difference was whatever the other person said made him stomp toward Jess and grab her arm.

"I'm going to send you a video. Show it to the asshole, and tell him if he doesn't do it, I'll pull the trigger." Miles held up the phone as he released Jess' arm and pressed the barrel of the gun against her temple.

He glared at her as he held up the phone and started to record her. Jess didn't know what was going on at the garage, but she was worried that if she disabled Miles, whoever he'd sent to the garage might hurt Wade. If she didn't do something, Miles might kill her and Monica anyway.

"You know, tell him that I might have some fun with this little thing before I put a bullet in her head. She's got one hot little body." Miles blatantly let his eyes travel down her body and back up again.

There wasn't a chance in hell that Jess would let Miles lay a hand on her. She'd made her decision. Miles Duggan was about to find out what happened when he tried to intimidate the daughter of Kurt O'Connor.

# *Chapter 28*

Wade stood next to the counter talking with Cory. The appointments for the day were light mostly because Wade had to stay out with Cory to greet customers and Harry was still in the hospital.

He wouldn't be any use in the shop anyway because he couldn't concentrate on anything. James arrived shortly after they opened to let him know George and his wife would be okay, and George confirmed the information Sandy had found about Timothy's family.

The problem was George didn't know where Reg or Oscar were, but he was concerned about his brothers. It was hard to believe that Miles would hurt his own family over money.

"I will never understand what turns someone against their family." Cory leaned on the counter.

"Me either but over the years with everything I've seen, nothing surprises me anymore." James shook his head. "I've got units out there looking for Duggan. We know he was responsible for the damage to your garage because when we picked up his son, the kid sang like a bird."

"What's going to happen to his daughter?" Wade asked.

"She's going to be sent to Gander with her mother," James told Wade.

"That's good." Kaylee was better off with her mother anyway.

"Lee Duggan confessed to the attack on you and Neil. He also confessed to hiring Morton Gibbons to attack Harry too. When Harry called the landlord, it was Lee Duggan he spoke with. The only thing Lee wouldn't admit to, was the attack on George and his wife and he didn't know where to find Oscar and Reg."

Wade shook his head in disgust. Miles Duggan was an evil man, and the sooner he was behind bars, the better. He was about to say the same thing when the main door opened and a familiar face walked toward him.

"Hey," Wade said.

"I need to talk to you." Sky's outfit, makeup, and hair were perfect as usual, but there was something in her expression that told him something was wrong.

"Sure." Wade nodded.

Sky glanced at James and Cory. She seemed uncertain about talking in front of them, but he had no idea why. She turned away, and he saw her shoulders rise and fall before she turned back to him.

"I need to talk to you. Alone," Sky said as she pointed to the Bluetooth attached to her ear and picked up the pen on the counter.

"Sky, what…" Wade snapped but she pressed her finger against her lips, telling him to be quiet as she tapped her ear.

James grabbed the pen and quickly wrote something on the paper. Wade didn't see what James wrote but he slipped it in front of Sky and she scribbled something and handed it back. The whole time she continued to talk to Wade but only about needing to talk about Ocean.

"We need to talk about your daughter," Sky said and nodded her head.

"Okay." Wade glanced at James.

"I think you should talk about this alone in your office." James held a paper up in front of Wade.

James hurried to the front door and locked it as Cory guided Wade and Sky to the office. When they got inside, Cory pulled out a set of earbuds and attached them to Sky's phone. He put one in her ear, and the other in his own.

"Wade, I need you to sign these papers." Sky slapped papers on the desk in front of him.

"What is this?" Wade shrugged.

"This is a legal document stating that all things left to you will be signed over to Miles Duggan." Sky shook as she pointed to the papers.

"I'm not signing anything over to Duggan." Wade shook his head.

"You have to. He has Jess at her shop with another woman." A tear ran down Sky's cheek.

There was something more to the whole situation than just Jess being held hostage. There was no way she was crying because she was concerned about Jess.

"He's on the phone with me right now and he's going to send me a video. He said if you don't sign this, he's going to kill her." Wade saw her swallow hard.

Sky's phone beeped, and she held it up in front of him. Wade's blood ran cold when he saw Jess with the gun to her head, but she didn't look scared. She looked pissed.

"You know, tell him that I might have some fun with this little thing before I put a bullet in her head. She's got one hot little body." Wade heard Miles' sick comment and shook with rage.

"You put one fucking finger on her, and I'll kill you," Wade shouted, but Cory grabbed Sky's phone from her hand and pulled out the headphones.

Cory hit the speaker on the phone, and they listened to a scuffle. Wade could hear grunts and Duggan cursed. Wade glanced up at Cory, but he didn't look concerned. If anything, he appeared amused by the sounds.

"What the fuck are you smiling at?" Sky squeaked.

"Because the grunts you hear is Jess kicking the crap out of that piece of shit." Cory grinned.

"You're damn right I did," Jess' voice echoed through the phone.

"That's my girl." Wade blew out a breath.

"No. No. You can't put him in jail," Sky shouted.

"What? Are you crazy? He's a nut job." Wade stared at Sky.

She was hysterically crying as she grabbed her phone from Cory. Her hand shook while she tapped and swiped her finger across the screen several times.

"He has Jonah locked up somewhere." Sky held up her phone with a picture of a badly beaten man.

"That's your partner." Wade glanced between her and the phone.

"He's more than that. He's my fiancée, and Miles told me if I didn't do this, he wouldn't tell me where Jonah is. He's a diabetic and hasn't had any food or insulin. I don't know where to find him." Sky sobbed and eased into the chair.

"Where is Jonah, asshole?" Wade heard Jess shout.

"He'll fucking die before…" Duggan's rant was interrupted by a loud slap.

"Where is he?" Jess sounded pissed, but Wade couldn't help but be proud of her.

"Fuck you, bitch," Duggan choked out.

"Someone needs to get over to her flower shop before she kills him." Cory turned to James.

"I've got cars on the way there now," James said.

"That still doesn't tell us where Jonah is." Wade crouched next to Sky.

"I can't lose him." She sniffed.

Wade tried to comfort her, but everything in his head was screaming at him to go be with Jess. Although, it seemed as if Jess was in a much better state of mind than Sky was at that moment.

"Jess, are you okay?" Wade leaned over the phone still in Sky's hand.

"Yeah, this guy is tied up with a big red bow right now. I'm searching his phone to see if anything can help us find Jonah." Jess sounded as if it was just another day.

"I'll stay with Sky. You go to Jess," Cory whispered next to Wade's ear.

Wade stood up and made his way to the door. Cory pulled another chair over in front of Sky and spoke to her softly as he took the phone out of her hand.

Jess' shop was only two minutes away from his garage, and he didn't give Hulk a chance to drive off before he was in the SUV next to him. Wade fisted his hands as they hurried toward Jess.

By the time they pulled into the parking lot, Wade jumped out of the vehicle and ran toward the shop. He was stopped by a police officer he didn't know and was annoyed when the man wouldn't let him through the barrier.

"It's okay. Let him through," Nick shouted to the young police officer.

Wade glanced around for Jess and was almost in complete panic mode before he finally spotted her talking to John. He blew out a breath as he hurried toward her.

"Jess," Wade shouted.

She turned and immediately ran toward him. He pulled her into his arms and held her tightly against him as he buried his face between her shoulder and neck. Jess wrapped her arms around his neck.

"I'm fine, Wade. That guy didn't know what hit him when I knocked the gun out of his hand." Jess laughed.

"I know you're a former cop, and you're proficient in Karate, but Jesus, listening to you fighting with that asshole scared the shit out of me." Wade lifted his head and held her face between his hands as he allowed his eyes to take in every inch of her beautiful face.

"I'm okay. We just need to find Jonah." Jess tried to pull away and turn around.

"Jess, that's not your job anymore." Wade tried to remind her, but from the way she narrowed her eyes and glared at him, he wanted to take the words back.

"I know that, but Nick says he knows where the picture was taken." Jess pulled from his grasp and dragged him toward where Hulk stood against the SUV.

"Where are we going?" Wade asked.

"Back to your garage," Jess said as she hopped into the back of the SUV.

When they arrived back at the garage, everyone was outside the building. Jess jumped out and took off into a full run. Wade cursed because he knew he couldn't catch her. By the time he got inside, Jess had disappeared.

"Sorry, I couldn't stop her if I tried." Everett shrugged as he pointed to the area they'd found in the garage.

"What's going on?" Wade followed Everett as he turned into the area.

He turned the corner as Jess was lowered into the hatch that had been blocked off earlier. Wade stared in shock as she disappeared beneath the floor.

"She's the only one that will fit down there now." James held up his hand as Wade approached him.

"Why is she going down there?" Wade looked down into the narrow passage.

"Nick said it looked like the area under the garage. The other side is secured with chains, so it was easier to pry this up."

James stuck his head into the opening and shouted to Jess. When Jess didn't answer right away, Wade's body tensed. James called out to her again, and when her sarcastic response echoed back, Wade chuckled in relief.

"Give me a chance to answer before you bellow, would you?" Her voice echoed up from the hole. "I found him," Jess shouted a few minutes later.

"Can you get him out here?" James yelled.

"Yeah, he's weak, but he said he can make it," Jess returned.

Wade stepped back as a couple of paramedics moved next to the opening in the floor. They waited until Jess appeared and helped Jonah out first. They dragged him up and settled him on the gurney while they assessed him.

Wade watched James help Jess up out of the hatch and shook his head when she gave him a huge grin. He didn't know if it was even possible, but at that moment, Wade fell more in love with her.

# Chapter 29

Jess stretched as she stared out the window of Wade's bedroom. It had been more than a month since Wade moved back to his house, and Miles Duggan was arrested. Miles was charged with so many crimes, Jess stopped listening at the courthouse. According to James, Miles and his son were going to be in jail for a long time.

Unfortunately, the bodies of Reg and Oscar were found in the basement of Miles' apartment building. Miles had plans to get rid of everyone who stood in his way of getting the inheritance to himself.

Harry, Jonah, George, and his wife had all recovered from their ordeals and were back to their normal lives. By the time Harry returned to the shop, Wade had the hidden room completely renovated into an office for his friend.

Jonah and Sky took a trip to the Caribbean and eloped while they were there. Sky was also spending time with her daughter, and surprisingly, Wade was okay with it. Ocean enjoyed the shopping trips with her mother and that made Wade happy.

Jess spent Christmas with Wade's family, and they rang in the New Year in Hopedale at *Jack's Place*. Her father also announced that he was stepping down as the Chief of Police to run for Mayor of Hopedale.

Jess stood in Wade's room listening to him discuss the closing of the house he bought in Hopedale. He was on the phone with Billie, and Jess didn't need to turn around to see him to know he was grinning.

"That's it. I now own a house in Hopedale," Wade said a few minutes later.

He picked her up and spun her around in a circle, making her squeal. The house he currently lived in was sold, and Wade had until the end of February to move.

"I don't know if you should be so excited. You do realize that living in Hopedale means you'll be surrounded by my family, right?" Jess giggled.

"As long as it's close to you, I don't care if the devil himself lives there." Wade put her back on her feet and held her head between his hands. "I love you so much."

"I love you too," Jess whispered as he lowered his lips to hers.

It was the one Sunday of the month that her entire family and extended family gathered for food and fun. Over the years, the gathering seemed to become larger with all the marriages and babies that had come into the family. There were also the extended family and close friends that had grown over the years.

Jess didn't know how the women in her family managed to make enough food to feed so many people but by the end of the dinner, everyone left with a full belly.

"I swear there has to be a thousand people here." Isabelle glanced around the large living room as she sat between Jess and Kristy.

"That may be a bit of an exaggeration, but give it a couple of years, and Aunt Kathleen will have to do this in shifts." Kristy leaned back on the sofa and smoothed her hand over her swollen belly.

"The way everyone is popping out babies, that may not be far off." Isabelle motioned to the six pregnant women around the house.

"Who knows, Jess could be the next preggy." Kristy grinned.

"Slow your roll there, girl. We haven't been together that long." Jess rolled her eyes, but the thought of having Wade's baby made her feel all warm and fuzzy inside.

She wanted a family, but Wade was already the father of a teenager. Jess wasn't sure if he wanted more children, and she was afraid to ask him.

Jess glanced to the other side of the room where Wade stood talking to Aaron, Nick, and Mike. Wade looked gorgeous in his light-blue dress shirt and black dress pants. He leaned casually against the wall holding a beer in one hand and the other in his pocket.

He turned his head and met her gaze and Jess winked at him. She loved that he got along with her family and hoped one day to marry him. It just seemed like that would be a long way off. They'd only been together less than a year.

"Pam seems quiet." Isabelle motioned to the kitchen where their cousin sat staring into a glass of wine.

"Damon left yesterday," Kristy informed them.

"I wish she'd tell us what the story is on the two of them. I don't care what she says, she loves him." Isabelle sipped her wine.

"Speaking of love, how's the hot chef?" Jess smirked at her cousin.

"Driving me crazy." Isabelle groaned.

"In a good way?" Kristy grinned.

"I don't want to talk about him here. If someone hints to Dad that Roman and I are together he'd have a cow," Isabelle whispered. "By the way, we aren't together."

"No, you're just dancing in the sheets." Kristy chuckled.

"Who's doing the mattress mambo?" Sandy said a little too loudly.

"Shush." Isabelle grabbed Sandy's hand and yanked her down on the couch.

"Oh, is this about Isabelle and how she's humping the help?" Sandy smirked.

"Oh my, God. Shut up." Isabelle groaned.

"Good luck with shutting her up." Stephanie eased down to the floor and blew out a breath.

"Please, stop talking about this. The last thing I want is Dad freaking out because I'm sleeping with Roman," Isabelle whispered.

"Has Cora met him, yet?" Bethany smirked as she sat on the arm of the couch.

"Stop." Isabelle groaned.

"No, but I think I might invite her to dinner at *A Taste of Hopedale* and tell her she needs to thank the chef." Lora grinned.

"Okay, I'm leaving." Isabelle stood up and started to walk away, but Marina and Billie stopped her.

"Leave the girl alone." Marina smiled.

"Yeah, we got to get Jess married off first." Billie winked at Jess.

Jess laughed because she loved getting together with her family. They teased each other, but there was never any doubt the family was full of love.

A couple of hours later, Jess looked around for Wade but didn't see him anywhere. With the number of people around the place, that wasn't surprising, but she wanted to spend the rest of the evening with him. They'd promised Ocean a movie night, and it was getting late.

"Hey, have you seen Wade?" Jess asked Renee as she walked up to the table where her mom and Renee were talking in a hushed conversation.

"Oh, I think he went outside to help your dad with something," her mother answered, and then quickly found the edge of her cup very interesting.

"I'm sure they'll be back in shortly." Renee smiled up at her and motioned for her to join them at the table.

Jess sat down but kept glancing at the door. If her father was giving Wade a difficult time because Jess was spending most nights at his house, she'd have to remind her dad that she was a grown-ass woman.

Jess sat in the back seat with Ocean and Renee as they drove back to St. John's. Wade would be moving into his new house at the end of February, and Jess couldn't wait until they could just walk up the road to get to his place.

"Your mom is planning a surprise party for your dad's retirement next week," Renee said.

"I know, although I don't really call it retiring if he's running for Mayor." Jess laughed.

"I think he'll make a great Mayor," Ocean said as she played with her phone.

"I agree." Wade glanced at Jess through the rearview mirror.

Jess agreed as well, but she was distracted and concerned. Wade had hardly spoken to her when he came in from outside with her father. She asked him what was wrong, but he told her everything was good.

Her father also had acted strangely when she was leaving. He'd hugged her so tight she thought he would strangle her. She could also swear she saw tears in his eyes, but he said he needed to sneeze.

Jess had the sudden feeling that maybe something was wrong with her father or mother. Perhaps they were sick, and her father had told Wade so that he could break the news to her. Jess' heart started to pound in her chest.

By the time they arrived at Wade's house, she was almost out of her mind with worry. She managed to get through the movie with Ocean and have a casual conversation with Wade's parents and sister before they excused themselves.

"What's wrong with my dad or mom?" Jess spun around as soon as Wade closed the bedroom door.

"What?" Wade looked confused.

"When you went outside with my dad, did he say something about him or Mom being sick?" Jess did her best to keep from bursting into tears.

"What? No, Jess. He wanted me to check something with his truck." Wade pulled her into his arms, and she buried her face into his chest.

"Are you sure?" Jess whispered.

"I wouldn't lie to you, Jess. Your dad and mom are fine as far as I know." Wade kissed the top of her head.

Jess blew out a breath and lifted her head to look up at Wade. He smiled and lowered his head to press a soft kiss against her lips. It quickly turned into a deep, toe-curling kiss.

"I love you, Blue Eyes," Wade whispered as he slowly undressed her.

"I love you too, Wade." She panted as he kissed his way down her body, bringing her to the brink of ecstasy and beyond.

# Chapter 30

Wade listened to Jess' deep and even breathing. She'd fallen asleep quickly after they'd made love, and Wade lay back thinking about his plan to propose.

He told Jess he'd never lie to her, but he did when they'd arrived home. His conversation with Kurt hadn't exactly been about his truck. The discussion was about her, and how he wanted Kurt's blessing to propose to Jess.

When he'd asked Kurt if he could speak with him, Wade thought he would refuse at first, but Kurt spun on his heel and motioned for Wade to follow him outside.

"We'll have this conversation outside, so I don't get overheated." Kurt stood on the front step and gazed to his left.

The Hopedale beach was visible from Kurt's front porch and Wade could see why so many people fell in love with the area. It was hard not to like a place where such beauty was apparent.

"Kurt, I want you to know, I love Jess with all my heart," Wade began, but when Kurt didn't say anything, he continued. "You know I'm a hard-working and honest person. I love my family and take care of my daughter."

"I know." Kurt's voice sounded choked.

"I can't imagine the day that some asshole comes to my door to take out my daughter or worse, want to take her away from me." Wade swallowed the lump that rose in his throat every time he thought about Ocean growing up.

"Yep, you'll want to rip the heart out of every man that even thinks about touching your daughter." Kurt turned to glare at him.

"I don't doubt that. So, trust me when I say I understand how hard it must be to see your little girl grow up, but I've seen how you are with Bull, and you seem to respect the hell out of him." Wade swallowed again.

"I do, but he didn't gain that respect easily. I still want to beat the hell out of him when I see him kiss my daughter," Kurt grumbled.

"I'm sure you do but you know he loves Kristy and he'll never hurt her." Wade smiled.

"Right, now what is it you want to talk about?" Kurt wasn't letting Wade beat around the bush anymore.

"I want to ask Jess to marry me." Wade wanted to be upfront with the man he respected.

"You do, do you?" Kurt smirked. "Do you think she wants to marry you?"

"I hope so, but I'd love to have your blessing before I ask. You gave my garage a chance when I was just starting out. You and your family are part of the reason my business is thriving. I respect the hell out of you," Wade continued.

"Sucking up won't work." Kurt deadpanned.

"I'm not sucking up, Kurt. I'm telling you the truth. As much as I love Jess, and want to make her my wife, if I don't have your blessing, it would be difficult, but I will still ask her because there's nothing I want more." Wade figured he might as well be honest.

"So, if I'm against it, you'll still marry her?" Kurt narrowed his eyes.

"Yes, if she agrees to marry me, but I don't think she'll be happy if you aren't supportive of our marriage, and I want her to be happy." Wade looked Kurt straight in the eyes. "I love your daughter, and I'll do everything to make her happy."

Kurt turned away and rested his fists on the railing as he gazed down at the waves crashing on the rocky beach. Wade shoved his hands in his pockets as he waited for Kurt to respond.

"She's the most like me between the three girls. She's stubborn and smart as a whip. Don't try to bullshit her because she'll kick your ass." Kurt turned back to him. "I'll give you my blessing on one condition."

"Anything." Wade held his breath.

"Treat her like the treasure she is." Kurt held out his hand.

"Always." Wade shook his hand.

"Oh, and you should do it at the surprise retirement party my wife thinks she's hiding from me." Kurt smirked as he pulled Wade toward him and slapped him in the back.

"You got it." Wade laughed.

Wade smiled to himself as he glanced down at the woman sleeping in his arms. He had a plan in mind and would put it all together the next day. In one week, he'd ask the woman he loved to marry him. Hopefully, she would say yes.

Wade stood on the side of the dancefloor and waited for Aaron to give him the signal. They'd worked on this proposal all night until it was perfect because Jess deserved perfection. She knew he wasn't comfortable with the fast dancing mostly because of his bum leg. He thought he looked like an elephant trying to balance on a high wire. Not that he'd ever been a good dancer, but Jess was content with the slow dances, and he was okay with that.

The song Nick and Aaron had picked to sing just before Wade's surprise was a Brad Paisley song called *Wrapped Around*. At first, he thought it might give the proposal away, but John assured him it would be the last thing she expected. They sang the song all the time.

Considering the party was to celebrate Kurt's retirement from the Chief of Police, and his appointment as Mayor of Hopedale. It was why *Jack's Place* was closed to the public for the evening. When Kurt asked him to surprise Jess at the party, Wade knew it was the perfect place for his perfect match.

Wade glanced over his shoulder and locked eyes with Kurt. Jess' father could be intimidating, but who could blame the man? Wade would be the same way when some guy came looking for Ocean. It was why he understood how Kurt felt, and knew what a privilege it was to have his blessing to marry Jess.

When he turned back to the dancefloor, Jess caught his eye and winked. She was so damn beautiful and made his heart flutter every time she smiled at him. He still couldn't believe she loved him, but he was damn well not going to let her get away.

"The song is almost over." Bethany nudged him with her very pregnant belly.

"I'm just waiting for the signal." He smiled down at Aaron's wife.

"She's never going to see this coming." Lora stood next to Bethany, equally pregnant.

It seemed as if there was something in the water with the O'Connor clan because Stephanie, Billie, Emily, Lora, Bethany, and Kristy were all pregnant. Jess had joked about staying away from them in case it was contagious, but he knew she envied them.

The previous night she'd mumbled in her sleep about wanting to be a mom, and how she couldn't wait to have his baby. He'd asked her that morning if she remembered talking in her sleep, but she told him he imagined it. He didn't.

Ocean may be a teenager, and most people would cringe at the thought of starting over with diapers again, but not Wade. He couldn't wait for the day that Jess' belly would be swollen with his child. She just had to say yes.

"Are you nervous, Wade?" Kristy linked her arm into his.

"Me? No, not at all." He glanced down at Jess' sister and tugged on the collar of his shirt.

"You're sweating. I think you may be telling me lies." Kristy laughed.

"It's being around all these hot pregnant women." he winked at Kristy.

"Oh, you're good." Lora snickered as she rested her hands on her belly.

Before he could answer, he heard the signal. Ian kept Jess turned with her back to Wade as the song ended. He strutted across the dancefloor as the crowd parted for him to pass. Jess didn't seem to notice as she stood next to Ian, clapping for the band. When he was behind her, Aaron winked and started to speak.

"Before we move on to the next song, I want to congratulate Uncle Kurt on his retirement and winning the election. We are all so proud of you. With that said, Jess, turn around." Aaron winked at Wade.

Jess twisted around and glanced at Wade. He could see the confusion on her face, but there was nothing that could take away from her beautiful eyes. Wade swallowed hard as he reached up and tucked her hair behind her ears.

"I think it's time to put a ring on the finger I'm wrapped around," Wade whispered.

"What?" Jess stared at him as he took both her hands in his.

"Jess, the first day I saw you in my garage with pretty boy up there," Wade said and motioned toward Aaron still at the microphone. "You took my breath away. I never thought for a second I would ever have a chance with you, but thanks to that wonderful car of yours that kept bringing you back, I fell in love with you."

"Wade, what are you doing?" She tugged him closer and whispered.

"Jessica O'Connor, you're the most beautiful, sweet, smart, kind-hearted, understanding, and courageous woman I've ever met. You even have that little bit of sass thrown in to keep me on my toes." He chuckled.

"You make me sound like a cocker spaniel." Jess rolled her eyes.

"There's a lot more but your dad's over there and I don't want to get the shit kicked out of me." Wade glanced at Kurt who didn't seem to think Wade's joke was funny.

"Probably not." Jess smiled.

"That right there. That smile takes my breath away every time I see it. For years it was just Ocean and me. I could never let anyone else in. Then you walked into my life and I was a goner. I knew at that moment this would happen one day." Wade reached into his pocket as he slowly eased down on his good knee.

"Wade," Jess choked out his name.

"I'm not a poet or good with words. I'm a grease monkey who fell in love with a beautiful woman. I'm not asking you this just for me because my daughter loves you as much as I do. Jess, there's nothing in this world I want more than this. It's why I'm down on one knee in front everyone we love." Wade dropped her hand and opened the small white velvet box he'd had in his pocket for a month.

"Harder to say no when everyone is watching," Mike shouted from where he stood next to his wife.

"I'm not perfect, and from talking to Kristy and your cousins' wives, neither are their husbands. John leaves wet towels on the floor. James hogs the blankets. Ian talks in his sleep. Keith snores. Mike always leaves dishes in the living room. Nick never puts his dirty socks in the hamper. Bull leaves his shoes in the middle of the foyer, and I'm sure A.J. has something that makes him not so perfect, but Bethany couldn't think of anything because they're still in the honeymoon stage." Wade glanced over his shoulder to where Aaron stood behind Bethany with his arms around her and his chin on her shoulder.

"Nope, I'm the only perfect one," Aaron shouted.

"That's so not true," Pam yelled.

"Even with all their imperfections, those women love their men. I'm hoping you can overlook my imperfections. I'm not sophisticated, I can't dance, my singing leaves a lot to be desired but the one thing I can do perfect is love you with all my heart. I will promise to do that until my last breath. Jessica O'Connor, will you make me whole and agree to spend the rest of your life with me? Jess, will you marry me?" Wade hadn't been able to look away once he caught the smile on her face.

A tear ran down her cheek as she cupped his face in her hands. His heart raced as she stared into his eyes, but it was only because she hadn't answered him, and he wondered if she was even ready for marriage.

"Are ya gonna answer da lad?" Nanny Betty yelled from the back of the room somewhere.

"It's hard to answer him when I can't speak." Jess sobbed.

"Holy shit, Jess is crying," Nick shouted.

"Shut up, asshole," Kristy yelled at her cousin.

"Well?" Wade tuned out all the voices around him except for hers.

"Yes. Yes, I'll marry you, but there's one thing you need to know." She tugged him until he was back on his feet.

"What?" Wade cupped her cheek in his hand.

"You are perfect. You're the perfect person for me." Jess wrapped her arms around his neck and lifted her in the air as her lips crashed against his.

He could hear the cheers around him, but the only thing he could see was her. When he lowered her to the floor, he took the ring from the box and slipped it on her tiny finger. Thanks to her mother, the ring fit perfectly.

"It's beautiful." Jess held her hand out and then lifted her teary eyes to him.

"You're beautiful." He cupped her face in his hands. "And I love you."

# *Epilogue*

Isabelle forced a smile as she watched Jess and Wade kiss in the middle of her mother's pub. Another of her sisters found the man of her dreams, and Isabelle was still single. She was also having issues with her restaurant.

In the last few months, she'd had several pieces of equipment either malfunction or crap out. It cost her more than two thousand dollars to replace or fix them so she wouldn't lose any money.

It seemed as if she had a streak of bad luck that may cost her the business she'd worked so hard to build. A year earlier, she'd finally received her five-star rating, but in the last three months, she'd lost it.

Isabelle didn't want to tell her family how bad it had gotten, but they would find out soon enough if she had to put the foreclosure sign on it. She'd barely made the bills in January, and from the way things were going, she would be out of business by May.

Then there was Isabelle's incapability to stay out of the sheets with Roman. All he had to do was flash those chocolate-brown eyes or give her that panty-melting smile, and her clothes vanished. The man made her lose all reason and it was ridiculous.

The fact that the sex was mind-blowing didn't help things. Roman was sexy as sin and could make her scream in pleasure every time they were together. The problem was, to him, it was just sex, and in the beginning, Isabelle tried her best to keep her feelings out of it. She couldn't, and she'd slowly fallen for her sexy chef.

"Cuz, we need to band together." Pam linked into Isabelle's arm.

"Yep, the only two single O'Connors." Isabelle chuckled.

"We're outnumbered." Pam sighed.

"I'm sure Damon would gladly take you out of the single status." Isabelle smirked at Pam.

"He's gone, and I'm fine with that. It was never meant to be." Pam tried to sound matter-of-fact, but Isabelle could hear the sadness in her cousin's voice.

"I'm pretty sure Aunt Cora said he was the one for you," Isabelle reminded Pam.

"I'm pretty sure she hasn't met that hot chef yet either," Pam returned.

"Okay, let's just call this a draw." Isabelle laughed.

Her humor soon vanished when she looked toward the bar and saw the issue she was trying to avoid leaning against the bar talking to Lora's brother, Ethan.

"What the hell is he doing here?" Isabelle said mostly to herself.

Then complete panic set in when she saw her Aunt Cora heading straight for Roman. When Cora turned to smile at Isabelle, she wanted to run out of *Jack's Place* screaming, but a little part of her wanted to know for sure. Was Roman Young meant for her? Only Cora could tell her. Then again, Isabelle didn't need her aunt's weird Cupid powers to tell her that she was head over heels for the sexy chef.

"I'm so screwed."

# About the Author

What does someone say to describe themselves? You could start with giving what others say about you. Scratch that. It doesn't really matter what others think about you. It matters what you think of yourself. So here we go.

First of all, I'm a wife and mother. I'm also a grandmother. That alone would fulfil any woman's life and to be honest it does. But.....

I'm also a writer. Someone who loves to tell stories of love, suspense, heartache and of course happily ever after. For most of my life, I've written those stories for myself. A type of therapy, I suppose. I love the characters I create. They become part of who I am because there's part of me in them.

So.... Now that you know this about me. I hope when you read my books, you fall in love with them.

You should also know that I'm a Newfoundlander. What is that you ask? Well we're a proud people who live on an island, off the east coast of Canada. Some people believe Canada ends with Nova Scotia. It doesn't. If you keep going east, there is a beautiful island full of amazing people and magnificent scenery. That is where my stories are set because let's face it. The best stories always come from the places you know and love.

If there is anything else you would like to know about me. Ask me!

# O'Connor Brothers Series

Read about the sexy O'Connor Brothers

In Books 1, 2, 3, 4, 5 & 6

Available on

Amazon and

Kindle Unlimited.

# Also Available

## Dangerous Therapy

### Book 1

Officer John O'Connor is giving up on life after a terrible accident. His family are at their wits end when he refuses any kind of therapy. The only thing keeping him sane is his dreams of a beautiful woman he pulled in for a traffic violation months before.

Physical Therapist Stephanie Kelly is healing from a broken heart. When she is hired by Nightingale's personal care and physical therapy, she's ecstatic, but she's shocked when her boss asks her to take on a new patient. Shocked because the patient is her boss's nephew and he's not exactly keen on therapy. He's also the cop who's been heating up her dreams.

As Stephanie helps John get back on his feet, they grow closer, but someone is out to hurt Stephanie, or worse. After multiple attempts on her life, John's family tries to figure out who's after the woman he loves and stop them before it's too late.

# Dangerous Abduction

## Book 2

Widower James O'Connor has been fighting his growing attraction to his brother's sister-in-law for four long years, but when someone breaks into her home, destroying everything she owns, James takes her and her young son into his home. The break-in wasn't random. Marina and her son are in danger, and James swears to protect them, but can he keep them safe?

Marina Kelly dedicates her life to caring for her sweet little boy, Danny. Since she broke free from her abusive husband, she's sworn off men, but when James O'Connor keeps entering her thoughts and her dreams, it takes everything she has to keep her feelings hidden. Now, her sister and parents are out of the province, and she's in danger, Marina has no choice but to accept James's help and try to hide her attraction and growing feelings.

The attraction between them impossible to resist. Only her ex's family secret may tear it all apart. Can Marina and James unravel the family's hidden mystery without losing each other?

# Dangerous Secrets

## Book 3

Ian O'Connor has everything going for him. He's got the O'Connor drop dead good looks, an incredible body and to top it off he's a doctor. Why wouldn't anyone want the man but none of that was the reason Sandy Churchill was head over heels in love with the man. After he had stood her up for their first official date, she was weary of taking another chance. When she ends up in the hospital because she turned her back on a criminal determined to get away from her, Ian admits that he loves her and wants another chance. A secret from his past throws Sandy into a tailspin, but she has a secret that she's hiding from everyone.

Ian's on cloud nine when he finally takes a leap of faith and tells the woman he's loved for four years how he feels and wants a chance to make up for his screw up. They have two weeks of bliss, but a murder and secrets come back to haunt him. Sandy's reaction tells him there's another reason why she's avoiding him. She's hiding something, but he has no idea what and to make matters worse there's danger coming from her past that could hurt the people he loves the most.

# Dangerous Beauty

## Book 4

When you come from a privileged family, you're expected to follow a particular path in life. Unless you're Emily Bradshaw. Defying her father, Emily turned down a full scholarship to Dalhousie University. Instead, she followed her dream and opened her own salon in the small town of Hopedale with her friend. She's happy. Then her mother vanishes. Her father receives threatening messages and hires Newfoundland Security Services to protect his children. Emily doesn't like the idea, especially when the man that walks into her salon dressed in a black leather jacket makes her weak in the knees. Emily knows she's in danger but not the kind her father is worried about.

Keith O'Connor isn't expecting his newest security job to be anything out of the ordinary. Then he walks into Snippy Gals, a beauty salon in Hopedale. Keith gets the shock of his life when an auburn-haired beauty turns to face him. Emily is defiant, sassy, and her sexy curves have him in a complete spin. Fighting his feelings for her becomes almost impossible, but when Emily's mother is found, a family secret is revealed turning Emily's life upside down. Can Keith help her cope and keep her out of the clutches of a vengeful stranger?

# Dangerous Silence

## Book 5

Mike O'Connor's reputation earned him the name Mr. Homerun, but after two hours with Billie, he's ready to change all that. There's one problem. She disappears before he can find out her last name.

Billie Carter had little choice but to leave when she received a desperate text from her friend. Peggy and her daughter have no family, both are deaf, and Billie wants to protect them from an abusive man.

When Peggy is brutally murdered, Billie is determined to protect Chloe. Like a dream come true, Mike walks through her door to help. They soon learn that the little girl is not the only one in danger, and it may take more than Mike to keep them safe.

# Dangerous Delusion

## Book 6

Lora Norris quits a great job and moved to Hopedale to escape an unknown stalker. Little did she know that finding employment at Jack's Place would lead her to some of the best friends she would ever have. Of course, there is also one man she wanted to be a lot more than a friend, but can't take a chance and put him in danger.

Nick O'Connor never thought the pretty waitress working at his Aunt's diner would give him a second glance. Especially with his playboy reputation. She's friendly toward him but doesn't seem the least bit interested.

When women show up dead and bearing a striking resemblance to Lora, Nick and his family do everything to protect her and her little girl. As they admit their feelings for each other, the danger moves closer than they even realize.

# Dangerous Witness

## Book 7

Aaron (A.J.) O'Connor is the youngest of seven brothers. His reputation for being a love 'em and leave 'em kind of guy is only a mask to cover the heartbreak he suffered at the hands of his high school sweetheart at the tender age of eighteen. Thirteen years later, she's still the one he dreams of.

Bethany Donnelly left Hopedale on the last day of high school and hasn't looked back since. Finding out the love of her life played her for a fool and only used her to win a bet broke her heart. Now her boss wants her to return to Newfoundland to investigate an employee he suspected of illegal activity. That means facing the one man who can destroy her. The one she's never been able to forget.

Now Bethany's back, and Aaron's determined to find out why she left. First, he's got to keep her safe from a killer intent on taking her away from him forever.

# O'Connor Girls

Book 1

Available on

Amazon and

Kindle Unlimited

# Hidden Betrayal

## Book 1

Kristy O'Connor never hid the fact that she wanted Dean 'Bull' Nash. He's kept her at arm's length since they met but he's pushed her away for the last time.

Dean loves Kristy more than he could ever tell her. He wants her desperately, but his family secrets could destroy them both.

When he can't stay away from her any longer, murder and a shocking betrayal shake them to their core. Can their new relationship survive?

# Rhonda Brewer

Keep up to date on all things new.

Follow me on

Facebook

Twitter

Instagram

Sign up for my newsletter and never miss another release!

http://www.rhondabrewerauthor.com/talk-to-me